Astonished,  a sheet dra priest. He w Elite and kne of the woode ... ...e top strained to see him better as his robes, which had been creased and folded while he knelt, now fell freely about him. Then she saw the great Eye motif across the priest's shoulders.

She drew in such a sharp breath that she feared she had given herself away. Ducking down as low as she could, she held her hand to her mouth. The Eye motif could mean only one thing: the priest was no ordinary priest *but Parnassas himself.*

Cautiously, she peered over the balcony. He was still standing, looking up at the great window. She wondered what he could possibly be doing down here, alone, while the City above – *his* City – was in turmoil. Why was he not on the battlements, rallying the soldiers?

When, across the vastness of the cathedral, the sound of sobbing reached her, Tugela could not at first believe what she was hearing. Curiosity got the better of her and she rose again, overcoming her fear. But she was not imagining it. The sobs were unmistakeable, soft and pitiful. The High Priest – mighty Parnassas – was crying.

By the same authors in VGSF

DOUBLE PLANET

JOHN GRIBBIN AND MARCUS CHOWN

REUNION

VGSF

VGSF is an imprint of Victor Gollancz Ltd
14 Henrietta Street, London WC2E 8QJ

First published in Great Britain 1991
by Victor Gollancz Ltd

First VGSF edition 1992

A catalogue record for this book is
available from the British Library

ISBN 0-575-05280-5

Printed and bound in Great Britain
by Cox & Wyman Ltd, Reading

Contents

Tugela caught sight of the Eye – way off across the plateau – a tiny black dot flying out of the bright dawn sky. She was hopelessly exposed, with no place to hide.

Instinct threw her to the ground, pressed her so flat against the rock that dust caught in her mouth. She twisted and spat. The involuntary movement brought the Eye back into full view, grown now to a silver disc, bearing down on her remorselessly. There was no opportunity to mutter even a few words of prayer. In the time between heartbeats, it was on her.

It skimmed across the plateau, wildly fast, a silver sphere as bright as a second Sun. As it flashed overhead (How high? It was impossible to tell.) it made no more than the faintest of hisses in the thin air, a sound so soft that Tugela would have missed it altogether had adrenalin not sharpened her senses. Then it was gone, streaking out over the precipice on a trajectory that would take it deep into the heart of the Forbidden Zone.

With the danger passed, Tugela's fear turned to perplexity. Never in her life had she seen an Eye at such close quarters. Nor did she know of anyone who had. In normal circumstances, Eyes kept to the very edges of space, appearing only as pinpricks of light in the night sky.

Cautiously, Tugela rose to her feet, keeping her eyes constantly fixed on the shrinking sphere. Her thoughts were in turmoil. What she had seen challenged everything she had been taught about Eyes. The elders said that the priests called the Eyes home to the City when their spying was done. *Then why was this one heading straight into the nightmare land?*

Book One
TUGELA

God's Window

It was extremely dangerous for Tugela to linger in this place, high on the exposed plateau. It was true that the Eye had gone but at just about any moment it could return. Worse still, another Eye might fly over even lower and catch her. Who could tell what might or might not happen in this time of turbulence and change?

Safety lay far below her in the embrace of the forest (what was left of it), and that was where she must soon return. But she had made the tortuous climb to the plateau for a reason and she might never return here again. Against common sense, and with her heart pounding violently (more from the achingly thin air than from fear), Tugela hurried on towards God's Window.

The place often figured as a backdrop in the Sagas, the tales told by old men round crackling fires during long dark nights in the Land. Because the Sagas were her father's private obsession, she had heard them repeated more often than most. But never, even while listening intently to the soft drone of his voice, had she dreamt that she herself might one day journey to the fabled lookout point at the edge of the world.

At God's Window, the Sagas told, the Land came to an abrupt end, like a conversation choked off in mid-sentence. Along a ragged boundary that was hundreds of klomters in length, firm ground simply ran out, and empty space took over. In the remote past, evidently, some monumental cataclysm had split the skin of the world, and raised up the ground on one side – or perhaps, depressed it on the other (depending on your point of view). As a result, the Land came to a sudden end in vertiginous cliffs, in places almost two klomters high.

Beyond God's Window stretched the wilderness of the Forbidden Zone – a grey nightmare place, empty except for demons and other vile creatures too horrible to contemplate. Whenever ordinary folk talked of the place, they did so in hushed and respectful voices, as if merely uttering the name of the place might somehow conjure it to life in their midst. And such was the power of the name, that even when it was whispered, the cold emptiness of that place did seem to reach out across the Land, a tangible thing, clutching with icy fingers at their hearts, impelling them to crowd in closer to any source of light, any source of warmth.

To restless souls, however, the Forbidden Zone acted like a magnet. It drew them from far and wide – those individuals who had yearned all their lives for adventure and unlimited horizons, for whom the Land had never been enough, had always seemed claustrophobically small. From the towering cliffs of God's Window, they could contemplate a land their imaginations had imbued with the colours of their hopes, and test the strength of their resolve to go on against the grey reality.

At this sight, most would wake suddenly, as if from a dream, and realise that what they really sought lay elsewhere. For not only did the nightmare land have the power to sober the most restless of men and women, it also had the power to hold a mirror to their lives, to show them what they had somehow missed in the confusion of their days: what was important and worthwhile.

For a short time, they would drink in the awful vista; then, resigned to the Land, they would turn their backs and begin the long journey home, to return only, perhaps, in their troubled dreams.

But not all.

Six men and women had reached God's Window and, because

they were insane or deranged in some other way, gone on. Each, in their turn, had found a way down the face of the precipitous cliffs to the plain below. And each had vanished for ever into the Forbidden Zone.

The names of the Lost Ones, Tugela, like every child in the Land, knew by heart. From Waymon Dart, the renegade priest from the City, to Aletta, the orphaned outlander, barely fifteen years old when she disappeared. Dart, the first of the six, had left the Land more than three centuries before; Aletta had disappeared at the beginning of the Third War of Independence, a conflict that was raging still across the Land.

In the Sagas, the names of the Lost Ones cropped up again and again. Their exploits were embroidered and embellished until it seemed they were more than mere mortals. Yet they had all been ordinary men and women. Tugela, perhaps better than anyone else, knew the truth of that.

For one of them had been her grandfather.

A bitter wind stung Tugela full in the face, tore at her loose hair. It sliced through the layers of her clothing as if they were made of the thinnest paper and struck deep into the very core of her body. But so far had she come and so close was she now to her goal that she could permit nothing to deflect her. With her head down, she pressed on into the hurricane.

The wind, for all its severity, was no more than the overspill from a much stronger draught of air. That air, Tugela knew, was rising up the wall of the world from the plain far below. Its roar, like the ominous rumble of deep thunder, had already drowned out every other sound.

Heedless of the danger, Tugela broke into a run. At first, it seemed a futile thing to do and she made next to no headway. The wind threatened to lift her off her feet and toss her back whence she had come. But, miraculously, and in the space of just a few strides, it slackened, and was suddenly gone.

It was as she had guessed it must be. The rising air, when it reached the level of the plateau, could not simply spill over the edge; its momentum would carry it on and upwards. In a great overhead arc, the air would descend on to the plateau, leaving the ground at the very edge of the cliffs calm, as at the eye of a storm.

Cold beyond caring now, Tugela covered the last stretch of ground to God's Window, and looked out on . . .

An ocean of whiteness.

It opened up before her like a vision from a dream. She had expected to see grey monotony, the rise and fall then rise again of bare, lifeless hills, but instead she saw endless banks of puffy white clouds marching away to infinity like waves on a frozen sea. Below her feet, a klomter down the sheer cliff face, the waves rolled in to the shore, breaking and eddying against the hardness of the Land.

It was a sight of powerful beauty but it provoked in the girl only a feeling of bitter disappointment. It was so unfair! She had come so far, risked so much, only to be cheated out of a glimpse of the Forbidden Zone at the very last step. Though she stood now, a god at God's Window, cold tears streamed down her face.

The Sagas lied!

It strained credibility to think that she was the first person to get to God's Window only to find the Forbidden Zone hidden from view. Yet, at no time, did the Sagas admit such a possibility. It was a reminder, if a reminder were needed, that the Sagas were stories – stories built around a kernel of truth perhaps, but stories nonetheless. How had she forgotten? Her father had stressed the point to her often enough.

Wearily, Tugela sat down on the cliff edge, allowing her long legs to dangle into space. She wiped the mist from her eyes and peered downward. Just below her vantage point, a thin waterfall spurted from the rock face, draining the last reserves of moisture from the plateau into the cloud layer far below. Where the waterfall turned to vapour, she picked out the tiny black silhouette of a glideagle, wheeling slowly, gracefully, on invisible currents of air.

With one hand anchoring her to the rock behind her, Tugela craned further forward. But looking straight down the vertical wall made her dizzy; her stomach heaved. To steady herself, she had to lie flat on her back and gulp great lungfuls of the thin air. *How, in the name of sanity, had her grandfather managed to climb down there?*

And this thought led to a host of others concerning her grandfather, all of which she had pondered on countless occasions before. What kind of man could he have been to have come to this place at the edge of the world and then to have struck out into the unknown?

As a young child, her mind cringing from the horror of his deed yet at the same time fascinated by it, she had imagined her grandfather as a giant among other men, a man who did not know the meaning of the word fear. But as she had got older, her unconditional awe had become tempered by a pragmatic realism. He had left a wife back in the Land, and children, too. What kind of man would do that? And why?

Tugela turned her attention back to the clouds, the endless banks of clouds. For an age, she stared out across that unbelievable ocean of whiteness, unable to focus on any portion, drawn down deeper and deeper into its depths. She had the disconcerting feeling that she was falling and could not stop herself. So disorientated did it make her that when, after minutes, after hours perhaps – time didn't seem to come into things now – the clouds began slowly to disperse, she did not notice. It was with a shock that she realised what was happening and sprung to her feet.

In a dozen separate places, the cloud layer was breaking up.

The Sun was burning it off. Here and there, the crests of hills, the tips of mountains, were beginning to show, islands breaking the surface of the white sea. Consumed by impatience, Tugela began to run along the cliff edge, as if this activity might, in some way, hasten the natural processes underway. As she stumbled on, a land was slowly unveiled before her. It was painted in greys and browns, and the blacks of deep, inpenetrable shadows. Nowhere were there trees or any other signs of vegetation. Strangest of all were the faint rings etched on the land. They were first to appear and seemed, to Tugela, like she imagined the great Circleberg, the mountain ring that enclosed the plain of the City.

And then no cloud at all remained. Tugela stopped running and stood, her lungs heaving, taking in the terrible vista of the Forbidden Zone. The Forbidden Zone, where nightmare creatures prowled the shadows. The Forbidden Zone, which had swallowed her grandfather, and five others. The Forbidden Zone, where at regular intervals the comets that brought air to the Land impacted. *Only they weren't impacting any more. The City had made sure of that.*

Time passed . . .

Suddenly, Tugela realised just how cold she was so high up in the thin air. She was shaking uncontrollably. She was dehydrated, her lips and face dried out by the cruel wind. Why, she wondered, had she not noticed these things before? The excitement, perhaps, or the fear. And how long had she been up here? She realised with a shock that she really had no idea at all. In the thin air, her thoughts seemed to be oddly fuzzy and sluggish. She had heard that altitude could have such a effect.

Then Tugela remembered her uncle, Kasteel! She had left him down in the valley, asleep by the wagon where he had passed out drunk. She had to get down. In a stupor, she stumbled across the open plateau and began the descent through the ranks of yellowed and dying shatterpines. When, finally, they petered out, and she emerged into bright sunlight, she saw the figure coming towards her. Even at a distance, something in his posture told her he was mad at her.

Shaking with exhaustion, Tugela stood her ground and braced herself for the inevitable storm.

Kasteel

By the time of the second seventh, the Sun should have taken the worst of the night's chill off the Land. But the thin air was still freezing and the ground was still hard with frost. As the wagon trundled across the valley floor, Tugela tried to shrink deeper into the cave of her cape and hood. But there was no place, it seemed, not even in the deepest folds and layers of her clothing, where the cruel wind could not reach.

Think warm, she told herself. But the sensation was now as alien to her as the colour of purple is to a man blind from birth. Try as she might, she could not breathe life into a single memory of balmier days. Warm was something she had simply never been.

In the Land, the nights were always cold, winter and summer. People expected that and got by the best they could. What helped them to survive the long night more than anything else was the promise of the long day which would follow. But now, in the middle of summer, when by rights the world should come to life at the first touch of the new Sun, the Sun was climbing the sky and it was still freezing. How long, the girl wondered, before the blanket of air that insulated the world was so depleted that night and day in the Land became indistinguishable?

Tugela glanced at the shape of her uncle beside her, hunched over the reins of the carriers. Only the fog of frozen breath, expelled from time to time in long measured exhalations, betrayed the existence of a human being beneath the amorphous mound of clothing. When he lifted the flask of liquor to his hood and gulped, she caught for a moment the wedge of his jaw, set hard in sullen fury.

When she had returned from God's Window, Kasteel had been more than merely furious; he had been apoplectic. Her misjudgment of his mood cost her a fierce beating. Even now, the pain of that punishment lingered. Only with the greatest of care was she able to shift in her seat atop the wagon without wincing from the bruises and she cursed the misfortune that had forced her to travel with him.

Tugela realised, with the benefit of hindsight, that she had been a fool not to have guessed that Kasteel would see her ascent to God's Window as the most heinous of crimes. Kasteel was the one whose life was most badly affected – shattered even – when her grandfather had vanished into the Forbidden Zone. Hadn't her own father told her that, often enough? For Kasteel, the trade route to Ironvale, which passed so close to God's Window, was a kind of living hell, re-opening an old and festering wound. That was why, immediately they made camp, he had begun drinking heavily. And that was why Tugela had been able to slip away, while he lay unconscious beside the campfire.

Kasteel's terrible misfortune was that he had been born the eldest of four brothers (her father, Bandon, was the youngest). When their father disappeared, therefore, it was Kasteel, a boy barely fifteen years of age, who inherited the responsibility of supporting the family.

According to her own father, who at the time of her grandfather's disappearance had been barely old enough to understand what was happening, his elder brother had been a quiet, studious boy who had shown academic promise early on and whom the family intended to send to the distant City to be educated into the ways of the priesthood. With the sudden departure of the family's breadwinner, the boy was thrust into premature manhood, all those dreams cruelly swept away.

To his credit, Kasteel discharged all of his duties to the family. Then, as suddenly as his father before him, he left. Perhaps in an attempt to free himself for ever of what he had found to be the crushing weight of responsibility, he became a freelance trader, buying metal goods in the City and selling them among

the more remote outlander settlements. It was a lonely occupation, which explained why Kasteel, at the best of times, was a
man of few words, but it was an occupation that left him
answerable to no one, and that suited him. Plying his trade at
the wild periphery of the Land, her uncle had found a kind of
peace.

At one time, the family had heard rumours of a woman he
had loved who had died, but the rumours had not been
confirmed and Kasteel himself, on his rare return visits, said
nothing. Those visits became rarer and rarer and, perhaps, the
girl would not have seen her uncle for many years had not the
City soldiers burned the farm at Boschendale and taken away
her parents. When Tugela had no one in the world, Kasteel was
suddenly there, as if summoned from afar by the glideagles that
rode the air currents above the Land. For that she was grateful
and for that she tried – she tried *so* hard – to understand the
man. To some extent, she had succeeded. But forgiveness was
quite another thing. At present, the bruises on her back were
too fresh, and she was certainly no saint.

The ground was smoother now, so she stood up a while to
stretch her legs. Like most people in the Land, Tugela stood tall
and slim with sun-darkened skin. When she walked she did so
with long, loping, easy strides. When she ran, she flowed
effortlessly across the ground. Her muscles, barely perceptible
at rest, could propel her like the wind when taut. Only in height
did she differ from the racial, having not quite reached that of
an adult.

Mentally, the differences were rather more marked. She had a
strong feeling of being unlike others of her age. Perhaps this
came from being the grand-daughter of a man who had entered
the Forbidden Zone. Or perhaps it was because, being a loner,
she deluded herself that she was important, setting herself above
others to provide a comforting explanation for why she did not
fit in.

How much further to Ironvale, Tugela wondered? The wagon

was climbing a steep rise now, the yellow, oxygen-starved trees of a dying forest to one side of them, and the carriers were finding it very hard going. Ahead, if she strained her eyes, she could just about make out a long line of hills, their summits dusted lightly with snow. Having never travelled at the Periphery before, she could only guess that those were the High Hills. If she were right, then they could not be far from their destination.

The journey to Ironvale had brought them out to the Periphery along a valley that ran along the back of God's Window. Now, ironically, they were headed back into the interior of the Land as if they had somehow ricocheted off the barrier obstructing their path. It was a curiously convoluted route but they had no choice, constrained as they were by the lie of the land and by the need to avoid patrols of the City, a few of which penetrated even this far into the outlands.

As far as Tugela was concerned, of course, the route was fortuitous. It had, after all, given her the chance to climb to God's Window. What she had glimpsed of the Forbidden Zone had been worth the beating, worth it a hundred times over. And the Eye ... that had been an unexpected bonus. Descending through the shatterpine forest, she had toyed with the idea of telling Kasteel about it. But now she was determined it would remain *her* secret, at least for the time being.

The wagon came to the top of the rise and began descending a stony slope to a place where a stream, now dried up, had once run. Without warning, Kasteel drew up the carriers. Tugela looked ahead, puzzled, and then saw what her uncle had seen: below them, by the dark stain of the stream bed, was a small homestead. At such a distance, it was difficult to make out any detail, but the tiny wooden buildings had the feel of a place abandoned. As far as the girl could see, there was no smoke rising into the air. No dwelling was habitable in the present cold without a fire.

Driving on, they came to a portion of the hillside which was neatly terraced on either side of the track and planted with some kind of cereal crop, now dead. Evidently, when the stream had disappeared, the crops had gone with it. Or perhaps the severe frost had killed them before that. Tugela found such matters depressing to speculate on.

It was rare to find a homestead out here on the Periphery. Only those outlanders to whom the dominion of the City stuck in the throat trekked this far from its power. But whoever they were had gone now. As the wagon passed the shacks, three in all, it became clear that they had been abandoned recently. The door of the largest swung mournfully in the wind, while the deep ruts cut by the wagons, heavily laden, stretched away into the distance.

To Tugela's surprise, Kasteel, instead of slowing to take a look, urged on the carriers. Had he known the people who had lived here? Had he stopped on his way to Ironvale to water the carriers and rest awhile? Yes, Tugela concluded, seeing the way he concentrated his attention on the horizon, he had known them. But what they had meant to him she could not guess.

It was a measure of how hard things had become recently that people who were so determined to live in freedom should feel no alternative but to trek back towards the enemy they hated so much, for that was where they must surely have gone. Already, on the journey to Ironvale, they had passed three or four abandoned farms. In all cases, the settlers, their crops ruined, had headed inward from the Periphery to the Great Depression. There, at the lowest point in the land, they must have reasoned, the air would be at its thickest and water might still be running free.

Kasteel never looked back at the farmstead, and neither did Tugela. Like her uncle, she kept her eyes fixed on the route ahead, willing Ironvale to come into view. And so, long before they ever reached the endpoint of their journey, Tugela spotted the tell-tale black smoke hanging like a shroud across the hills. Forgetting herself for a moment, she pointed and shouted excitedly, but her uncle was still in a black mood and continued to stare ahead doggedly, pausing only to take occasional swigs from his flask of liquor. She shut up abruptly and sat still. But, inside, she was jubilant.

Soon she would be among people again, in a place throbbing with life.

Man of Iron

The road that formed the final approach to Ironvale wound down through hills entirely stripped of forest. For the most part, the slopes of the hills were littered with the severed stumps of trees but, in places, not even these sorry remnants poked from the barren ground. Ugly grey scars had opened up on several slopes, carved by avalanches of mud that had swept all before them. Against the devastated landscape nothing moved, not a single small creature on the ground nor a glideagle in the air, and it was eerily quiet apart from the constant *crump, crump, crump* of the wagon as it jounced and bounced on the rutted track.

Tugela had never seen such destruction before in the Land. Seeing it all about her, and the pall of smoke which hung above the hills ahead and which, so far, was the only visible sign of Ironvale, she trembled. Was it perhaps Hell that Kasteel was heading for and not the town that promised to deliver the outlanders at long last from the tyranny of the City?

Below them on the road, a giant wagon was ponderously negotiating a hairpin bend. It was loaded with the slender trunks of shatterpines and led by a great team of carriers, numbering perhaps a dozen in all. Kasteel, in no time at all, had caught it up and was cursing loudly because there was no room to pass. Tugela gazed upward with awe at the great logs piled high on the wagon and hoped fervently that they could not break loose from their thick chains. Telling her uncle that she would walk the remainder of the way to Ironvale and meet up with him there, Tugela jumped down on to the track. Kasteel grunted his assent and dug into the layers of his coat for his flask.

Quickly, Tugela skirted the giant wagon and came to a boy who was standing on the bend of the road, signalling to the three men atop the wagon. One of them, the youngest, saw her and waved. But before she could exchange a word with him, the urchin on the ground suddenly became animated and the older men yelled "Brake, brake!" Promptly, the young man complied, throwing his full weight on a stick of wood that protruded from the front of the wagon. The wheels screeched in mechanical pain and Tugela passed on by.

Further on, another giant wagon, this one empty, trundled past her, going up the track. She watched it go by and then her thoughts turned back to the pall of smoke ahead and to the town that lay beneath it. Soon, around the next bend or the one after that, Ironvale would be revealed in all its glory. Her heart beat faster in anticipation and she quickened her pace.

For a while, there was no other incident as Tugela walked. Then, as the road veered sharply yet again, a sudden commotion to one side caught her attention. Instinctively, she reached for the knife beneath her cloak. But before her hand could close around it, she recognised the shape of a small boy. He was standing on the steep hillside, about twenty metres above her, grinning. As she watched warily, he made his way, slipping and sliding, down the muddy bank. He ambled across the track and thrust out a grubby hand.

Tugela estimated he could be no more than eleven or twelve years old. He had long hair that was black as soot and unkempt; his clothes, a jerkin and gaiters, were the colour and texture of old sacking. The only thing out of keeping with his dishevelled appearance was a necklace of polished metal pieces, a product, Tugela guessed, of Ironvale. He was smiling, with a toothy grin as he held out his hand. "I've been following you," he said.

"Ever since way back up the road." And, at this, he motioned, the links of his heavy necklace clattering.

She ignored the dirty hand. "Why?" she asked, suspiciously.

"Thought I might be of help to you," he said. He peered at her quizzically, tipping his head to one side, then the other.

"No," he said, apparently coming to a conclusion. "I can see you don't trust me." He withdrew his hand but not his toothy grin. "Look," he said. "I mean you no harm. What I said's the truth, swear to you it is. Thought you might need a guide who knows his way about Ironvale. Well, miss, do you?"

"I might," she said, grudgingly.

"Right," the boy said with a decisiveness that knocked her back. "Then, we're in business." He started off down the road.

A dozen paces further on, he twisted round and grinned back at her. She did not move but watched him, her hands planted firmly on her hips. The bare-faced cheek of the boy! If he thought for one moment that she was going to follow him . . .

Suddenly, Tugela laughed loudly. It was the first time in a long while she had laughed and she found she could not stop herself. Miraculously, the weight of the long journey with Kasteel seemed to lift from her shoulders.

"Wait!" she shouted. A guide might not be a bad idea, after all. While Kasteel went about his business in Ironvale, Tugela would undoubtedly have time to herself. With someone who knew the place well, even this pushy little boy, she might see things she might otherwise miss.

But watch your pockets, she thought as she caught him up.

"What's your name?"

"Tugela," she told him.

"Mine's Tolly Hoopa. Pleased to meet you." This time she took his hand. "For a krown, I'll show you round Ironvale. How's that sound?"

She hesitated. "Gotta make a living," Tolly said. "Showing visitors around the sights is one of the only ways I've got."

"Okay," she said. "Half now and half when I'm satisfied

you've done a good job." She dug into her pockets and brought out a battered coin.

"Done," the boy said, catching the coin. "You're a hard one, miss. I can seen there's no messing with the likes of you."

"Get away, Tolly Hoopa," she said. "I'll be watching you. Any funny business and . . ." She drew her finger across her throat and grimaced. "I won't hesitate, don't think I will."

"Do anything funny, miss?" The boy echoed, aghast. "*Me*, Tolly Hoopa, as honest as the day is – "

"All right, all right," Tugela said. "I get the idea."

They continued on down the track, past a handful of shatter-pines which, for reasons unknown, had been left standing alone on the blasted slopes.

"So, tell me why you were following me, Tolly Hoopa?"

"I was up by the top of the road and I saw you with your father – "

"My uncle."

"With your uncle then. Saw you atop your wagon and thought I could do you a service. Told you that already, miss. I often come up here. I can get a krown or two from the lumberjacks for guiding a wagon down to Ironvale. I get off at the tight corners and signal to the driver."

"Like the boy I just saw back there?"

"Jossie? You must have seen my mate Jossie. Sometimes, we work together – if the load's a big 'un, that is."

"So there's no school in Ironvale, then?" Tugela asked.

"We're on a war footing," the boy said. "We've all got to make sacrifices. Peet Stel says – "

"You *know* Peet Stel?" Tugela broke in.

"'Course I know Peet Stel. 'Course I do." Seeing how the name had affected her, the boy grew tall with pride.

So the Man of Metal was no fiction.

For so long, Tugela had had her doubts. Oh, she had heard the stories all right, the stories outlanders liked to tell of Stel in hushed, reverent tones round their camp fires. But her fear had always been that they were just that: stories. Perhaps, she had thought, the Man of Metal was no more than the collective wishful thinking of the outlanders. So great was their need for a champion to help them break the chains of the City and give them back their pride. Perhaps, just perhaps, it was strong enough to have created a mythical man to embody all their hopes?

But the boy was saying that Peet Stel was real, made of flesh and blood. *Then there really was hope for the outlanders.* Tugela's heart leapt with joy.

"Peet Stel," she mouthed silently.

"He can make metal just like Parnassas and the priests of the City," crowed Tolly. "The priests have got their recipes, Peet Stel says, but he's got his science. Chemistry not recipes, that's what he says. Chemistry . . ." And the boy repeated the slogan over and over again, as she had heard it so often across the Land, until it became a chant, which she could almost believe was as potent in its power as the sacred litany of the priests of the City.

And so Tugela turned the final bend in the road to Ironvale and saw the town for the first time, spread out beneath her like a black stain on the Land. But already she could see beneath its surface ugliness. For now she knew in her heart that Ironvale held the power that could change the world.

Ironvale

"This bridge is really made of *iron*?" Tugela said. She stood at the highest point of the graceful arch, peering down into the nacreous waters that flowed beneath.

"Sure is, miss," Tolly said, grinning with pride. He kicked the rail hard with the toe of his boot, causing its substance to ring out dully. "Every last rivet."

A bridge made entirely of metal. It was a revelation. Tugela
had never seen anything like it. When Tolly led her through the
gates into Ironvale, the bridge was the first thing she saw. (It
was the first thing *anyone* would see, for that matter – and
surely that was no accident.) Immediately, she had told him:
"That's where I want to go."

"But your uncle . . ?" the boy had reminded her.

Kasteel! She had clean forgotten she was supposed to wait for
him. Frantically, she scanned the hillside above the palisade of
Ironvale. On the twisting road, a large group of carriers was
descending (she could clearly see the clouds of dust they kicked
up) but she could see no sign at all of Kasteel's wagon. If he had
met an obstruction on the road, or had broken a wheel or
worse, he might not arrive for hours. Should she wait or could
she go on with the boy? She bit on her lip and dabbed absently
at her hair.

"Look, miss," Tolly said, seeing her uncertainty. "When your
uncle gets to Ironvale, he'll be bound to go to the inn." He
pointed to a squat wooden building which Tugela had not
noticed before. Carriers were tethered outside and smoke curled
from two tall thin chimneys, one at either end. "Come on,"
Tolly said. "We can leave a message there for him." Obediently,
Tugela followed along the main thoroughfare, past men hurrying about their mysterious business, their clothes streaked with
grime, their faces lined with exhaustion.

Tolly vanished inside the inn. She decided to wait outside.
The wind was beginning to gust strongly. Above her, a sign
creaked as it was buffeted back and forth. She backed away a
little and, looking up, was able to read the words "King of
Ironvale" emblazoned in gold letters on a black background.
Painted below was a portly man, built very differently to the
average outlander, whose face was lit by the yellow glow of a
fire and who was brandishing a hammer from which sparks
splashed all about. Without doubt, the man was Peet Stel. But
before she could examine the figure more closely, Tolly appeared

once more. "Done," he said, pleased with his efficiency. "Let's go."

They had been standing on the bridge for some time peering down into the polluted waters, and the cold wind was beginning to chill both of them to the bone. Tugela had pulled her cloak tight around her shoulders but it was not enough to prevent her from shivering visibly. "Right," she said, letting go of the rail suddenly. "I'm ready to see the rest of Ironvale." With obvious relief, the boy led her off the bridge.

It wasn't until the sound of metal had ceased to ring at their footsteps that a thought struck Tugela, a thought so obvious that she wondered why it had not occurred to her before. In all the time they had stood on the iron bridge, *no one else had crossed it.*

Upstream, she could plainly see several other bridges, each made of wood, and they were more than adequate for the traffic to and fro across the stream. The iron bridge was, quite simply, redundant. In fact, now she looked back at it from some way off, the bridge seemed a little incongruous, spanning, in such a huge arch, a stream that could have been no more than a trickle even before the comets stopped coming and the air above had begun to leak away. The bridge clearly was no practical solution to a problem. Then why . . ? She turned to Tolly but before she could open her mouth to ask a question she knew the answer.

Practical considerations had nothing to do with it, nothing at all.

The bridge was not a bridge designed to be *used.* No, no. It was clear to her now that its purpose was far more important than that. The bridge had been built as a symbol, an embodiment of the new optimism of the outlanders. It was a statement of their bullish confidence, of their newfound self-belief. It screamed out, loudly and clearly, to all who beheld it: *This is what we outlanders can do. Now we are a force to be reckoned with.*

The thought that the iron bridge, and indeed all of Ironvale, existed in defiance of the City simultaneously exhilarated Tugela and terrified her. It was good that, after so long, the City's monopoly on metals was being broken. It was good also that the outlanders, after centuries of domination by the City, at last had the means to fight back. But the City possessed a power against which the outlanders were no more than insects. It was, after all, taking away their air, and suffocating the Land. With its Eyes, it must be watching Ironvale even at this moment. Might not Peet Stel succeed only in bringing the wrath of the City down on all of them? Who knew what terrors the City might unleash if they provoked it.

Tugela's gloomy thoughts were interrupted by a sudden commotion. When she looked up, she saw carriers bearing down on them fast. Deftly, Tolly steered her out of their path. A score of men rode past, led by a gaunt young man with the purple arm badge of a general. Their carriers snorted and spluttered noisily, steam rising from their glistening flanks. It occurred to Tugela suddenly as she watched the Kommando go – for that was clearly what it was – that these were the men she had seen earlier on the road. She turned to Tolly to mention it but if she had spoken, he would not have heard her. He was staring open-mouthed at the receding men. "Mandelbrot," he whispered to himself.

"What?" Tugela asked.

"That was General Mandelbrot," Tolly said.

The name at first meant nothing to Tugela. But at the back of her mind a vague memory stirred. Way back along the route they had travelled to Ironvale, Kasteel had conversed briefly with another trader whose route had crossed theirs. The name of Mandelbrot had come up in the exchange, she was sure. In fact, now the memory was sharpening, she was certain that the name had been mentioned more than once.

"Mandelbrot," she said, as they walked. "He is the Unappointed." It was half statement, half question.

Her ignorance evidently surprised Tolly. He looked at her oddly, as if to say: *You really do not know*? Instead, he said patiently: "Things're moving fast, miss. Perhaps on your journey in the Periphery you didn't hear . . ."

"I heard the name of Mandelbrot," she said.

Tolly nodded sagely. "It's a name that's been on people's lips for a while now – ever since the battle at Winterberg when General Mandelbrot routed the City's soldiers. That's a lesson they won't forget. He taught them another one at Two Bridges on the Ochre River, and that's within spitting distance of the Circleberg itself." The boy was now puffed up with pride. "Some people say they were small victories," he went on, now defensive. "But they were victories all the same – no one can deny that. He's shown everyone that the City can be beaten."

They walked on, past strange mounds of earth from which smoke issued without fire. Beside each mound was a neat pile of shatterpines. Tugela's guess was that she was looking at kilns of some kind. "Charcoal," Tolly said, confirming her suspicion. "It's needed to make the iron hard. It's why there are no trees on the approach to Ironvale."

"Oh," she said, distractedly.

"Everyone loves Mandelbrot," Tolly continued, undeflected from the subject of his hero. "They say that his men would follow him anywhere – into the Forbidden Zone itself, if he should command it." He shook his head in admiration. Tugela, shocked at such an unexpected reference to the nightmare land, felt the chill of that place brush against her. She held back a shudder. If Mandelbrot's men were willing to follow him even *there*, she thought, then truly he must be a formidable leader.

A giant wagon had now drawn up beside one of the kilns. Men jumped down, undid chains, and began to discharge its cargo of wood.

"Even the old guard have now given him their support," Tolly said as they watched the men carry out the unloading. "When General Zennor stood down in his favour, others followed.

Now everyone agrees that General Mandelbrot should be the one to lead the massed Kommandos against the City."

To Tugela, learning so much in such a short space of time, it seemed at first as if a man had been conjured out of thin air to lead the outlanders. When Kasteel had rescued her from the ruins of Boschendale, the news of the skirmish at Winterberg was still fresh (Two Bridges had not yet happened), and there were few details of that fight, certainly no reports of a new champion among the outlanders. Now, suddenly, there was a new leader of leaders, to whom all, even the stubborn old guard, had apparently deferred. This new man, this Mandelbrot, reed-thin and in appearance barely older than Tugela herself, now held the fate of the outlanders in his hands.

Though she reeled a little from the speed of events, deep down she did not doubt that they had taken the right course. If Mandelbrot did not have the total trust and respect of his men, they would not have chosen to follow him. That was the Way. Among the outlanders, there was no formal procedure to elect a leader. A man became the leader of a Kommando, naturally, spontaneously, *because he was followed*. No one appointed him, hence his name; Mandelbrot had been followed, the men of his Kommando had willingly placed their lives in his hands. And now, so, too, had the leaders of every other Kommando across the Land. How could such a choice, which was made naturally, by common consent, be the wrong one?

"Look, iron ore," Tolly said suddenly, breaking into Tugela's thoughts. Wagonloads of the black material were now approaching them in a convoy. They had to step aside to avoid being run down.

Tugela had never seen iron ore before. To say it was unprepossessing was an understatement. *That stuff*, she reacted with incredulity, *that stuff* can be turned into hard, shiny metal you can see your face in? It seemed miraculous to her. But then Ironvale itself was a miracle, the biggest miracle of all.

"Purest stuff outside the Circleberg itself," the boy told her.

"Comes from a rich deposit called the Crescent Formation about a day's wagon journey across the hills. Peet Stel says there's even more than beneath the plain of the City."

On Tolly's suggestion, they followed one of the ore wagons. It juddered unsteadily down a rutted track to one of a cluster of large wooden sheds. Through the open doors of the shed, Tugela saw men with picks, smashing the black rocks into smaller and smaller chunks. None of the men, all of whom were shirtless and sweating despite the outside cold, looked up for a moment from their toil. The work looked back-breaking.

It struck Tugela suddenly and forcibly that it was here, in these sheds, and not on the field of battle, that the conflict between the City and the outlanders would ultimately be decided. If the men of Ironvale worked harder, put in longer hours, than their counterparts in the City, then the outlanders had a chance. If not, then their revolt was futile.

Now that her eyes had become used to the gloom of the shed's interior, Tugela saw that at the far end other men shovelled the pounded rubble into yet more wagons. These wagons carted it further along the valley. Their destination was a complex of squat buildings, made of stone not wood. Though they were some distance away, Tugela could see that within them fires burned fiercely, issuing showers of sparks. The din, even at this distance, was clearly audible.

Tolly had noted the direction of her gaze with mischievous satisfaction, and he had also seen the fear in her face. He made no attempt to allay it, however. Instead, he just grinned. When Tugela saw his expression, she promptly stiffened. "I'm ready," she said, barely managing to conceal a tremor in her voice. "Let's go." She struck out along the track towards the noise and the fire. The boy skipped along beside her, and began an off-key rendition of a song:

"Swart smutted smiths, smattered with smoke,
Drive me near death with the din of their dints,

Such noise on nights ne heard men never,
Say, hey for the metal mad man o' the myrre."

By now Tugela was acutely aware that the boy was watching her every move and taking a sadistic pleasure in observing her reaction to sights which were, to him, not in the least bit unfamiliar or threatening. It was a relief, then, to hear someone call out Tolly's name. They turned together to see the small boy Tugela had noticed earlier on the road above Ironvale. He was waving at them, beckoning. "Jossie!" Tolly yelled back enthusiastically. Then to Tugela, he said: "Sorry, miss. But I've got to go." Without any further explanation, he shot off towards his friend. "Be back in a moment," he shouted over his shoulder. But he wasn't, and for that Tugela was thankful. It saved her any further humiliations as she continued her tour.

Finally, she arrived at the stone buildings which contained the fire. The din was terrible. Peering inside one, she saw four men shoulder four horizontal poles and lift a huge pot from a furnace. They staggered a little under the weight, and white fire splashed over the sides of the pot, exploding in sparks before it touched the ground. Even in broad sunlight the brightness of the fire was so intense that it nearly blinded her. By squinting, she could see the men pouring the molten liquid into moulds of some kind. She continued on her way, dazed by what she had seen, her senses overloading fast. The noise coming from within the next building overwhelmed her, a wall of sound so terrible that she hardly dared look in. The urge to run became powerful but, with an enormous effort, she held it at bay. When she did pluck up enough courage to venture forward, she saw rows of men beating dull red ingots with hammers and other unidentifiable implements.

The sight occupied her attention so exclusively that she did not notice when she was no longer alone. With a start she registered the presence of a man standing beside her. He was an unusually short, dumpy man, balding, with cheeks that were clearly florid from the heat but probably, she suspected, red underneath, too. Red cheeks would have been in keeping with his overall good-natured appearance. The man asked her who she was and where she had come from, and she told him, but he clearly wasn't too interested in her answer, though it was evident that he knew the name of Kasteel. He was apparently taking a short break away from the heat of the furnace. The pipe, which he took from his pocket and lit casually, confirmed this.

The man was clearly not a workman. There was something in his nonchalant manner that said he was master here, and his clothes were not grime-smeared like the other men she had seen. She didn't have time to puzzle over this because the man reached beneath the folds of his shirt and, to her surprise, brought out a shiny new dagger. He proffered it, saying: "On your travels with the trader, be sure to show people what Ironvale can do." Then, without a backward glance, he left her, gaping, in a cloud of pipe smoke. She hadn't even had a chance to thank him.

The whole incident threw Tugela into confusion. Strangers, in her experience, simply did not present her with gifts. But the dagger was something special and she secreted it beneath her cloak, resolving to hide it from Kasteel. These days, there seemed to be more and more things she had to hide from her uncle.

Back at the inn, she saw that her uncle's wagon had arrived at last. But, inside, her worst fears were confirmed; he was already drunk. Kasteel was with a group of men, all roughly dressed, and he glowered at her from their midst, a tankard in his hand.

She found a corner that was quiet and where she could sit and sift through her bewildering images of Ironvale. It was there, much later, that Tolly burst in. "There's going to be a big meeting," he told her, excitedly. "Mandelbrot's riding on the City!"

Mandelbrot

Already, a large crowd had gathered at the approach to the iron bridge. The mass of people pressed hard against a cordon of men who were straining to keep them back. Beyond, at the apex of the great arch, stood an empty wagon. Tugela guessed, and the boy confirmed it, that this was the platform from which Mandelbrot would speak to the people. If she had taken a moment to think on the matter, while hurrying from the inn with Tolly, she would surely have concluded that there was no place more fitting in all of Ironvale for such an address.

At the fringe of the crowd, Tugela stopped to catch her breath. But Tolly was already searching for a gap that he could exploit. After a moment, he yelled: "Here, Tugela." When she reached the spot, he had already partially vanished into the throng. "Let me through. Let me through," he yelled. To her surprise, people obeyed. She did not hesitate; she followed him quickly, before the path could close again.

Rapidly, they worked their way through the press of bodies. Only when they neared the front, where everyone was packed together most tightly, did progress become more difficult. The people Tolly was trying to displace snarled and cursed at him. But the boy expertly deflected it all with the charm and cheek he possessed in abundance. Finally, the two of them burst through to the front. Pressed up hard against the cordon of men, they could go no further.

As she looked about her, Tugela noticed that the front ranks consisted almost exclusively of men with swords and knives in their belts – obviously fighters. Very likely, they were men who had seen combat with Mandelbrot.

A murmur rose from the crowd. Tugela noticed that a dozen or so men on carriers were riding towards the bridge's far approach. Tolly pointed but she did not need to follow his finger to know that at the head of the group, taller and straighter in his saddle than the rest, was Mandelbrot. The carriers came to a halt and Mandelbrot was the last to dismount. The other men, his personal guard perhaps, quickly took up positions on either side of the empty wagon.

All around her, the fighters raised their weapons high in the air, cheering loudly. Turning about, Tugela saw this action spread back through the crowd like a wave on the surface of water. The men at the rear, it struck her, would be raising their weapons in salute before they had even caught a glimpse of their leader.

Mandelbrot strode towards the makeshift dais. Using the hub of a wheel as a step, he climbed up. A chant began spontaneously from the rear of the crowd, and propagated forward. "Mandelbrot, Mandelbrot . . ."

The object of this adoration made a lonely figure on the dais. Dressed drably in a manner no different from his men, he was set apart only by the purple armband of his office. Tugela was so close that she could even make out his eyes – a penetrating blue. They were the eyes of a young man, though they peered from the shadows and lines of a much older face. Mandelbrot was only twenty-eight years old, according to Tolly. But on his shoulders rested the weight of all the outlander hopes. And the strain of it showed.

For a while, Mandelbrot stood motionless, his feet planted slightly apart, apparently taking in the scene before him. He waited a while, perhaps expecting the chanting to die down naturally. But it showed no sign of doing so. Finally, imploringly, he gestured for quiet. There were a few more sporadic shouts while the noise died away, then all was still.

Mandelbrot took a deep breath.

"People of Ironvale," his voice boomed out. It was much deeper and carried further than Tugela had expected. It was a voice that commanded attention. "People of Ironvale. At last, we are strong enough to challenge the tyranny of the City." At this, an enormous cheer rose up. Tugela found herself cheering, too. Mandelbrot, now impatient, signalled for it to stop.

"For generations . . ." he went on. "For generations, we, the outlanders, have depended . . ." (He stopped and corrected himself, deliberately) ". . . have been *forced* to depend on the City." All around, people muttered agreement, turning to each other and nodding emphatically.

"But no more!" Mandelbrot roared.

Another enormous cheer, but, this time, the crowd contained its enthusiasm, eager to hear more. Mandelbrot strode from one side of the dais to the other, planted his hands on his hips and renewed his address.

"Centuries ago . . ." he began. Tugela noticed that the tone of his voice had changed subtly. "Centuries ago, our forbears had a dream. They dreamt that somewhere, far from the stifling influence of the City, there existed a land where they could be free – free to live in peace and to run their own lives. And because of that dream, they left the City. With their wagons piled high with everything they owned, they passed through the great mountain ring of the Circleberg and set out across the vast waste of the Thirstland.

"In the Thirstland, when it was the children that suffered most, it was the dream that kept our people going. In the wilderness beyond, where men had never set foot before, it was the dream that gave them courage to face the dangers of the unknown. The dream. Always the dream: that, one day, some-where, someplace they would find a home – *beyond* the power of the City."

Tugela was getting impatient. These were things she knew better than her own name. His speech had become a history lesson, like the ones she and every other outlander child were given from the time they were able to walk. But, though she was impatient to hear things that were new, a part of her understood what Mandelbrot was doing. He was reminding people of their past. History was important. In the wilderness lands, it had been the collective memory of the hardship that they had suffered that had been the bond that held the outlanders together. And now, each time the story was repeated, it served to reaffirm that bond.

"Out here ..." Mandelbrot continued, motioning with a grandiose sweep of his arm. "Out here, on the very rim of the Land, we believed that we had put enough distance between us and the City." As he spoke, imperceptibly, the "they" had become the "we"; there was complete identification with the past. The outlanders were their history. It defined them, it gave them their identity as a race.

"Out here, in the wilderness, we planted our shatterpines to break the hard bedrock into soil. Then, we sowed the seeds of our crops. And as our crops put down their roots, so, too, did our people. From the wilderness of the outlands, we wrested a hard and meagre living. Through our toil and through our sweat, we made a life in the barren wastes.

"But the dream – the dream of finally being free – remained always a dream. Never, not for a single instant, has the City relaxed its stranglehold on the economy of the Land. Never has it allowed us to break free of our stifling chains."

In the crowd, a collective anger rose to the surface and began to boil over. Someone shouted "Death to the City!" and the crowd drew in its breath, appalled and at the same time exhilarated that someone had dared to utter such a blasphemy in public.

"For generations ..." continued Mandelbrot. "For generations, we have been forced to sell the produce of our farms to them. The City, despite all our efforts, has held on to its position as the major market in the Land. It sets the prices – and we all know what prices they are!"

"They cheated me!" a man immediately behind Tugela shouted.

"And me!" came another angry voice, this time some way off

to one side. "A pittance, that's all I got for a whole year's crops."

Mandelbrot paused until there was quiet again. "The City's prices have kept us poor and downtrodden, barely able to cling to our lands. By cheating us of what our produce is worth, the priests have prevented us from developing our own markets — markets which might have competed with the City's own.

"But the stranglehold is tighter even than this. For generations, we have been forced to buy all our metal goods from them. The priesthood — Parnassas and his Elite — has jealously guarded the secret of metals. When we have needed tools and farm implements, we have had no choice but to buy them from the City — and at grossly inflated prices. And as for weapons — of course, they would not sell those to us at all.

"But now, my friends," Mandelbrot roared, his face suddenly flushed, "things are changing!"

At this, the crowd went mad. Even Tugela, who until this moment had been little more than an observer in the crowd, was caught up in the euphoria. Tolly danced up and down, screeching at the top of his voice. A stranger hugged her and she hugged him back.

"At last . . ." Mandelbrot shouted, fighting to be heard above the din. "At last we have smashed their monopoly on metals. Now, slowly but remorselessly, we are breaking the stranglehold they have on the economy of our Land. Already, hundreds of farmers, across the length and breadth of the outlands, are defying the City by refusing to sell it their produce.

"The price of our defiance is high. In this struggle, farmers — their wives and their children — stand on the front line just as surely as soldiers. But our action is biting hard, I assure you. With each passing seventh, the City becomes more desperate. Witness how it lashes out at us in ever more brutal acts of retribution . . ."

"They burnt our farm!" Tugela shouted. Mandelbrot's words had struck home. Her face was suddenly red, and tears were streaming down her cheeks. "My father wouldn't sell to the City, and they sent their soldiers . . ." The floodgates opened. The horror that she had buried in her mind in the interests of her plain day-to-day survival overwhelmed her, she could hold it back no longer . . .

Black smoke lies writhing and twisting in the sky above Boschendale.

Riding alone in the hills, she looks down to see the ugly spiral rising from the tiny huddle of buildings in the valley. At first (incredibly), the sight merely puzzles her. Who can have lit such a large fire so close to the farm buildings? But full understanding is only an instant away. She sees the line of soldiers kicking up dust as they ride away across the fields and her world explodes.

No!!!

She is leaping dry ditches and thorn hedges in the glutinous slow motion of a bad dream. If it takes her any longer to reach the valley bottom, she will surely go mad. The smoke column grows thicker, orange flames erupt inside. As she bursts through the last line of hedges and leaps to the ground, her senses are overwhelmed. The heat is terrific, the crackling roar of the flames deafening. The smoke stings her eyes until she can barely see. Stumbling, she weaves her way past the outbuildings to the farmhouse. But the heat is too much for her and she is forced to retreat. Everything she knows, the miniature landscape of her childhood, has been transformed into a roiling inferno.

She screams for her parents. She screams the names of the farmhands. And she goes on screaming, though the din of combustion makes it quite futile, though she knows that nobody could survive for a moment in the heart of that ferocious fire. From as close as she can bear, she watches as the farm is consumed. Never has she considered that it would come to this. Never. The war she has heard so much about was to happen someplace else, far away across the Land. Not here. Not at Boschendale . . .

She catches a movement in the periphery of her vision. She turns. Through the curtain of flames, she catches it again.

Someone is alive!

Flames lick across the ground she must cross. She has no choice but to skirt around them and approach from another direction. In the dirt, she finds Jed, the stable boy. He is barely alive. His clothes are blackened by the fire. Beside him in the dust a large purple stain is spreading slowly. He is dying from a sword wound. She has never seen so much blood.

There is nothing she can do but cradle his head on her lap. "My parents," she says, "they're dead, aren't they?" For a moment, she gets no response, and she thinks that perhaps he is already too far gone to hear her. But then, Jed lifts his head a little. He shakes it before falling back, exhausted. "They're alive?" She cannot believe it. How could they have survived? He points feebly and she realises that he is pointing in the direction of the soldiers. "They took my parents away? Back to the City?" But he does not answer. Nobody has ever died in her arms before.

"Now, now, you poor dear." Tugela came back to the present to find an old woman with her arm around her shoulder. Tolly was holding on to her sleeve, looking at her with genuine concern. All around her, people were comforting her with kind words, with gentle pats on the back. She was awash in a sea of sympathy.

Mandelbrot, who had clearly stopped his address at her interruption, began again. One by one, the people turned back, until the boy alone was watching her. She wiped her tear-stained face on her sleeve, stuck out her chin, and looked straight ahead. But she found that she could not concentrate. She could not stop thinking of her parents, probably held in the deepest dungeons of the City and being subjected to who knew what tortures. God, she couldn't bear to think what might be happening to them . . .

Mandelbrot was saying: "One man alone has brought about this miracle. First, he discovered the secret of making metals, then he built the forges of Ironvale, which are already outproducing the City." As he spoke, Mandelbrot strode to the edge of the dais. Stooping, he helped someone up to join him. The man, who was short and stocky, clambered on to the stage. When he stood up straight, he was dwarfed by the tall, thin figure of Mandelbrot. The two men embraced before the crowd.

Tugela gasped surprise taking her out of her reverie. "That man," she hissed, grabbing Tolly by the arm. "He's the one! He's the one who gave me the dagger!" Swiftly, she pulled it from the folds of her cloak and passed it to Tolly. He fingered its hilt gingerly. Astonished, he looked first at the stocky man on the dais, then back at Tugela.

"This is the man . . ." Mandelbrot was saying. "This is the man who will ensure our victory." With this, the crowd began chanting again. But this time the chant was not for Mandelbrot. "Stel. Stel. Stel . . ."

Peet Stel himself had given her the dagger. And she had not recognised him!

Tolly gave back the dagger. For a moment, Tugela was too stunned to notice what was happening on the dais. When she looked again, she saw that Mandelbrot was no longer visible. He had left centre stage to the shorter man; to the Man of Metal, to Peet Stel.

Stel's voice was not as powerful as Mandelbrot's and Tugela was certain it did not carry as far. Luckily, being so close to the front of the crowd, she heard every word.

Reiterating what Mandelbrot had earlier, Stel said that the outlanders were now outproducing the City in metals. But, he insisted, this was merely the beginning. The priesthood – Parnassas and his Elite – understood none of the processes that went into the creation of metals. Instead, they followed blindly recipes passed down from generation to generation, recipes enshrined in their sacred litanies. Stel, on the other hand, had

developed what he called a "science of metals". He relied, as
Tugela had heard said before, on "chemistry not recipes". Like
the City, he knew how the rocks could be made to yield their
precious metals. But, more importantly, he knew *why*. That was
power, Stel said, power of a sort the City had never possessed.

Stel finished his address, and there was uproar once more. He
bowed several times, and Mandelbrot embraced him; then the
short man jumped down from the stage.

"Now, we, the outlanders, have the advantage," Mandelbrot
declared. "Soon, we ride on the City!"

Tugela expected that that was the last note of Mandelbrot's
address, that the crowd would now begin to disperse. But when
the cheering had at last died down, she became aware of a
stirring behind her. "Wait!" And then again: "Wait!" She
turned, along with the people around her, but, as yet, she could
see no one. On the dais, Mandelbrot waited patiently.

Finally, a man broke through to the front some distance from
Tugela. The cordon of Mandelbrot's men parted and the man
climbed on to the dais (without Mandelbrot's help, Tugela
noticed). There was a short exchange between them, which was
inaudible. But she saw Mandelbrot nod, then stand aside with
his arms crossed on his chest. The man turned to face the crowd.
Tugela could see nothing remarkable about him, except his eyes.
They burned with an intensity that was disturbing. Silence
descended and the man announced himself.

"My name is Toover and I speak for the League of Reason."
Mandelbrot stiffened noticeably. "Is there not something we
have forgotten, something we have perhaps overlooked?" The
sarcasm was not lost on Tugela. Toover scanned the crowd,
fully expecting an answer. When it did not come, he went on.
"The City controls more than simply the technology of metals
and the economy of the Land. It summons the comets, too, the
comets that bring air to the Land." He paused again, to let his
words sink in. Tugela knew what was coming.

"By making *these* . . ." (and he pulled a sword from his cloak and held it up), "By making these things of metal, we are committing the ultimate blasphemy. Already the City is punishing us for our sins by taking away the air we breathe. If we march against the City, we will increase its ire. What more will it do to us? What other punishments will we provoke?"

"What more can they do to us than they are doing?" a woman shouted not far from Tugela. "Is there anything worse than death by suffocation?"

Toover fixed her with his gaze, the gaze of a fanatic. "There are many things worse than death by suffocation," he replied. "Many things." The man knew enough about the fears and superstitions of the outlanders not to say any more. Their imaginations would be more than enough to do the rest. Even Tugela, though she would not have admitted it, felt a terrifying sense of unease about defying the City.

Toover continued. "Every one of you has seen the Eyes abroad. I ask you, can anyone remember a time when there were more of them in our skies?" There was silence. "Be warned, the priests of the City watch our every move." With that, Toover left the stage.

"Toover is right," someone shouted. "We will burn for ever for our sins." There were other mutterings in the crowd. The people had been unnerved by Toover's words. They were no longer as certain of themselves and their cause as they had been only moments before.

Mandelbrot watched Toover go, then held up his arms to quieten the audience.

"This is my answer . . . For generations, we have been powerless in the face of a tyrant. Now, at last, we have the power to overthrow it. Can we really pass up the chance to break our chains and finally be free?" He paused. "Today, we stand within a hair's breadth of victory and only one thing holds us back. Yet that one thing is the most difficult thing of all to change. It is the way we think about ourselves. We may have a hundred times as many men as the City, a hundred times as many weapons. But if we believe, here, in our hearts, that we are mere mortals and they are gods, we will never prevail. The City will hold us in bondage for ever.

"Are they gods or are they men? In the end, that is what it comes down to. At Two Bridges and at Winterberg, we faced soldiers who were men not gods. Their blood flowed as freely as any outlanders' and my men were witnesses to it. I believe that their masters in the City are made of flesh and blood, too. I can say no more than this."

And with that, Mandelbrot jumped down from his makeshift platform. With the crowd cheering ecstatically, he collected his escort and strode towards his waiting carrier. As they rode away, the crowd began gradually to disperse, leaving Tugela and Tolly at the great iron bridge, still a little dazed by it all.

Clearly, Mandelbrot had managed to carry the crowd with him; the cheers he received were proof enough of that. But he had not been unopposed. Tugela was now aware of the two factions among the outlanders. The faction led by Toover was in a minority. But would it stay that way, she wondered? Toover had planted a seed of unease in the minds of the outlanders. As Mandelbrot rode towards the City at the head of his Kommando, that seed would have ample time to take root and grow. Long before the conflict with the outlanders and the City, there might be another conflict which would determine whether it would take place at all: a conflict between the power of Mandelbrot's personality and the power of superstition. Tugela suddenly felt the urgency of her situation.

She turned to the boy. "Tolly," she said, clutching his arm tightly. He was still in a daze after the speech.

"Yes, miss?" he said.

"Tolly, I must talk to Mandelbrot." Suddenly, the boy came back to life.

"Talk to Mandelbrot! What about?"

"My parents . . . in the City. I want to ask him whether . . ."

She broke off. "Look, all I want to know is, can you take me to him? *Can you?*"

Tolly looked at her, dubiously.

"To Mandelbrot?" he repeated, as if it had just dawned on him what she was asking.

"To Mandelbrot," she insisted. "*Please.* I have to speak with him."

For a moment, Tolly considered the request. Then he said: "All right, all right, miss, I'll try."

In retrospect, it was surprising how far they got: past the corral for the carriers, past the men cooking around fires, and a large part of the way to the largest tent which, Tolly claimed, had to be Mandelbrot's. It was inevitable, however, that they would be stopped. When they were, and it looked as though the guard who had caught them would throw them out immediately, they knew what to do. They made as much noise as possible. It worked. Men got to their feet all around to see what the fuss was. And Tugela saw Mandelbrot's tent flap lift up. The General walked towards them, eating a piece of bread.

"What is it?" he asked the guard.

"These two, General. I caught them prowling. Perhaps they are spies for the City."

"No!" Tugela protested. She made a direct appeal to the thin man. "General Mandelbrot, I am no spy. I was the one who cried out during your address. Your words, they brought it all back to me. The burning of our farm at Boschendale, the capture of my parents . . ." Her voice faltered. Mandelbrot's frown deepened.

"We will punish the men who did it, I promise you that."

"I am sure that you will, General Mandelbrot. But that will not get my parents back. Will you . . ." She hesitated a moment, then, screwing up her courage, spat it out: "Will you take me with you to the City so that I can find them?"

Mandelbrot's fierce expression lightened in surprise. One or two soldiers sniggered.

"I cannot take you to the City, girl. We are riding to war."

Tugela's voice rose in desperation. "If you cannot take me to the City, then take me as far as you can – to the Circleberg, even. That will be enough."

Mandelbrot chewed thoughtfully at the bread. Then, he said: "Who is your guardian in Ironvale?"

"My uncle. Kasteel, the trader." The General nodded distractedly.

"Get his permission and I may take you."

With that, Tugela's brief audience was over. Mandelbrot strode back to his tent to finish his meal and Tugela and Tolly were unceremoniously thrown out.

Kasteel's permission! Tugela thought, bitterly, as they walked disconsolately along the river. *He'd have to be sober to give that.*

Much later, they stood gloomily on the iron bridge and watched the Kommando ride out of Ironvale. As the knot of carriers dwindled, so did Tugela's hopes of ever reaching her parents. She left Tolly and went back to the inn to sleep. It was there, later, that a loud commotion outside the building woke her. A wagon had run over a man, trapping his leg. The man turned out to be Kasteel. He had been drunk, of course.

The leg was not as bad as it looked, the doctor had said. Kasteel had been fortunate not to suffer a break. It might take only a day or so before he was back on his feet, sore and limping, or it might take much longer; the doctor could not say.

Faced with the prospect of being stuck with Kasteel in Ironvale for any length of time, Tugela came to a sudden decision. While the doctor tended to her uncle's leg, she collected up her bag of things. Outside, she headed for their wagon, where, carefully, deliberately, she unhitched the lead carrier. In a swift motion, she swung herself on to its back.

Much later, she thought to glance back at Ironvale, but by then it had already vanished behind high hills.

Kommando

They flew like glideagles across the Land, and all that they passed was a grey-green blur. How long they had been riding, Tugela could no longer tell; they might have been in motion for ever. Grimly, she clung to the neck of her mount, fighting back waves of fatigue. If she let down her guard and revealed her exhaustion, even for an instant, Mandelbrot might see. And she dared not give him an excuse to send her back to Ironvale.

Tugela glanced across at the rider called Faro, who had been her shadow since she had joined the Kommando. Wrapped tightly in his cloak and the mantle of his thoughts, he was infinitely remote from her. Like most of the men, Faro had done his best to completely ignore her presence. She was a nuisance to them, a burden they could do without. They suffered her because Mandelbrot said that they must. But no one could make them like it.

To Tugela, it still seemed something of a miracle that Mandlebrot had allowed her to stay. Even to her own ears the lies she had told him had sounded hollow.

She remembered the first sight of the dust on the horizon as she had finally caught up with them. The sight should have brought relief but it only filled her with dread. On the long, lonely ride through the Thirstland, with cold wind chilling her through and through, doubts had set in where only certainty had dwelt before. She had an infinity of time, during the flight from Ironvale, to reflect on the rashness of her impulse, and on the feebleness of the story she had rehearsed over and over.

"My uncle," she had blurted out to Mandelbrot. "He got drunk, and a wagon filled with ore . . . it crushed his leg. They say it's badly broken and it'll be weeks, longer even, before he can ride again. But I just have to get to the City, to find my mother and father. I have to. So I rode after you across the Thirstland, I rode without stopping . . . You will take me with you, won't you? You will . . ?"

Mandelbrot had listened impassively while, all around, a tight knot of carriers snorted noisily, their hot flanks steaming in the bitter cold. Weathered men glowered at her from beneath the hoods of their capes. "It's true, sir," she had gone on quickly, before the silence could accuse her. "My uncle . . . I have to get to the City."

Mandelbrot only looked past her, not at her. He scanned back along the path the Kommando had travelled, then twisted in his saddle to peer at the other horizon, below which lurked the City. He did not betray any emotion. Not a word of anger passed his lips, not a word of any kind. But he emanated power and authority. It was the casual, nonchalant power of the predator secure in the knowledge that it has all the time in the world, because no creature exists that is its match. For the first time, Tugela understood why men followed Mandelbrot, and she felt not a little afraid of him.

Without warning, Mandelbrot snatched up the reins of his carrier and wheeled it round. "Faro," he called out sharply. "You, look after the girl. She rides with us – for now."

And so she had succeeded in joining the Kommando.

Had Mandelbrot really believed her story? She very much doubted it. Later, she came to learn the real reason why she had been allowed to remain with them. The Kommando had passed close to a City patrol. It did not veer from its course, and the patrol, never more than a line of specks along a distant ridge, soon vanished. Faro, in a rare moment of shared confidence, told her it was not the first patrol that they had come across, and that their progress was being monitored closely by the City. Clearly, then, her story had been immaterial. Mandelbrot had let her stay simply because it was too dangerous to send her back. That was all there was to it.

The Kommando consisted of roughly eighty men. That made it large by any standards; it was certainly the largest that Tugela could ever remember. It was formed, as was the custom, from a group of local farmers, men who already knew each other well and probably had done so since boyhood. Tugela noted the odd manner in which the men pronounced a handful of common words and was able to place the Kommando's origin firmly in the Transochria, beyond the Blue Mountains, a region not more than two days' ride from her own birthplace at Boschendale. When she had asked him, Faro confirmed her suspicion with a grunt.

The Kommando, of course, would have formed quite spontaneously. That was the custom, too, in the Land: the Way. Men simply came together, when they perceived a common threat, to their farms, to their way of life itself. The Kommando was the articulation of a collective need. It was an organic thing which had a life only as long as there was a collective will to keep it together. Then, at no discernible signal, and just as spontaneously as it had formed, the Kommando would begin to fall apart, melt back into the landscape from which it had formed, to coalesce and reform again when next there was a need.

Mandelbrot's Kommando would be just one of dozens converging on the gap in the Great Circleberg which ringed the plain of the City. It would be the greatest show of force from the outlanders the City had ever seen. What could stop them now?

But Tugela knew that there were indeed many things that could stop them. And chief among them was not the might of the City but the outlanders' perception of its might. The enemy within, eroding their courage, feeding on their tiredness. She could feel the apprehension in the air. With each hour that passed, the warnings of Toover and the League of Reason gained more solidity in her mind, and, without doubt, they did so in the minds of the others, too. Even those who, back in Ironvale, had dismissed those warnings as the ravings of the superstitious, must be wondering, as the City sped towards them, whether they were not about to commit the ultimate blasphemy.

If they thought the enemy invincible, then it was invincible. Mandelbrot had said that. She only hoped that he had a plan to defeat the enemy that lurked deep in their hearts.

On the ride, though, there were distractions, which kept them from too much dangerous introspection. City patrols continued to shadow them, appearing without warning in the distance and vanishing before the Kommando could close on them. There were wagons, too, some solitary, some in despondent columns of up to ten or twenty, all heading for the Great Depression with its thicker air and the promise of running water. Some passengers, mostly children, waved and cheered enthusiastically as the Kommando passed by, others barely raised their heads, perhaps still seeing in their mind's eyes the parched and suffocated farms they had left behind. And, of course, there were the Eyes, difficult to pick out in the brightness of the sky but ever-present, nonetheless. Tugela could not remember a time when the sky had been filled with so many of the City's silver spies.

Once, in the Thirstland, the Kommando stopped. Enormously relieved, Tugela dismounted and found herself a place to rest in the lee of some large boulders. While she watched distractedly, several of the men had begun digging with spades in the bone-hard bed of a river and, very soon, found muddy water. All, including Tugela, drank their fill. Then, to her horror and dismay, Mandelbrot gave the curt order to ride on. There was no protesting. As she clambered back on her carrier, her limbs felt made of iron.

Now the Kommando was slowing again. This time, she prayed, they *must* make camp. The column veered sharply away from the line that led to the City and, for a while, rode up a gentle incline. Abruptly, the slope ended. From a ridge which swept round in a great arc, Tugela found herself looking down on a great natural bowl. Mandelbrot directed guards, six in all, to distribute themselves at regular intervals around the periphery. So they were to make camp! Tugela gave silent thanks. Mandelbrot had obviously decided that, within the bowl, the Kommando would be hidden from City patrols. As the six rode away in clouds of dust, he led the bulk of the Kommando down into the great hollow. They were now close to the Circleberg, Faro told her.

Even before they drew to a halt and dismounted, Tugela realised that this was a curious place that they had come to. The floor of the great amphitheatre was punctured by holes, not unlike the post holes that might be left in the ground long after a house had crumbled to dust. The holes were regularly spaced in the pattern of a grid. Most were filled almost to the brim with dust and, consequently, not easy to pick out. They were about ten strides apart.

Even the place Mandelbrot chose to camp was studded with the mysterious holes. Evidently, most of the men in the Kommando had seen this place before for none of them remarked on it. She asked Faro what this place had been but he just shrugged. "No one knows," he said, taking food from his saddle bags. After she had eaten, curiosity got the better of her despite her exhaustion. She set off to explore.

No shatterpines had been planted in the bowl to break the hard rock into usable soil but the diurnal variation in heat had fractured it sufficiently to allow some wind-borne seeds to grow. Wiry bushes grew in clumps, some as tall as a man, and she was soon out of sight of the men and carriers. Ahead, on the ramparts of the bowl, she spotted the silhouette of one of the lookouts against the watery pink of the sky.

She turned her attention again to the post holes at her feet. Kneeling, she put her hand into one and began scooping out the dust. The hole was deep. She dug on. When her fingertips finally struck hard bedrock, her face was pressed flat against the ground and her arm was buried up to her shoulder. With an effort, she strained to scoop out the last handful of dust.

Beside her a small conical pile had now grown. She sat on her haunches to rest. It was only after a while that it dawned on her what was so startling about the pile. *It was a different colour to the surrounding ground.* Instead of being white, it was much darker, almost a reddy brown. Intrigued, Tugela peered back in the hole. Sure enough, the lining was the same dark, reddy brown. To Tugela, the conclusion seemed inescapable: whatever had filled the hole had rusted away until nothing at all was left. But what could it have been?

If a building had stood in the great amphitheatre, it must have been enormous. Not even the priests of the City could have built something *this* large. If not a building, then what? Tugela could not think. Anything built on such a vast scale would surely have been talked of across the length and breadth of the Land. Wouldn't it? Then why had Tugela never heard people talk of this place?

Another thought sprung into her mind. A thing of metal as large as this would have taken a long time to rust into non-existence. Then this place had to be old, very old. Where were her thoughts taking her? Suddenly, she did not like where they were going at all. They were forcing her to conclude that this place was much older than the City, much older than the Land itself. By now, she seemed to be piling impossibility on impossibility. The Land and all its people had been created five hundred years ago. Before that was . . . was, well, nothing. How could there be anything that was older?

Fatigue rose in her like a tide, threatening to submerge her. She stumbled groggily back to the camp. As she bedded down beside the others, many of whom were already asleep, her mind was full of unsolved puzzles. There were more things in the Land than had explanations. Already, on this trip, she had seen an Eye venture into the Forbidden Zone. Here was another mystery. Could there, perhaps, be a connection? It was her last dying thought as she gave in and tiredness finally overwhelmed her.

Her sleep was fitful and filled with ugly dreams. In one, she had reached the City but it was blazing out of control. From the bowels of the world, her mother was crying out: "Help me, someone. Help me, please!"

"Mother!" Tugela was paralysed by indecision. All around her, buildings were disintegrating and falling. "Where, Mother? Where?"

The heat was terrible, the noise and the smoke. Far beneath her feet, came a cry like that from a wounded animal. "Father!"

Tugela plunged into a maze of burning streets. Fire rained down so hard she could hardly see ahead. But her mother's sobbing was getting closer. Once more, her father cried out.

"I'm coming, I'm coming!" Ahead, an iron grating was set into the road. She knew beyond any doubt that it led to the bowels of the City. But suddenly the street had filled with people. They stampeded past her in blind panic, and she had to fight her way through them.

She pulled at the grating with all her might. But it would not budge! "Help me! They're torturing my parents!" She grabbed a man's arm, but he yanked free of her grip and continued running. "The outlanders are coming!" he shouted back at her. "Got to get away." She grabbed at another man, and another, but they all pulled away.

"Help me!" It was a cry of awful, gut-wrenching despair.

She awoke, suddenly, her face wet with tears. Several of the Kommando were looking at her queerly but none got up from his blanket to comfort her. Ashamed of her involuntary show of emotion, she hid her face while she wiped away the tears.

Later, fatigue drew her back into the land of nightmares.

Circleberg

"This is where our ways part. I'm sorry."

Mandelbrot's words were still ringing in Tugela's ears as she picked her way down the steep slope to the valley floor below. Opposite, on the far slope, a thin ribbon of white smoke twisted above the ranks of densely packed shatterpines. All the girl's hopes were now pinned on the source of that smoke. Please, she prayed, her lips moving silently, let me find someone there who knows a way through the Circleberg. Mandelbrot, by refusing to allow her to travel any further with the Kommando, had left her with no alternative but to find her own way to the gates of the City. But that was impossible without the help of a guide.

By now the Kommando would have made camp by the entrance to the main pass through Circleberg. Mandelbrot had made the decision not to move on the City until other Kommandos arrived to reinforce him. He had also decided, as they approached the pass, to shed all non-combatants. Tugela alone of his company fell into that category.

She understood well Mandelbrot's reasons for leaving her behind, and bore him no ill will for his action (how far, after all, would she have travelled without his help?). The battle, when it came, was likely to be a bloody one — she had no illusions on that score. Since she had no desire to die just yet, it was best she was out of it. Nevertheless, she had come too far to be denied a sight of the City. If a way existed to cross the Circleberg, she was determined to find it.

It was a hunch, no more, that she might find help in the foothills of the Circleberg itself. From Steenscamp, the tiny settlement on the Ochre River where he had abandoned her, she had struck out on foot towards the great ring of mountains, careful, of course, to give Mandelbrot's men a wide berth. Her plan – if that wasn't too grand a label to attach to it – was to seek out someone who possessed an intimate knowledge of the mountains, a shepherd perhaps. If there was another way through, maybe only a track used by goats, such a man would, surely, know of it.

Wheezing a little under the weight of her belongings, which she carried in a rough sack across her back, Tugela at last reached the foot of the slope. A stream had once run along the valley but, like countless others across the Land, it had now dried up. Its bed was strewn with boulders, some as large as a full-grown man. In Tugela's mind, they conjured up an image of the stream each spring, when the melting snows on the High Circleberg transformed it into an irresistible torrent, sweeping all before it.

One of the smaller boulders made a good place to sit and Tugela took the opportunity to rest a while. High above, a glideagle wheeled against the watery pink sky. Its cry, shrill and plaintive, reached her on the back of the thin wind. Something it carried in its talons caught the Sun – once, twice, a third time. Then the bird flew out of the sunlight and into the shadows. For a while, Tugela waited, but it did not reappear. With a sigh, she got to her feet, slung her sack across her shoulders and headed for the trees.

The climb proved a lot easier than she had expected. Though the path upwards through the forest was steep, it was well-trammelled. From the droppings scattered liberally along its route, it was apparent that goats made frequent use of the track. This raised her hopes immediately. As luck would have it, she had stumbled on the dwelling of a hill shepherd.

The clearing, when it finally came, caught her completely unawares. One moment, she was slipping and sliding on what was the steepest portion of the track, using her hands to steady her, the next moment she had burst into bright, dazzling sunlight after the track had made an abrupt change in direction. Not unreasonably, she had expected the track to begin to level out

as it neared the clearing. As she blinked, she could immediately
see why her intuition was wrong. The house, little more than a
large hut really, far from being built on a level piece of hillside,
had been erected on a rather steep portion. What Tugela hadn't
reckoned on was the terracing. Shallow steps, a score or more
of them, had been cut in the side of the hill.

She advanced into the clearing.

Nobody seemed to be about. Besides the single-storey house,
there was nothing there apart from a rough lean-to stacked with
logs, newly cut. The house itself, through necessity, was built on
more than one level. The door seemed to be ajar but she would
have to approach closer to peer in. Cautiously, she edged
forward.

"Who are you?" A gruff male voice startled her. Tugela
turned on her heels. Facing her now, at a distance of several
paces, was a man, unarmed except for a large knife tucked into
his belt. (Experience had taught her to notice such things first.)
The man, who was perhaps forty with a grizzled countenance,
was wearing a rough shirt over loose, ill-fitting trousers. Though
he was chronically under-dressed for the cold, he did not seem
to notice (perhaps he had been working). The man looked her
up and down in a way that unsettled her. The thought that she
might have to run crossed her mind. But he made no attempt to
come any closer, so, she eventually decided to trust him. What
option did she have, after all? In a voice that she tried to make
firm and confident, Tugela told him who she was and what she
wanted. He listened but said nothing.

"I can pay," she said, hurriedly. At this, the man seemed to
show a modicum of interest. "In my bag, here . . ." Throwing
her bag down on the ground, she delved for a moment and
brought out the dagger. When she proffered it, the man came
closer but did not take it. He looked at her queerly as if to say,
how did someone like you ever come to own such a thing? "Peet
Stel gave it me," she said. Clearly, the man was impressed,

because he repeated the name Peet Stel to himself as if savouring the flavour of the words.

"So, my girl," he said, "you've travelled out by the Periphery. Is is true what they say, that the Man of Metal can duplicate the science of the City?"

"Is this dagger not proof of that?"

The man took the dagger from her. He turned it slowly in his hands, examining it closely. "Yes," he said. "I'll grant you, it's as good as anything made in the City." He gave back the dagger and then went silent as if thinking. After a while, he said: "I know a pass through the mountains, yes."

"You'll take me then?" She tried not to sound too eager.

He smiled. "Too fast. First, come inside, and join us for supper."

Did that mean, yes – that he was going to take her? Tugela did not like to push her luck. Be patient, she told herself. She followed the man into the house, into a large kitchen where she was met by steam and marvellous smells from bubbling pots.

"Tannie, we have a visitor."

A large, robust woman with rosy cheeks who emanated good humour shouted a welcome from a corner of the kitchen. She was cutting vegetables of some kind on a chopping board.

"Your name?" the man asked.

"Tugela."

"Her name is Tugela, Tannie, and she has been to the workshops of Peet Stel out on the Periphery."

"Peet Stel!" the woman echoed. The name seemed to have as big an effect on the woman as it had done earlier on her husband. Immediately, she dropped what she was doing and swept over to Tugela. She grabbed her hand and pumped it heartily.

"Then you are doubly welcome, my girl. Sit yourself down. Over supper, you will tell us all you know."

"Show Tannie the dagger," the man said. Obediently, Tugela took it out.

"Peet Stel made this?" the woman exclaimed incredulously. She held it to the light and admired it. "Then there *is* hope for us, is there not? An end at last to the tyranny of the City."

Supper was wonderfully good. Tugela could hardly remember the last time she had eaten so well. Between mouthfuls of hot bread and goat stew, she told of Peet Stel and Ironvale and the ride with Mandelbrot through the Great Depression and across the Thirstland. At intervals, Tannie topped up Tugela's tankard with a hot, mulled wine, which made her head spin. From a huge pot on the table, her husband scooped meat and vegetables, heaping them on to Tugela's plate until she protested that if she ate another mouthful she would very probably explode. On and on, she talked, goaded constantly for more details by her onlookers, until the muscles of her face ached from the strain of conversation, such a novelty after the long ride with Mandelbrot's taciturn men.

The curiosity which her audience displayed was like a thirst Tugela was unable to quench. They wanted to know more and more of the events among the outlanders on the Periphery. Her answers were never enough to satisfy them. For the first time, Tugela began to realise just how little news had penetrated this far in and what a stranglehold the City had on the channels of information in the Land.

Finally, when it seemed to Tugela that if she talked any longer her voice might disappear altogether, Tannie rose to her feet and began to collect up the empty plates. On her signal, her husband (who, Tugela gathered from the conversation was called Rant) also got to his feet. Wiping the wine from his chin with the back of his hand, he announced: "Tugela, if you're ready now, I'll take you through the Circleberg." Tugela went for her bag, but before she could get to it, the man's voice rose suddenly in annoyance. "No, Tugela," he said. "I'll take no payment for it. The news you bring of Peet Stel is enough for us. You have cheered our hearts in this time of troubles."

While Tannie disappeared in the kitchen, Rant put on a heavy coat made of skins and lifted a stick from a peg on the wall. His wife returned with a parcel of food and a canteen of water which Tugela accepted gratefully. At the door, she embraced Tugela and wished her luck. Tugela was astonished at the warmth of these people who she had known little more than a few hours. She kissed the older woman and thanked Tannie for her kindness. Moments later, she was straining to keep up with Rant as he climbed a steep path through the forest.

It was impossible to remember in detail the route that Rant followed through the contorted mountains of the Circleberg. Later, all that remained in Tugela's mind were visual fragments, the correct time sequence of which she could never quite recall. At one time, she remembered looking down on an abandoned farmstead, clinging desperately to a bare hillside, with shatter-pines lying like matchwood all about, flattened by a recent avalanche of mud or snow. Another time, they were in the gloom of a deep canyon, with sheer walls rising on either side. Only a thin sliver of pink sky gave illumination as they clambered across rockfalls which would have choked off the river if there had been any river left to choke. Once, Rant saved her when she lost her footing, once she saved herself, grabbing at a branch as she careered down a scree slope on her back. She broke no bones, fortunately, but afterwards her back felt like raw meat.

The Circleberg, being just a thin annulus round the plain of the City, did not take long to cross. But it was hard going every step of the way and Tugela lost all sight of her goal. Instead, her attention became focused exclusively on the ground at her feet and the immediate challenge that it posed. It was for this reason that she failed to notice that Rant had stopped abruptly on the brow of a hill. Consequently, she almost bumped in to him. "What is it?" she asked. He was staring, his hands planted on his hips, at a gap in the mountain range ahead. Tugela saw something glinting on the horizon.

"What do *you* think it is?" Rant asked rhetorically.

"The City?" she ventured. Rant confirmed it with a nod.

Nothing had prepared her for the reality of what, until now, had been merely a construct of her imagination, pieced together from eyewitness accounts and tales she had been told on her father's knee. It had been a fantasy. Now the fantasy had come to life. When, finally, it sank in, really sank in, that she had reached her goal, she let out a whoop of joy; When Rant laughed at her, she felt a little silly. "Come on," he said, and he led her on. Suddenly, her tiredness had gone, she was walking on air.

She had succeeded. She had made it to the plain of the City. And, what's more, she was ahead of Mandelbrot.

It was amazing how easy their progress became now that her goal was at last in sight. In no time at all, Tugela was looking down from the inner ramparts of the Circleberg on a thin black column which emerged from a gap in the Circleberg and stabbed out across the Great Plain. The column was heading straight for the City. Rant took her lower still and the column resolved itself into men and women and children, into animals and wagons. Tugela even saw a detachment of City soldiers, riding their carriers at full pelt.

When she descended further, however, it was without Rant. He wished her luck and departed. For a while, she had stood watching his figure dwindle and then disappear. Somehow her thanks had seemed inadequate for the kindness he had shown. But there was not much she could do about it now.

She descended the hillside alone. Quietly, and without any fuss, she joined the column marching towards the distant City.

City

It seemed as if the whole world was going her way. Tugela had never been in the middle of so many people on the move. If she stopped now and sat herself down in the road, she had no doubt that the current of people would simply lift her up and sweep her along with it. She would be deposited, whether she liked it or not, at the gates of the City.

As she followed the road across the Plain, Tugela passed entire families, struggling under the weight of their belongings. She passed wagons, too, piled to toppling point with supplies of food. The City was evidently preparing for a long siege. The realisation of this cheered Tugela immensely. In her head, she had always known that the outlanders had a chance of victory but in her heart of hearts she had never really believed it. Too many stories of the power of the City had sown in her the expectation that the outlanders would be crushed like insects under foot (the enemy within again). But the wagons piled so high told Tugela a different story.

The City does not believe that it is invincible.

As she inspected her companions on the road, Tugela found more evidence to support her conclusion. These people were quite clearly ordinary farming folk, indistinguishable from the outlanders. (Hadn't it been easy for her to blend in with them, after all?) They were afraid. Tugela could smell their fear – and it smelled no different from her own.

Many of the wagons that Tugela passed were festooned with people who clung to their sides at all possible angles. Hanging on in this way, however, was a risky business because the road over which the wagons trundled was badly rutted. On more than one occasion, Tugela passed a wagon which had broken an axle or shattered a wheel, spilling its produce, together with its passengers, across the road. Invariably, City soldiers had arrived promptly on the scene. With shouts and dire threats, they warned against looting.

And all the time, more refugees came, swelling the ranks of the column. They converged on the road from farms all across the Great Plain of the City. And in all their minds a single thought had gained ascendancy, driving away all others, repeated over and over. No one articulated it but Tugela could see it in the eyes of people as surely as if those eyes were windows on to their minds: *The outlanders are coming. The outlanders are coming.* And that terrifying thought compelled them onwards, always onwards, to what they presumed would be safety, within the walls of the City.

At intervals, Tugela watched detachments of soldiers ride by, their carriers kicking up great clouds of dust which settled on the column and got in her eyes. Some of the soldiers were riding towards the City and some were riding away, but the net flow, Tugela observed, was in the outward direction, towards the gap in the Circleberg where the outlander Kommandos were gathering.

At the head of one tight phalanx of soldiers, Tugela caught sight of her first priest, his white and purple robes billowing behind him as he rode. Around her, a handful of people dropped to their knees, and made the sign of the Eye. But only a handful of people showed such deference. In more stable times, Tugela knew, such disrespect would have earned an instant fine, perhaps even a beating.

The priest was the first of many Tugela saw as the column neared the gates. Figures in purple and white seemed to appear with increasing frequency, all engaged in supervising the refugees. Now, when people made the sign of the Eye, Tugela noticed, they did it wearily, almost resentfully. She made the sign, too, as they passed each priest, careful not to draw attention to herself.

They were now approaching the shanty town which ringed

the City. As far as Tugela could make out, few of the dilapidated buildings had been evacuated. Dirty children played among mounds of rotting rubbish, the stench of which was terrible. Their parents, insubstantial as ghosts, stood motionless amid the rubble of their lives, watching the column pass with faces devoid of any expression. Was this group of people, this underclass, excluded from protection even in this time of danger? Tugela wondered. Or did they have so little to lose that they feared no one, least of all the outlanders who might, just might, give their masters a hiding?

Tugela had no time to reach any conclusion on this. Ahead, a priest had dismounted from his carrier and was striding towards her. For a moment, she felt panic rise in her, but when he veered to one side and she saw that he had stopped not to question her but to check the load on a nearby wagon, she relaxed. Just what he was checking for, she did not know or care. That he was occupied with some task other than her arrest was all that mattered.

She came abreast with the priest and, along with the others around her, made the sign of the Eye. This was quite the closest she had been to a priest on the road, and she was shocked at the state of his robes. They were crumpled and stained with dust. There was even a gaping tear in the material across one shoulder, and bare skin showed through.

This was not at all what she expected. Before, on those occasions when she had seen priests travelling among the outlanders, she recalled them as clad in dazzling finery. Their power seemed to come from being so untouched, so unsoiled by the world of ordinary men. Aloof, infinitely remote, to Tugela they had seemed almost godlike. This priest, on the other hand, was soiled. Could men like him really control the air above the Land?

She could see now why the priests were engendering less respect in their subjects. It was because they were showing signs of panic as the outlander Kommandos closed on the City. They were revealing themselves as mortals not gods. But there was something else, Tugela realised, that ran even deeper than this. It fuelled the resentment she had felt so clearly in the refugees who walked with her. By withholding the air from the Land, the priests were not only suffocating the outlanders.

They were suffocating their own people, too.

The priest with the torn robes finished examining the wagon. Stepping down on to the road, he shouted angrily at those people who had stopped – more to rest their weary limbs than to gawp. The people began moving again but it was as if they were considering carefully whether to obey or not because they did not move instantly. Enraged, the priest strode back to his carrier and climbed on to it. As he had passed her, Tugela had caught a glimpse of his face. She saw rage but, beneath it was uncertainty and real fear.

The wall of the great City rose higher and higher until it seemed to blot out the sky altogether. It was a vast wall of grey stone that had been battered and sculpted by the wind of centuries. Tugela found her gaze drawn upwards now to the battlements so far above where tiny silhouetted figures stood gazing across the Plain to the great natural wall of the Circleberg.

Behind the figures black smoke rose in thin plumes high into the air. It came from the great foundries of the City, which must be working flat out in order to match the output of Ironvale. Already, Tugela could feel the ground beneath her feet trembling and shaking and there was a distant rumble like thunder. The air was becoming thick and dense with particles of soot and some people were beginning to cough.

At the entrance, the only passageway Tugela could see in the great stone wall, soldiers were standing guard. As each person went through, the soldiers examined them, poking their garments and looking into their loads. Beyond them, framed in the gateway, Tugela could see tongues of flame rising from tall towers. She remembered her thought when approaching Iron-vale with Tolly Hoopa, that maybe it was Hell that she was heading for. That time, she had been mistaken. But this place fitted the bill more closely.

When it was her turn to pass through the gate, the guard did not even look in her bag. Instead, he leered at her, looming close and until she could taste his breath, warm and stale. The next instant, his hand plunged deep inside her clothes and she went rigid. Turning away, she fought back a wave of nausea and an overwhelming urge to go for her knife and kill him. She looked about, desperate for help but no one else seemed to have noticed.

Her indignity was cut short, though, by a sudden cry from among the crowd. "Spy!" Tugela looked round to see a small grey-haired man with a cart. He was being held at the point of a sword. Although he was vigorously protesting his innocence, it seemed to be doing him no good. "Traitor! Traitor!" The guard's face was jubilant. Tugela was flung aside. In the confusion, she took the opportunity to slip away.

Suddenly, she was inside the City.

The sight that met her was one of such complete turmoil that Tugela could only stand rooted to the spot. She was on the edge of a large open square, surrounded on three sides by stone buildings of monumental size. The square was filled to bursting point with people, more than she had ever seen together in one place before, even in Ironvale. They scurried back and forth, shouting above the din, merchants, peddlers, beggars, priests, soldiers, women of the street, and people Tugela could not identify. Among them all were animals, carriers, wagons. All of her senses were assailed, even her sense of smell. The stench, which she identified as rotting vegetables and animal dung, overwhelmed her.

When she had calmed down a little, it began to sink in, really sink in, that she had made it at last to the City. But before she could savour that thought or its implications, the flow of people and wagons in through the City gate, suddenly started up again.

She was swept by the pressure of people behind into the throng before her and the City proper.

It was difficult going, but she worked her way across the square to a sidestreet. It was crowded but not as crowded as the square had been. Still, people were in a state of panic. Without warning, a detachment of soldiers rode by, scattering people in their wake. An old woman fell, the vegetables in her bag spilling over the road. But before she could pick herself up, most of her produce was gone, stolen. She stood in the road among the remnants shaking her fist and trembling.

Tugela wandered randomly among the streets and alleyways, avoiding only those that led in the direction of the fire and smoke of the City's foundries. In another street, she came on yet more soldiers. This time they got down from their carriers and broke down the door of a house. Moments later, they pulled a man and a woman, kicking and screaming, from inside. Tugela backed away and fled down a narrow alley.

In a small square, she found a cafe of a sort. She sat among the throng of people and drank a mug of viscous black coffee unlike anything the outlanders had ever drunk. Two men approached her, but she managed to discourage both of them by the simple tactic of ignoring them; they cursed her and went away.

From the snippets of conversation around her she was able to piece together a picture of what was happening in the City. There was turmoil, of course, because of the large influx of refugees, and the general panic at the approach of the Kommandos. But there was another reason, it seemed. There were widespread rumours of outlanders infiltrating the City, and of traitors among the City's own people. Now, Tugela understood why the man with the cart had been stopped at the gate. Soldiers were also rounding up everyone who was suspected of being an outlander or an outlander sympathiser.

Out in the square, Tugela wandered among the crowds. A huddle had formed in a far corner. A man (or perhaps it was a woman) was addressing the people from a platform of some kind. Curious, she began working her way over to the orator.

Suddenly Tugela became aware that the square was clearing. Where it had been crowded only a few minutes before, now there were only scattered clumps of people barring her way, and even these clumps were in the process of breaking up. Like a shoal of fish, the people seemed to be reacting en masse to some unseen danger. Suddenly, Tugela felt very exposed. She decided to get out of the square and quickly. But her decision came too late.

From a side alley, soldiers on carriers burst into the square. Tugela stood, stunned, unable even to goad her legs to carry her away. With a deafening clatter of hooves, and shouts of "Stop, traitors!" the soldiers bore down on the huddle of people around the orator, mostly men, that were now almost the only occupants of the square.

There was confusion, people running everywhere, swords flashing in the sunlight. Tugela was running, too, as fast as she could. A soldier came after her. She changed direction abruptly, just managing to dodge the hooves of his carrier. Another soldier had seen her. She changed direction again to avoid him. Suddenly, there was a woman, running beside her. "Quick," she shouted. She pulled Tugela down a narrow alleyway. The soldier followed, slashing air with his sword. "Here," the woman yelled and they ducked through an archway into a tiny courtyard. There was a low wall facing them and the woman clambered on to a barrel and over. Tugela did not wait to follow. Behind them, she could hear the soldier swear loudly. He wheeled his mount round and galloped away to head them off. They turned down a sidestreet, through another archway, and descended a staircase which led out to a deserted street again. Two houses down (Tugela almost ran past), the woman shouted "In here". Tugela dived through a door after her, landing up in a cellar of some kind.

Slumped in the gloom, their lungs heaving, the two women listened to the clatter of hooves die as the soldier passed by.

Jamilla

"We're safe now. The soldier's gone."

For an age, Tugela had sat with her back pressed hard against the cellar wall, hardly daring to draw breath, though her lungs were at bursting point. The woman's words came as a release, and she began immediately to gulp great mouthfuls of wonderful air. After a while, the agony in her lungs began to subside.

In the gloom of the cellar, Tugela peered at the stranger slumped opposite her. Her hair was long and dark but it was impossible to make out much more in the dim light. "Who – ?" Tugela asked.

"Jamilla," came the reply. The voice was that of an older woman. It had a noticeable tremor. "And you?"

Tugela told her.

There were so many urgent questions Tugela needed to ask. But her mind was in such turmoil that she could not think of where to start. For a while, the silence in the cellar stretched. Then Tugela became aware of something she had not noticed before. The woman was crying softly. Tugela got up and moved closer. "Please. What is it?"

Crouching before the woman, Tugela saw Jamilla's face clearly for the first time. She seemed to be in her late thirties. Her long dark hair was tinted red. Clumsily, she wiped at her eyes with the back of her hand. "My friends," she said. "They're all gone now."

Tugela recalled the people she had seen in the square, the speaker on the platform and those who had crowded round. She asked Jamilla whether they were her friends. The woman nodded, dabbing at her tears.

"Your friends – " Tugela began. She hesitated for a moment but finally plunged in. "The soldiers called them traitors. Why?"

Jamilla wiped away the last of her tears and her features hardened suddenly. "*Who* are you?" she asked, suspiciously.

"My name is Tugela. I told you."

"Yes. But that does not tell me *who* you are. Where do you come from? You are not from the City."

The statement, and it was a statement not a question, stunned Tugela. Until now, she had been convinced that she had blended in. For a moment, she considered lying to Jamilla. But the woman had saved her life. Honesty was the least she owed her in return.

"You're right," she admitted. "I am not from the City."

"Then you are an outlander." Again, it was a statement not a question. Tugela nodded.

"Tell me, just how did you come to be here?"

Tugela made a quick decision. She decided to trust Jamilla and tell the woman her story (really, she had little choice). But she could not risk telling her everything. She dare not reveal to anyone, for instance, the movements of Mandelbrot and the other Kommandos. On the other hand, Tugela felt that she must tell enough to gain Jamilla's trust. Then perhaps the woman would answer some of Tugela's own questions. Quickly, without dwelling too long on any of the details, she told of the main incidents on her journey out from Ironvale.

When she had finished, Jamilla rose suddenly to her feet. Looking down at Tugela, still crouching on the floor, she said: "Prove to me that you are not a spy planted by the priests. Prove to me that this story of yours is true."

"But how – ?"

"*Prove it.*"

Getting to her feet, Tugela faced Jamilla. She felt utterly helpless. What proof could she provide that would possibly satisfy the woman standing before her? "I . . . I can't," she stammered finally.

"Then I must go," Jamilla said.

"No. Wait!" Suddenly, Tugela remembered her bag. She rushed across the cellar to the place where she had dropped it and rummaged through the contents. "Here!" she cried, triumphantly, pulling out the dagger and holding it out for Jamilla to see. Curious, Jamilla approached and took the knife from her. "It was made by an outlander," Tugela told her, and then she added: "By Peet Stel himself."

"Peet Stel!" Jamilla said. Evidently, even here in the City the name of the Man of Metal carried weight. Jamilla turned the dagger over and over in her hands, inspecting it closely. "Yes," she agreed finally. "It is not like anything forged here." She fixed Tugela with an enquiring look. "Peet Stel?" The intonation of the question convinced Tugela that Jamilla had been won over. Quickly, she told the woman about her fortuitous meeting with Stel in Ironvale. Finally, Jamilla handed back the dagger.

"Well," she said. "You have told me how you came to be in the City. Now tell me why you came."

With relief plain in her face, Tugela told her the story. She shook with the effort of holding back the tears as she described the burning of Boschendale by the City's soldiers, and the capture of her parents. "My father's only crime," she finished up, trembling, "was to sell the produce of our farm to Ironvale instead of the City. With the air leaking away and the crops failing, we outlanders are hungry, too. We need to keep all the food that we grow.

"Now, my father and mother are prisoners. And I don't know what they've had to suffer. I have to find them. You must help me, if you can."

As Jamilla listened, her expression softened. "Your parents," she said, "will be held in the deep caverns beneath the Inner City, where my friends are too." She stopped a moment and looked intently at Tugela. She seemed to be considering something. Abruptly she came to a decision. "You asked who my friends are. Well, now I'll tell you. They are sympathisers with the cause of the outlanders."

"Sympathisers? But why?"

"Is is not obvious? Your people are not alone in needing air to breathe. We, in the City suffer, too, at the hands of the priests. When they cut off the air to the Land, they began to suffocate us as well. Already, there are many who think like us. My friends were telling people what the priests are doing to them."

"Inciting rebellion?"

"If you like."

"Can you help me find my parents?"

At first, Jamilla did not answer. She seemed to be considering the request carefully. Then she strode over to the door of the cellar. "Follow me," was all she said. "And, stay close."

Tugela blinked in the strong light of day. She followed Jamilla up a short flight of stairs to street level. The street was empty, the soldier long gone. Jamilla remained cautious, nevertheless. The route she led Tugela on was a contorted one, which took them through the narrow twisting alleyways of the City. Whenever they came to a major road which they had to cross, Jamilla checked first that it was free of soldiers before signalling for Tugela to follow her. It was a sensible precaution and, because of it, they ran into no trouble. Eventually, they reached the chaotic main square where Tugela had first entered the City. At an inn on the square, Jamilla darted in a doorway and up a narrow staircase.

"Tarragon!" she shouted, while still climbing the stairs. "Tarragon!"

A young man appeared on the landing above. He had long blond hair and a substantial scar along his jaw. "Tarragon, the soldiers . . ."

It didn't matter that she had choked off before finishing. The blond man understood what she was saying. A shadow passed across his features. When Jamilla reached the landing, he took her in his arms. She was sobbing.

"Now, now . . ." he said, consoling her. For a while, he held her tightly, then he pushed her away a little so that he could see her face. "Jamilla. The soldiers, tell me – they took *all* of them?"

"All of them, Tarragon."

He bowed his head. The shadow did not lift from him. When he raised his head again, he did not look at Jamilla, but past her, at Tugela, standing on the stairs.

"Who – ?"

Jamilla turned round. "Tarragon, this is Tugela." The woman had now stopped crying. "She was in Amaryllis Square. When the soldiers came, she got caught up with us." Tarragon regarded Tugela suspiciously. "No," Jamilla said, sharply. "She's no spy. I'm convinced of that. She's an outlander, Tarragon. Her parents defied the priests and are held in the tunnels beneath the Inner City." She let out a long sigh. "Oh, it's a long story . . ."

Jamilla's assurance was evidently enough because, immediately, he broke away from her to shake Tugela's hand. "Welcome to the City," he said. There was real warmth in his greeting and Tugela managed a weak smile in return. It was the first time, after all, that anyone had welcomed her to this place.

"Come."

Tarragon ushered Jamilla and Tugela into a room off the landing. It had a bed and a table and a large window which overlooked the square. He made them sit at the table, then disappeared. When he came back, it was with a tray piled high with food and drink. While Jamilla and Tugela ate – she had forgotten, in the excitement of the last hour, just how hungry she was – Tarragon stood by the window, looking out across the crowd in the square. He said nothing. In fact, no one spoke until the last mouthful of food was chewed, the last drop of drink downed. Then, Tarragon turned from the window abruptly. He said: "There is a way to get to our friends – and to your parents, Tugela."

"*There is*?" Tugela was immediately on her feet.

"Whoah, whoah. Not so fast. Sit down and listen." Reluctantly, Tugela obeyed and sat down.

"How?" Tugela asked Tarragon. But the answer came not from the blond man but from the woman sitting beside her. "No one knows the deep caverns under the Inner City better than Tarragon," she said. "As a boy, you see, he was trained for the priesthood – "

"Before I was thrown out," Tarragon interrupted. "I didn't take to the discipline. They called me a 'disruptive pupil'." He said this with some pride, Tugela noticed. The image of Kasteel flashed suddenly into her mind. Her uncle, too, might have been trained for priesthood. But he had fallen at an even earlier hurdle than Tarragon, when her grandfather had run off into the Forbidden Zone.

"When Tarragon was a novice," Jamilla continued, "his chief entertainment was exploring the caverns under the Inner City."

"My only entertainment, Jamilla. Those years of instruction were five of the most excruciatingly dull years of my life." Despite his words, however, Tugela detected a certain nostalgia for those lost days. "It'll be difficult," he said, "but the City is in total chaos at the moment. That's the one thing that we have on our side."

Tugela was on her feet again. "Then we will go there now?"

"Tugela!" Tarragon said. "You are an impatient one! Do not fear, though, we will go to the Inner City. But, in a while, when we have had time to catch our breath. There are things I must discuss first with Jamilla." With this, the older woman rose and joined Tarragon at the door. "You – you sleep if you wish," Tarragon said, motioning at the bed in the corner of the room. Then, the door closed and Tugela was alone.

Surprisingly, Tugela did manage to sleep, almost immediately she laid her head down. That she did so was a measure of just how exhausted she was, because her mind was consumed with a terrible impatience to be on the move again, to leave straight away for the Inner City. Her parents were there. And it made her shudder to think what the priests might be doing to them.

Though she slept, however, she did not sleep long. The noise of the crowds outside the window woke her after only a short while and she got up and began pacing the room. Finally, Jamilla and Tarragon returned. Tugela scooped up her bag. "Now?" she said.

"Now," Tarragon replied.

Inner City

With her, Jamilla carried a basket which was filled with newly baked bread and fruit. The reason for this, she told Tugela, was that if the soldiers saw her carrying supplies which seemed destined for the priests they might be less likely to stop the three of them. Tarragon had no food with him, but carried instead a bundle of torches wrapped up into a parcel. There was no time for Tugela to ask him why he had brought the parcel before the three of them were swallowed up in the turmoil of the square.

It seemed to Tugela that the crowd was in a state of even greater agitation than it had been when she had first entered the City. Clearly, rumours of the outlander movements were running rife in the streets. Half way across the square, Tarragon stopped a man, who blurted out an answer to his question before hurrying on. Tugela did not catch the exchange but, as they pushed through the remainder of the crowd, Jamilla told her what she had overheard. There had been a preliminary clash out by the Circleberg. The result had been inconclusive.

To Tugela, the clash sounded no more than a minor skirmish, with each side probing the weaknesses of the other. But the response of the people around her, who were barely able to control their hysteria, belied this. Tugela wondered how they would react if and when Mandelbrot broke through the ring of the Circleberg and set up his camp within sight of the great walls.

To reach the compound of the Inner City, Tarragon led them on a route that passed close to the great foundries. Once again, the air became thick with soot particles and, as they hurried on, the buildings, too, got blacker and blacker. Above the rooftops, Tugela saw the smoke curling skyward, and a cold wind brought with it the terrible din of the place.

Long before they could reach the foundries, however, Tarragon veered away and plunged them into a maze of narrow and gloomy streets. When finally they emerged into sunlight, looming before them, across a no man's land of cobbled ground, was a great wall built of blocks of stone of a reddish-brown colour. The wall was twice the height of a man and stretched away in both directions as far as Tugela could see. All activity seemed to be concentrated at a large gateway in the wall. People and wagons streamed along a wide road which led from the gateway. After only a short moment of hesitation, Tarragon led them towards it.

As they neared the entrance, a detachment of soldiers emerged. Paying no regard whatsoever to the crowd, they scythed through them, scattering them in all directions. A wagon, whose driver manœuvred it out of the way too hastily, overbalanced and tipped clean over, spilling its load. In the pandemonium that followed, Tarragon steered them quickly towards the guardhouse by the gate. Glancing inside, Tugela saw that it was empty. The guard had joined those out on the street who were engaged in helping the wagon driver.

Hissing at them to speed up, Tarragon shepherded the two women through the gate into the compound of the Inner City. This was the most ancient part of the city, the kernel about which all the rest had accreted over the long centuries. They emerged into a large cobbled courtyard from which radiated several narrow streets. The courtyard was momentarily empty, but Tugela could see the silhouettes of distant figures down at least two streets.

For a while, Tarragon seemed to hesitate over which way to go, as if trying frantically to dredge up a memory that he had stored away long ago. Then he set off across the expanse of cobbles.

They crossed the courtyard rapidly and dived down one of the streets leading away. Almost immediately, a group of foot soldiers, six or seven in all, appeared up ahead, their boots thudding on the cobbles, their swords clattering noisily. Tugela, who could see nowhere at all to run, froze in the dead centre of the roadway. It was only when Tarragon yelled at her, then yanked her arm forcibly, that she jumped out of the way.

The soldiers ran past, taking not the slightest bit of notice of the three of them. They were headed instead towards the commotion at the gateway.

Relief plain on his face, Tarragon led them on.

Not far ahead, on the left-hand side, Tugela could see a huge, ornate porch, with wide steps leading up to it. As they approached, a group of boys, dressed in the white robes of novitiates, descended the stairs on to the street, pushing and shoving at each other in the way that boys do. High above them, on the face of the crumbling building, tall windows were flung wide open. From within, came the drone of other boys, chanting.

As they came abreast of the group, Jamilla signalled to Tugela not to hurry past. Tarragon and Jamilla bowed their heads and made the sign of the Eye. Tugela was quick to follow their example.

One of the boys detached himself suddenly from the group and walked boldly up to Jamilla. His eyes daring her to react, he pulled a fruit from her basket. After several defiant bites, he turned and threw it hard at one of his companions. Tarragon took advantage of the scuffle that broke out to chivvy them on.

The sound of the chanting was louder now. Tugela looked up

to see that they were immediately below the open windows. She caught up Tarragon, who was also looking upwards. "This was the school where you trained for the priesthood?" she asked, though there could be little doubt that it was.

"Guilty," he replied with a smile. "I was one of those boys. Just as arrogant, just as rude. More so, maybe. After all, I failed to make the grade."

At this instant, the commotion behind them died abruptly. Turning, they saw why: a priest-instructor had arrived suddenly on the scene.

They turned into another street, leaving the school behind. But the drone of the chanting followed them. There was little doubt in Tugela's mind what it was, but she asked all the same. "Is that the litany?"

"That's the litany."

"But the boys don't . . . I mean, they can't learn it complete."

"The priests are not that stupid, Tugela. No, they with hold crucial stanzas of the litany from the novitiates. You learn them only when you are finally accepted into the order, when your loyalty to the priesthood is beyond any doubt."

So that was the way in which the priesthood kept the secret of metal. Now, of course, taking such care over who knew the formula was a quite futile act. The secret was well and truly out. Peet Stel could recite his own version of the sacred litany to anyone he cared to, and, what's more, he understood what it meant.

Tarragon led them down several more cobbled streets. But, thankfully, there were no further incidents. Finally, they came to an area which was not built up at all. In fact, Tugela was astonished to see rising before her a barrier of shatterpines, ringing what appeared to be a park. She was astonished because she could not remember seeing a single one of the trees in the City before.

There was traffic — a wagon moving up ahead, flanked by two priests, but this was all. Tarragon had stopped abruptly in the road and seemed to be considering what to do next. Without being told Tugela realised that they had come to the very heart of the Inner City.

Tarragon came to a decision. He told them that they must leave the road and continue using the cover that the park offered. They did so, zig-zagging quickly after him across the bare earth and through the curtain of shatterpines. Once in the park, they were screened by shrubbery, which though dry and without any leaves to speak of made a thick enough shield nonetheless. They skirted ornamental gardens and empty pools which had once, apparently, been fed by a battery of fountains. Even in its present run-down state, Tugela could only marvel at what a sight it must have been before the comets stopped coming, when water was abundant in the Land!

Keeping at what he deemed to be a safe distance, Tarragon was following the course of the road as it struck deep into the park. As she peered through the gnarled shrubbery, Tugela spotted the wagon they had seen before. It had now stopped up ahead at what seemed to be a guardpost. The guards — two of them — were in conversation with one of the priests. Tugela almost bumped into Jamilla as Tarragon came to a standstill. The exchange between the guards and the priest ended and the wagon began moving again. It was now that Tugela noticed something very strange: the wheels of the wagon were gradually disappearing!

As she watched, the wagon got lower and lower on the road, until finally only its driver, perched high on his seat, was still visible. Then, he, too, disappeared from view. In a distance that could have been no more than fifty paces, the road had dived completely underground.

Jamilla, who had seen the look of astonishment cross Tugela's face, nodded at the ground. "The caverns," she whispered. "They're right beneath our feet." Tugela looked down at the bare earth she was standing on. She was unable to really take it in and could only shake her head in disbelief.

The soldiers had now returned to their guardpost and there was no more traffic in sight. Tarragon turned to the two women. "This road," he explained. "It's one of three identical roads. They extend in from the perimeter of the park like the spokes of a wheel."

"How identical?" Jamilla asked pointedly.

Tarragon managed a wry smile. It was clear what Jamilla was asking. Nodding in the direction of the guardpost, he said: "So identical that they all have one of *those*."

"Then how – ?" Tugela asked.

"Tugela, have faith. Would I have led you this far if I did not know of a way?" Tugela made no answer. She thought it unlikely that Tarragon would, but she really did not know the man well enough to make a judgment. "There is a small maintenance shaft," Tarragon said finally. "It was the route we novitiates would use to get into the caverns. In my day, the shaft was abandoned. Pray that it still is."

"Then what are we waiting for?" Tugela demanded.

Suddenly, Tarragon looked uncomfortable. He hesitated. "The park has changed," he said. "It's been a long time . . ." He looked about him, distracted. He seemed to be searching for a familiar signpost, something that would jog his memory. Finally, as if trying to convince himself, rather than his companions, he said: "No. No, I'm sure I can find it."

Tugela was aghast. It had not occurred to her when Tarragon spoke of the maintenance shaft that he might not remember where it was. But even as she reeled at the news, she realised that it was stupid of her to be shocked. Tarragon was quite obviously returning to this place after a long time. She didn't know how old he was but Tugela would not be surprised if it was twenty years or more since his days as a novitiate.

She looked at Jamilla. She was clearly as shocked as Tugela. "Tarragon," Jamilla said firmly. "Tell us what we must look for?"

But Tarragon could not tell them. In his day, he said, the

entrance to the shaft had been overgrown and unrecognisable. He had no reason to believe that it would be any different today. They asked whether there was some marker nearby, a tree perhaps, by which they would recognise the spot. But Tarragon shook his head. All he would say was that he would know the place when he saw it.

The two women had no option but to trail helplessly behind him as he searched, unable to be of the slightest use. Their frustration was unbearable, compounded by the fact that, while Tarragon scoured the park for a sign only he would recognise, the three of them were sitting targets. Tugela expected, at any moment, to hear the shout of a soldier ring out behind them. Until now, luck had been running with them, but there was no telling when the tide of their fortune might suddenly turn.

Jamilla was increasingly nervous, shooting glances warily in all directions as she followed Tarragon. "*Come on*," Tugela heard her hiss. "*Hurry!*" Tarragon, thankfully, did not hear. He was too engrossed in the task at hand.

One moment, he would be crouching to examine an anonymous piece of ground, tapping the compacted soil, perhaps, or clearing away dead leaves. Then he would rise, shaking his head glumly. "Perhaps behind that clump of trees," he would mutter, half to himself, or "Maybe over there where the ground begins to rise." And they would follow him, obediently – because there was nothing else they could think to do – until the new place, like all the others they had inspected, turned out not to be the right one after all.

Then, suddenly Tarragon stopped dead. "These trees . . ." he said, his face creased into a frown.

"Yes?" Jamilla asked, grabbing his arm. "Yes!"

"I'm not sure but I think . . ." He was nodding to himself now, as if something solid was finally coalescing out of the fog of his memory.

"You think *what*?" Jamilla said. She shook him hard.

"Look out for a stone path," he barked suddenly, relief

present in his voice. "I remember now. The path leads straight to the shaft entrance."

They needed no more urging. In a moment, Jamilla had split the search area between them, and the two women, at last, were able to throw themselves into something useful.

Despite all their efforts, though, it was Tarragon who found the path, half buried. When he called out excitedly, they joined him, clawing at the dirt with their hands until an entire flagstone was revealed, then another. When several more had been uncovered, the direction of the path was clear. It extended towards dense undergrowth, no more than a dozen strides away.

Tarragon tore at the tangle of bushes, and the woody growth, dry and dead, broke away easily. The undergrowth formed no more than a circular screen, effectively hiding the shaft entrance from view. They burst through quickly and stood on bare ground. Up ahead, the path, now easy to see, ended abruptly.

Tarragon was ecstatic. He rushed forward, Jamilla and Tugela close behind. They reached the end and stood in a ring looking down. A crumbling staircase led to a rough wooden door, which was battened shut. It was clear that no one had come here in a long time.

Tarragon went down first. Jamilla abandoned her basket at last and joined him. They began pulling at the battens. With Tugela helping, too, they managed to wrench one free, then another; leaving two, which were nailed more tightly, and harder to remove. Only when Tarragon thought to use one of the battens he'd already freed as a lever, did he make further progress. With a grunt of effort, he tore away the last batten.

The door, of course, was locked, but it was makeshift and flimsy. Getting the two women to stand well back, Tarragon kicked at the lock, once, twice. On his third attempt, something gave. One more kick brought the sound of splintering wood. The door swung inwards, revealing . . . blackness. Tarragon was smiling now. "The maintenance shaft," he announced unnecessarily. "From here on, I think I'll remember."

"I'm praying that you do," said Jamilla. Her voice was devoid of any humour and, hearing it, Tarragon's smile faded a little. He took a deep breath. "Well?" he said. "Ready?"

"The torches – ?" Tugela asked, perturbed that Tarragon had made no move to take one from his pack.

"Not yet, Tugela. It's too dangerous. If you need to, feel your way along the walls of the shaft. The floor is smooth and it slopes into the ground." He stepped over the threshold, and was soon swallowed in the darkness.

Tugela hesitated. "After you," Jamilla said.

Caverns

At first, Tugela made slow progress and the sound of Tarragon's footsteps on the stone floor receded rapidly. Then, principally because Jamilla was close behind and urging her to hurry, she overcame her initial caution and began to descend a little faster through the darkness. Though the floor was quite dry, a distinct smell of dampness was coming up from the depths.

To begin with, blocks of rough stone lined the walls. They had been fitted together untidily without the aid of any cement. But they soon ended. As the shaft burrowed deeper into the ground, Tugela felt bare rock beneath her fingers. The surprise was how incredibly smooth it was. The shaft had been hewn through solid rock yet its walls revealed no sign whatsoever of the tools that had cut it. It dawned on Tugela suddenly that the lining of rough stones, and the flimsy door Tarragon had broken down, were late additions.

Tugela had not been mistaken in smelling water. It was dripping slowly from the ceiling and, as she passed under the place, she felt the iciness on her face. It reminded her of rain in the Land. And how long ago was it that she last felt that?

In the pitch darkness, it was easy to hallucinate. So when

Tugela saw a faint glow ahead, she managed to convince herself that it was nothing but her imagination playing tricks. But the glow got gradually brighter and Jamilla's hand, squeezing her shoulder, told Tugela that she had seen it, too. They were nearing the end of the shaft.

Sure enough, the figure of Tarragon soon came into view, a fuzzy silhouette against the strengthening light. Tugela broke into a run, at last completely confident of her step. When she reached Tarragon, he had already slowed to a standstill and the end of the shaft was barely a dozen strides beyond him. Tugela peered round his bulk but the light, which seemed to flicker and dance, was still too dazzling for her dark-adapted eyes.

They were now far below ground. Tarragon, a finger pressed to his lips, signalled them to follow him carefully. Standing in the shadows behind him, hopefully concealed from the view of anyone who might be about, the two women looked out.

When the light no longer made her blink, Tugela saw that the shaft had brought them to the floor of a huge dome-shaped chamber. The lofty ceiling of the chamber was blackened by the smoke from a ring of yellow torches, burning high up on the rocks walls. The place was larger than anything Tugela had dared to imagine when Tarragon had talked of the caverns.

The chamber was empty of both people and objects of any description. Around its circumference, however, and immediately beneath the torches, was a ring of what seemed to be metal doors, each of which was flush with the rock and quite feature-less. In all, Tugela counted nine doors. What made the doors noteworthy was not that they seemed to be made of metal – which Tugela found astonishing enough – but their sheer scale. They were doors for giants. Each seemed large enough to admit several wagons, side by side.

The doors were not equally spaced around the chamber. After every third door, there was a gap, as if the builders of this place had, for some unknowable reason, missed one out. Substituted instead around the chamber were the gaping mouths of three shafts, each far larger than the one the three of them had come down. It took a moment before it dawned on Tugela that one of these was the road they had followed part way through the park.

"What is this place?" Tugela whispered.

"The priests call it the Hub," said Tarragon.

"The Hub?"

"Because of those," he said, pointing. "The three access tunnels that radiate from this chamber."

"But what is it used for?" Tugela insisted.

"See the giant doors," Tarragon said. Tugela could hardly have failed to see them but she nodded all the same. "Behind each one is a vertical shaft which connects this place to the lower levels – the deep caverns beneath the City."

"Then this place ..." Tugela said. "It isn't where my parents – ?"

"Good God, no. We're barely below the surface here. The caverns where they're holding your parents are nearly a klomter beneath us."

"A klomter!" Tugela was stunned. She had never imagined that the caverns beneath the City were that deep. This chamber was something extraordinary to behold, a place which none of her experiences in the Land had prepared her for, and yet ... and yet what Tarragon was saying was that it was merely the entrance hall to the caverns. Would they ever find her parents in this incredible warren? She forced her mind away from such despairing thoughts.

"Tarragon," Tugela said. "Who built all this?"

But there was no time for an answer. "Shh!" Tarragon hissed.

Tugela became aware of a gentle hum, which was rising steadily in pitch. It was coming from across the chamber. "What – ?"

"The priests call them elevators," Tarragon said. "They connect the Hub to the lower levels. Now, shh!"

"Elevators?" The word meant nothing to Tugela. Also, looking about the Hub, she could see nothing that the word might apply to. She noticed, though, that the hum from across the chamber had stopped abruptly. Did that mean something?

There was a sudden movement opposite.

One of the giant doors grew a seam down its centre! Before Tugela's eyes, it split into two halves, each of which slid back. What this revealed was a multitude of people: priests and soldiers. Even before the door had opened fully, they had begun flooding out into the Hub, tiny figures, dwarfed by the immensity of the chamber. For an instant, she entertained the hope that among those figures were her mother and father. But it was a ridiculous hope, born out of desperation, and she chided herself for such wishful thinking.

Who, Tugela wondered, had slid back the door? And where did the light come from? The interior of the *elevator* seemed to be lit by a diffuse white light which did not flicker, quite unlike torchlight. She tried to locate its source but failed. And she had so many other questions . . .

In the chamber chaos reigned briefly, with people rushing about apparently randomly. Most, though, headed straight for one access shaft in particular, while the remainder split themselves between the two others. Evidently, panic still ruled in the City, and Tugela gave thanks for it.

When the Hub was clear again, which didn't take long, Tugela turned her attention back to the amazing elevator. But, infuriatingly, she had now missed her chance to look inside. The doors had closed again, and the hum which had accompanied its arrival was already fading.

Then Tarragon shouted "Quick!" and, before Tugela knew what was happening, she was propelled out of the maintenance shaft and into the bright glare of the Hub, Jamilla at her side. In the middle of the chamber, Tarragon hesitated, before heading towards one of the giant doors. Surely he didn't intend that they use an elevator? But then Tugela realised that he did not.

Between two of the giant doors was a much smaller one, which she had not seen from across the chamber. Tarragon was heading straight for it.

In a moment, they were safely through into a dimly lit circular room. Tugela slumped for a while against the wall, regaining her breath. Tarragon and Jamilla had carried on into the centre of the room where they appeared to be looking down into a hole in the floor.

Tugela joined them, and saw that the floor of the room did indeed contain a hole, a circular opening about as wide as a man is high. By the light of the room, Tugela saw the metal rungs of a ladder. It clung to the interior and reached almost to the lip of the hole. Within the space of half a dozen rungs, however, the ladder was swallowed in darkness.

"An emergency shaft," Tarragon explained. "It descends vertically all the way to the lower levels."

Jamilla looked at him, eyes wide. When she spoke, she took the words straight from Tugela's mouth. "You want us to climb down a klomter of ladder in total darkness?"

"If necessary, yes."

"My God!"

"I said 'if necessary'."

"What does that mean?" Tugela asked.

"There is another way – if it still works." With this, Tarragon lowered himself into the shaft. He climbed down until his head was just below the level of the floor. "It's a long time since I last did this," he said. "I only hope it hasn't run down . . ." He had bent over and was groping around the wall of the shaft. "Somewhere around here I remember . . . oh, here it is!"

In the gloom, it was difficult to see precisely what Tarragon was doing, but he seemed to have retrieved something from a compartment recessed in the wall. Tugela heard him clip something metallic on to the ladder. The next moment she became aware of a faint whirring sound and, to her astonishment, Tarragon began descending smoothly and without any apparent effort into the shaft. She clutched at Jamilla's sleeve. "He's gone!" she gasped.

But a moment later Tarragon was back, rising effortlessly out of the gloom, and grinning from ear to ear. He climbed out and showed the two women a linen sling. Apparently, this had been what he had been sitting on. Attached to it, by strong cord, were two metal clips. One, he said, fastened to each side of the ladder. He gave the apparatus to Tugela and reached into the shaft to retrieve two more, identical to the first. Tugela, peering at the clips in her hand, saw that each contained a small metal wheel.

"Right. Who's going to be first?" Tarragon said. When neither woman volunteered, he pushed Tugela, reluctantly, to the edge of the shaft. He showed her how to fasten the clips to the ladder and how to position herself on the sling. Then he repeated the demonstration for Jamilla. Minutes later, he had all three of them seated on their respective slings in the shaft: Tarragon lowest, followed by Tugela, then Jamilla. Both women looked decidedly nervous.

"Now, to stop and to start, this is what you do," Tarragon said. "Take your feet off the rungs of the ladder and the sling will start moving down. Put your feet back and you will stop. Simple. Ready?"

When they began moving, Tugela found that her first instinct was to jump instantly back on to the ladder, thus stopping the sling dead. For this reason, progress down the shaft was at first painfully slow, until she gained a little confidence – or rather until she managed to drive from her mind the fact that she was suspended above a klomter of empty space. In fact, this proved easier than she expected, because of the sheer novelty of the ride and because of other distractions.

In particular, she became fascinated by the soft illumination in the shaft. Near the top of the shaft, they had been surrounded by darkness. But now, as they descended, a light would flick on below them, triggered by their passage, then flick off when they had passed. The light seemed to come from the substance of the wall itself. It was a soft, diffuse light, and when Tugela reached out to touch it – and she did this with the utmost caution – she found, to her surprise, that it gave out no discernible heat. The texture of the walls was odd, too. It wasn't stone, or metal, or any other material Tugela had ever touched before. She wondered what Peet Stel would make of this.

"Tarragon," Tugela said, peering down between her feet. Tarragon did not bother to look up. "The light . . . How – ?" She had so much she wanted to ask, and she had to start somewhere.

"The answer to that, Tugela, is, I simply don't know. It's not made by fire, that's all I can tell you. It's like everything else down here – the elevators, the ventilation in the deep caverns, these slings – it's all been running for centuries. I never met anyone who knew how it all works."

"But the priests – ?"

"The priests say they run everything, they say they built it five centuries ago. But . . ."

"You don't believe them?"

"I have my doubts . . ." He took a deep breath, as if preparing to utter something that had been on his mind but that might be a sacrilege in this place. Tugela waited, the only sound in the shaft the soft whirring of the slings creeping steadily downwards. "This 'artificial' lighting," Tarragon said. "It doesn't operate in all the deep caverns. Most are in permanent darkness and no one goes there. Oh, the priests can light them with torches – but only where there's ventilation. That doesn't operate everywhere either."

"Why?"

"Because it's run down. The lights, the ventilation, all of it." Tarragon looked up at her. "You saw the elevator, Tugela?"

"Of course."

"Well, very probably that's the only one still working. Once, centuries ago all nine worked. In my day as a novitiate, though, all the elevators had broken down, except for two."

Tugela was bewildered. "So why don't the priests mend them? Why don't they fix everything that's run down?"

"Tugela, Tugela, don't you see? They can't."

It was too much for Tugela. Tarragon, far from answering the questions she so badly needed answered, was succeeding only in filling her head with yet more pressing questions. His final revelation left her in such a state of confusion that she could hardly get straight in her head what she should ask next.

"Be thankful," Tarragon was saying.

"Thankful," Tugela mumbled. "For what?" If Tarragon had been making no sense before, he was making even less now.

"That they can't fix things," he said. Then he explained: "We can use the abandoned tunnels to get to your parents."

"Oh." Tugela said. Clearly, the idea of using the tunnels to avoid detection was a good one. Nevertheless, the prospect of moving through unventilated tunnels in total darkness was not something that Tugela instantly warmed to.

For a while, they descended in silence, apart from the gentle background whine of the slings. Progress seemed painfully slow and there was ample time for her to worry about her mother and father. She dreaded to think what they had gone through. She prayed that she would find them, and that they would be unharmed.

Tugela, wondering why Jamilla had not spoken for a while, looked up to check that she was still there. Of course, she was. Her feet were dangling no more than a metre away. Evidently, she was wrapped up in her own thoughts.

It was not long before the cauldron of Tugela's thoughts boiled over again. "I never knew — I never even guessed — that all this existed in the Land."

"Few do," Tarragon said.

For a while, they descended in silence again. "Tarragon."

"Yes."

"If the priests can't fix things, if they didn't build all this . . .
then – "

"Then who did?"

"Yes, who?"

Tarragon did not reply immediately. Tugela realised with a
sinking feeling that he had no answer.

"When I was a novitiate," Tarragon said finally, "I thought
about that a lot. How could I come here exploring with my
friends and not wonder who built all this? But if your head is
full of questions and not a single answer is forthcoming, sooner
or later the frustration of not knowing gets too much. You turn
your mind to more productive things. That's what I did. I simply
gave up wondering."

"But, the priests – do they know?"

"There was a time when I thought that they did, and that they
were keeping the secret to themselves. Now, I'm certain that
they do not know. Perhaps they did once, but they've long since
forgotten."

"Then do you know how old this place is?"

On this question, Tarragon did not hesitate. With conviction,
he said: "Older than anything else in the Land."

"You mean all this was here before the City?"

"Before the City, before even the Land itself."

"Before the Land! But who – ?"

"I told you before, Tugela, I do not know."

"But we were the first in the Land. God created it for us five
hundred years ago. Before, there was nothing but darkness and
the void. Is that not what the priests . . ." She trailed off,
realising suddenly that she was reeling off automatically things
that she had been told. Until this moment, she had not thought
to question them, but now, seeing all this around her, all these
wonders she had never even suspected existed and which the
priesthood concealed from the people, she began to harbour
doubts. The foundations of her world, which, until recently, had

seemed to be so sure, were beginning to crumble. There was nothing she was sure of any more.

"It's simply a story, Tugela."

"A story!"

"There was another people here before ours there had to be, in order to build this place. I don't know who they were or why they dug caverns so deep beneath the ground, or even how they did it. But there was another people, of that I'm sure. And whoever they were, they knew more than us. Much, much more."

"But where did they go?"

Tarragon only laughed. "Tugela, Tugela, if only I knew. A thousand times I've asked myself that question. A thousand times, and I'm still no nearer to answering it. Have you ever tried to assemble a jigsaw with most of the pieces missing? If you have, you'll have an idea of what it's like trying to put together a picture of this place."

"No more questions then," Tugela said. She understood now the futility of continuing to ask, for Tarragon, by his own admission, had none of the answers she sought.

The walls, slipping by steadily, now became a blur of light. The slings, whirring reassuringly in the background, became a murmur Tugela was less and less aware of. She fought to make sense of all things she had learned from Tarragon. But it was quite impossible, Tarragon was absolutely right about that. Without warning, though, her thoughts took an unexpected turn and she remembered the great amphitheatre where Mandelbrot had made camp on his ride to the Circleberg. Instantly, she realised that she had in her possession a jigsaw piece that Tarragon did not have.

The amphitheatre, with its post holes set out in their inexplicable grid pattern, had been extremely old – she had been certain of that because the posts had rusted away leaving no remnants. The deep caverns, too, were extremely old. Both places were built for unknowable purposes. Then perhaps the simplest explanation was that the two were the same age. Whoever had built the bowl, for whatever reasons, had also been responsible for excavating the caverns beneath the City.

True, she had more to go on than Tarragon. But where did it get her?

Before she could decide, Tarragon broke in on her thoughts. He wanted them to stop their slings, he said. Tugela obeyed immediately, relieved to feel the reassuring solidity of the ladder beneath her once more. But when she peered down, past the bulk of Tarragon, she could see no sign of the bottom of the shaft. Before she had an opportunity to ask, though, Tarragon explained. They were indeed close to the bottom, he said, but that made it simply too risky to continue to use the slings. They must complete the descent by ladder.

This they did, in darkness. It had been the slings, after all, which had triggered the lighting. Without them, the luminescence of the walls quickly faded and died.

There was still a long way to go. Tarragon had been overcautious in stopping the slings so early and he apologised, blaming it on his faulty memory of the place. Finally, though, a point of light appeared down below, which expanded slowly into a circle. They were very close to the end when Tarragon signalled to wait. Alone, he climbed down the last stretch of the ladder. Tugela saw him pause a while at the lip of the shaft, then he jumped down. He looked up and waved for her to join him and, moments later, she, too, was at the bottom. The ladder extended beyond, down into another circular room. "Right, Tarragon," she said shakily. "Lead the way."

The chamber beyond the door was almost identical to the Hub a klomter above, except that it was lit artificially. Through the door, which Tarragon opened just a crack, Tugela was able to make out three of the elevators and the mouth of one of the tunnels, which was illuminated, leading away. People were about – a handful of them, waiting patiently before the closed doors of one of the elevators. But Tugela could not see any soldiers standing guard – at least not in the portion of the chamber that was visible.

Tarragon closed the door and waited. A little later, he opened it again, shook his head and pushed it shut once more. "We'll just have to wait," he told the women. Then, to Tugela in particular: "You saw the tunnel with the lighting? That leads directly to where your parents are being held. If I remember rightly, it's a chamber about half a klomter along the tunnel – on the level below."

"There's another level?"

He nodded. "The tunnel splits into two – just out of sight. One arm stays level, while the other one dives downward. It happens a lot in this place – you'll see. Don't ask me how many levels there are. I don't suppose anyone's ever counted."

"Surely, we're not going to use the direct route?"

"No. We'd be stopped right away. There's an alternative. Remember the Hub above with its three radial tunnels?" Tugela nodded. "Well, it's just the same down here. The other two tunnels – which you can't see – are in darkness and abandoned. We'll be using one of them." He opened the door again but closed it quickly. Tugela was finding it difficult to hide her apprehension. Tarragon put his hand on her shoulder. "Don't worry," he said.

"How will we find our way?" she said.

"Tugela, it's not the maze it seems. There's a definite pattern to the tunnels. The three radial ones are connected at intervals by tunnels which form concentric rings. It's the same on all levels. All we have to do is take a radial tunnel, then, when we judge we're about half a klomter out, follow round one of the circular tunnels."

"And you're sure they'll all be deserted?"

"I told you – most of this place is abandoned."

He opened the door again. When he closed it, he let out a sigh of relief. "The elevator's arrived from above," he said. He turned to the two women. "When I give the word – run." He opened the door, this time more than he had dared before, and looked about. "Right," he said. "Now!"

They flew headlong across the floor of the empty chamber. Tugela had time – just – to note that two of the three tunnels which led away were indeed in darkness, as Tarragon had said, then they plunged into the gaping mouth of one of them. There was no shout of alarm. No one had seen them. They kept on running, even when the light was so dim that they could no longer be sure of their footing. Finally, Tarragon told them to stop.

Doubled up in the darkness, fighting for breath, Tugela heard Tarragon scrabbling about. A moment later, a brilliant light flared up nearby and, for the first time, Tugela saw her surroundings. Up ahead, the tunnel split into two – just as Tarragon had said it would. He lit another torch, which he handed to Jamilla, and finally a third, which Tugela took gratefully.

"Down," Tarragon said, pointing with his torch. They moved quickly and soon the tunnel levelled out. Again it split, but this time they took the branch that remained horizontal. Presumably, the other branch sloped down to the level below. As she hurried to keep up with Tarragon and Jamilla, Tugela wondered how many more branches there were. Perhaps the tunnels extended for klomters more down through the rock beneath the City. Nothing would surprise her any more.

Tugela longed to examine the walls, which were smooth and white, and clearly not stone. But, of course, there was no time to stop. Above, on the ceiling, a broad dark strip ran along the tunnel. Tugela knew enough of this place now to guess that the strip had once been the source of the tunnel's light.

They came to a kind of crossroads. The tunnel to both sides was unlit but, to the right and in the distance a bright light shone. "That's where the direct route crosses," Tarragon explained. Immediately, Tugela realised that they had reached the first of the concentric rings Tarragon had spoken of. Further on, they passed another, then another. At the fourth ring,

Tarragon stopped. "This is the one," he said. Evidently, they had covered the required distance.

Tugela took a last look along the radial tunnel they had been following. She would never know now where it was heading. Turning sharply to the right, she followed the others along a tunnel which she could see already was curving gently into the gloom. There was no sign yet of the light ahead.

They had a long way to go. The circumference of a circle half a klomter in radius was more than three klomters, which meant that there was a klomter of tunnel to cover before they reached the next radial shaft. Long before that, though, they came to an interruption in the tunnel.

For a long time, Tugela had been wondering why such a vast network of tunnels apparently led nowhere. This was something that she found hard to believe and which she intended to quiz Tarragon about. But when the tunnel emerged suddenly into a huge hollowed-out space, there was no longer any need to ask.

They were on the axis of a giant half-cylinder, almost half a klomter long. The ceiling arched high above them, so high it was barely illuminated by the light from their torches. On the far side of the cavern, their tunnel continued, a faint light visible in its depths. Cautiously, Tarragon led them out onto the floor of the cavern.

"W-what?" Tugela stammered.

"Who knows. Some kind of storage place, perhaps." It was easy to understand Tarragon's reasoning. The entire length of one wall of the cavern was lined with metal racks, now empty. From markings on the other wall, Tugela could see that it, too, had once held racks. Twisted metal and other rubble piled at the foot of the wall suggested that perhaps the racks had collapsed.

When they were half way across the floor of the cavern, Tarragon motioned to either side with his torch. At first, Tugela could not see what he meant. "More tunnels," he said. Then she saw their mouths, one on either side.

"Where do they lead?" she asked.

"To other caverns just like this one. You may think this place is extraordinary, but it's only one of at least ten, all identical, side by side."

"Ten!"

"Some of the caverns are empty like this one," Tarragon said. "But others are knee deep in rubble – some of the strangest objects you've ever seen." But he did not elaborate.

They left the giant cavern and continued towards the light. From now on, there were many small side tunnels, some with lights and some without. Tarragon, more cautious now, slowed their pace to a crawl. Clearly, they were nearing the areas that the priests used.

Tugela tried to keep close to the others, but there were now more and more things to distract her. Down one side tunnel, for instance, she saw a strange vehicle in the gloom. It seems to have *eight* wheels. She hurried on, though, not daring to lag too far behind. It was unfortunate then that the next time she was distracted it was at precisely the moment that a soldier appeared suddenly from a side tunnel.

Tugela had stopped briefly at a small pile of metal objects, none of which she could immediately identify, and this had allowed Tarragon and Jamilla to get some way ahead. When the soldier appeared, and shattered the silence in the tunnel with his blood-curdling order to stop, he split them. Immediately, Tarragon and Jamilla began to run full pelt. Tugela had no choice but to run, too – but in the opposite direction. She dodged down a dark turning, running as fast as she could. On the right was another tunnel, also in darkness. She plunged into that, too. She had no idea whether the soldier was on her tail or had chosen to pursue Tarragon and Jamilla. She was propelled by blind panic alone. Very soon, though, she realised that she had not been followed. But, by then, she was well and truly lost.

Parnassas

How could she have been so stupid?

Catching her breath at a bend in the darkened corridor, Tugela fought to hold back the tide of her tears. Tears of frustration, of self-loathing. She felt like screaming she was so angry with herself. She had come through so much, braved so many dangers to be here, and for one overriding reason: to find her parents and somehow set them free. She had made it to within striking distance of the chamber where they were being held. And now she was separated from Jamilla and Tarragon and hopelessly lost. Why had she allowed herself to be distracted by a stupid, meaningless pile of junk?

She didn't deserve the luck she had had in reaching this place. Well, perhaps it was ending now . . .

The sound of voices ahead in the tunnel stopped her in her tracks. She turned and fled. When the tunnel split, one side lighted, the other in gloom, she took the darkened branch. But she realised immediately that it was the wrong choice. Up ahead, torches were moving towards her, and there were voices, too. Consumed by panic, she backtracked and plunged into the lighted tunnel. The bright illumination coming from the ceiling dazzled her. No one was about but she was totally exposed. If anyone came . . .

There was a door to one side. It was large and featureless, and set flush in the tunnel wall. She ran towards it, convinced even as she got close that there would be no way of opening it. But as she reached it, ready to push against it with all her might, something miraculous occurred. The door grew a seam, just as the elevator in the Hub had done, and the two halves slid silently into the wall! Some other time, Tugela would reflect on her

good fortune. But not now. She dashed through and the doors
slid shut behind her.

She was in a square room – some kind of atrium. It was
artificially lit and the light hurt her eyes. On the far side, was
another door, just like the one she had come through. She ran
to it, hoping that it would part just as the other had done. It
did, opening the way to a large cavern. Even before she stepped
through, she sensed that the chamber was far larger than
anything she had yet seen. Standing on the threshold, transfixed,
as the door hissed shut behind her, she knew immediately where
she was. She had stumbled into the great Cathedral of Light!

It was all Tugela could do to prevent herself from dropping
to her knees to pray forgiveness for her sins. She stood, a tiny
figure, dwarfed in the immensity of the place. Above – impossi-
bly high – a vaulted ceiling, hewn from the solid rock, spanned
the giant chamber. But nothing was as astonishing or as awe-
inspiring as the source of the cathedral's light. It flooded into
the chamber through windows!

Arranged around the walls, they were great kaleidoscopes of
phosphorescent colour. Round ones, oval ones, arched ones,
pouring forth artificial sunlight in a place where the sun had
never reached. Some were completely illuminated, others only
partially, mutilated by great blacked-out stretches.

Tugela walked forward a few paces, then stopped. The most
complete window was straight ahead of her. It comprised a
collage of jumbled panels. In one, stars like diamonds studded
the blackness of space, and a curious misty patch lay at the
centre. In another nearby panel, the misty patch had grown to
become the head of a comet, its multiple tails, tenuous and
shimmering, a veil drawn across the background stars. It was
not difficult for Tugela to guess what came next. In a final panel,
the head of the comet slammed into the face of the Forbidden
Zone, and ice and rock rained down across the length and
breadth of the nightmare land.

Other scenes depicted in the windows made little or no sense to her. On one window, which was half obliterated, human figures in ridiculously bulky suits seemed to be floating against the stars. Others, also in bulky suits, were emerging from something huge and blue which partially occulted the Sun itself. In another, people in brightly coloured clothing worked among lush vegetation, the like of which Tugela had never seen in the Land – even before the comets stopped coming.

She walked to where seats began, banks of them, sloping gently downwards. For the first time, she gained some idea of where she was. She had emerged on to a large balcony, high above the floor of the cathedral. The balcony obscured the floor from view. Above her, was another, smaller, balcony, presumably also filled with seats.

She walked down some steps, aware for the first time of smoke from burning candles, out of sight. Looking up at the vaulted ceiling, now that her eyes were completely adjusted, she saw that it was coated with black soot.

The balcony was empty but the floor of the cathedral might not be, so Tugela was cautious as she approached the edge. The Cathedral of Light was the holiest of holy places for the priests and discovery here would mean her death, she was sure. She came to the edge, and leaned over.

At first, all she saw were candles – thousands and thousands of them. The smoke, rising directly upwards, stung her eyes, so it took her time to focus properly. The candles were concentrated immediately beneath the window that depicted the comets. Tugela assumed that there must be an altar of some kind there.

When her eyes began to sting less, Tugela saw that below, too, there were seats – rank upon rank of them, leading up to the altar. Nobody was seated there. Why should they be? The time for services was now past. Up above, Mandelbrot might be advancing towards the walls of the City.

Now that the candles were no longer distracting her, Tugela tried to make out the altar. Something was very strange about it. It seemed to be a conical mound, shrouded in darkness, many times the height of a man. Wooden steps led up to its summit, where a white and purple sheet was draped. Tugela peered harder. The mound resolved itself into an untidy pile of junk — metal objects of unknowable purposes — not unlike the stuff she had seen in the tunnel. Incredibly, it seemed as if it had just been tipped there. Near the base of the pile, half poking from the rubble, Tugela was sure she saw an arm! But, when she squinted, she saw that it was part of a bulky suit, half buried. Immediately, she looked up at the window above the altar. There was no doubt about it. The suit was identical to the ones worn by the men in the window. Higher up the untidy pile, Tugela made out several small wheels. They could have belonged to another of the eight-wheeled vehicles she had glimpsed down a side tunnel. But it was impossible to be sure.

Tugela suddenly grimaced. She was doing it again! She was allowing herself to be distracted by the wonders of this place. What kind of fool was she to be taking in the scenery around her? She had to find Jamilla and Tarragon, and quickly. She made to turn and leave the cathedral. But then the mound moved.

Astonished, Tugela saw that what she had taken for a sheet draping the altar was in fact the back of a priest. He was dressed in the purple robes of the Elite and kneeling, apparently in prayer, at the top of the wooden staircase. As she watched, he rose shakily from his kneeling position and stood. He was a tall man — that was clear enough, even from this distance. She strained to see him better as his robes, which had been creased and folded while he knelt, now fell freely about him. Then she saw the great Eye motif across the priest's shoulders.

She drew in such a sharp breath that she feared she had given herself away. Ducking down as low as she could, she held her hand to her mouth. There could be no doubt about it. The Eye motif could mean only one thing: the priest down there on the altar was no ordinary priest *but Parnassas himself*. She had stumbled into this place and found the High Priest of the City at prayer!

Cautiously, she peered over the balcony. Parnassas had not heard her. He was still standing, looking up at the great window. As she watched, she wondered what he could possibly be doing down here, alone, while the City above – *his* City – was in turmoil. Why was he not on the battlements, rallying the soldiers?

When, across the vastness of the cathedral, the sound of sobbing reached her, Tugela could not at first believe what she was hearing. Curiosity got the better of her and she rose again, overcoming her fear. But she was not imagining it. The sobs were unmistakeable, soft and pitiful. The High Priest – mighty Parnassas – was crying.

Tugela was both shaken and bewildered. But before she could begin even to grope for an explanation, there was a commotion not far from the altar. Someone, a soldier it looked like, had come into the cathedral. Instantly, Parnassas rose to his full height. "Get out!" he roared. Even Tugela cowered at the sound of his voice. "Get out of here!"

When the soldier had gone, Parnassas turned back to the window. He raised his arms in the air. He was a tall man, as Tugela had seen, but, in his voluminous robes, he now seemed to grow larger than a man ought to be. That was the power of this great cathedral, focusing the attention on just one figure at its centre. He raised his arms above his head and began to shout. His voice boomed, a voice of thunder to silence an army of unbelievers.

"I, Parnassas, High Priest of the City, command the comets to come!" And he repeated this several times. But, with each repetition his voice seemed to waver a little more, to get more desperate, as if his belief in himself were evaporating. "I command the comets to come."

Finally, his demand was no longer a demand, it was a plea: "Please bring the comets. We must have the comets." And then

Parnassas was sobbing again. It was appalling, pitiful to hear. "They must come, they must . . . Don't forsake me. Please! The people, they will not believe that I have the power. Give me a sign, I beseech thee. I must show the outlanders now or the City is lost. Everything is falling apart . . . Everything . . ." But, by this time, Parnassas had dropped to his knees again, his body in convulsions.

Tugela was stunned. It took some time before it quite sunk in. *So it was all a monumental lie.* The priests of the City did not have the power to summon the comets. They were just as weak and frail as other mortals. Every year, a handful of comets fell from the sky into the lap of the Forbidden Zone, and whoever sent them – or whatever sent them – was as deaf to the entreaties of High Priest Parnassas as it would be to Tugela's own voice.

Parnassas was climbing down from the altar now. While Tugela watched, he stepped down on to the floor. Then, dejected, defeated, he walked past the rows of burning candles and out of the cathedral altogether.

Tugela did not move. She remained staring at the place atop the altar where Parnassas had been, replaying in her mind all the things she had seen and heard. If Parnassas and his Elite did not control the comets, then who did? Her mind raced. The conclusion became inescapable. In the Land, there had to be another power – greater even than the priesthood itself. It must control the comets. It must control the Eyes. But where was it?

Her thoughts were running away with her. She was sweating, even her breathing was ragged. If there was another power, for five centuries it had remained hidden; the priesthood had ensured that. For five centuries, it had been watching them, sending forth the Eyes to spy on the People. Watching and waiting. But for what, and why?

It was futile. Tugela realised this immediately. And what about the comets? Why had they stopped coming? The obvious answer was that they had been stopped deliberately, as a punishment for the sins of the people. If this were the case, then they were helpless. All they could do, as the last vestiges of their atmosphere drained into space, was to wait and repent and pray for forgiveness. But there was another possibility, one which filled Tugela with even more dread than the first: perhaps the power behind the Eyes was as helpless to stop the air leaking from the Land as they were.

But no, that was something she could not, would not, admit. It would be tantamount to giving up life altogether. She was still young. She had not even begun to live. It was just not fair.

Tugela stiffened and rose. She started up the steps to the back of the cathedral. Half-way to the top, she stopped, and turned back to the great window above the altar. But her gaze was not focused on it, her thoughts were elsewhere, clean across the Land. She was remembering that day, an age ago, when she had stood on the ragged cliffs of God's Window and watched the silver sphere of the Eye disappear into the Forbidden Zone.

Being a witness to that event had provided her with a piece of a puzzle no one else possessed. At the time, she could not begin to guess where her piece fitted; after all, she had had no reason to suspect that the priests did *not* control the comets. But now, in the light of what she had learnt here in the Cathedral of Light, she understood the significance of what she had seen at God's Window.

Whoever, or whatever, controlled the Eyes and the comets was in the Forbidden Zone.

The answers to all her questions lay in there, suddenly she was convinced. But she had no time to dwell on the implications of her conclusion. She had to rejoin Jamilla and Tarragon, and free her parents. Then, somehow, she would have to find a way to get back to Mandelbrot to tell him what she had witnessed. If the outlander Kommandos were hesitating out at the Circleberg, convinced that the priesthood was invincible, she had the one piece of news that would change everything.

But Mandelbrot would need some proof that what she had seen and heard in the cathedral was true. Tugela had no immediate thoughts on what would constitute proof but it occurred to her suddenly that she might find something on the floor of the cathedral. Hurrying to the back of the balcony, she found a staircase. She flew down it, two steps at a time. At the bottom, she waited in the shadow of a pillar, while she peered along the aisle of the cathedral. When she convinced herself that she was safe, she took a deep breath and quickly hurried along the ranks of empty seats.

At the altar, Tugela stopped. What should she take? Her eyes darted back and forth between the pile of metal junk and the door through which she had seen Parnassas leave the cathedral. Her only thought was to pull something, anything, from the mound of the altar, and hope that it would convince Mandel-brot. She crouched by the base of the altar and tried to free a piece of peculiarly twisted metal. But, as she struggled to pull it away, something else caught her eye. Above, on the wooden staircase, a band of white material had caught on the handrail. When she saw it, Tugela's heart leapt. She could hardly believe her good fortune. It was Parnassas's sash of office!

She retrieved the sash from the rail and stood for a while absorbed in studying it. There could be no doubt that it belonged to Parnassas. The Eye motif, repeated at intervals, confirmed it. Quickly, Tugela folded the sash, and stuffed it into her waist-band. Then, overcome suddenly by panic, she ran full pelt back up the staircase. Recovering on the balcony above, her heart pounding in her chest, Tugela's thoughts turned to her next problem: how to get out of this place.

The outer door slid back to reveal the lighted corridor. Thankfully, no one was about. But, Tugela was aware immedi-ately that the level of activity in the tunnels had increased while she had been in the Cathedral of Light. From one direction came the sound of distant voices and of running feet, from the other unidentifiable sounds, further away.

She chose the latter as the safest choice. She turned off into an unlit tunnel but, because she no longer had a torch her progress soon became painfully slow. Still, the sounds she had heard seemed to have faded, so she relaxed a little. She came to a crossroads and took a turning which led towards some kind of light. But, when she heard people again, she turned off before she reached them.

In the blackness of the tunnels, time and space seemed to lose all meaning. Tugela could neither tell how long she had been walking or how far she had travelled. She began to feel that rather than moving towards the exit, she might be succeeding only in penetrating deeper into the network of tunnels. It was all that she could do to fight back down the panic that rose in her. If she had not come suddenly to a place that seemed familiar, the panic would probably have got the better of her.

Even in the darkness, Tugela sensed that she had emerged into a much larger cavern. Both the sound of her footsteps and of her breathing had suddenly diminished. If it was the half-cylinder she had passed through earlier with Tarragon and Jamilla – and Tugela prayed that it was – then she might be able to find her way to her parents. The only way to tell for sure would be to work her way over to one of the walls and feel for the metal racks she remembered had lined them. It was while she was attempting to do this, that the sound of running feet reached her from a side tunnel.

Escape

Light exploded as three shapes bearing torches burst from the side tunnel. Tugela froze. She braced herself for her inevitable capture. But to her astonishment the three torches stopped dead. Silence descended. The torches began to advance. A woman's voice came, querulous, uncertain: "Tugela?"

She could hardly believe her ears. "Jamilla!" she shouted, overcome with relief. She ran to her friend. But before she reached her, two other voices echoed her name in the vast cavern. "Father! Mother!"

Tears of joy were streaming down her cheeks as she threw herself into her father's arms. "Thank God you're all right. I was so afraid they'd hurt you. I was so afraid . . ."

"Tugela, my little girl!" Her father swung her off her feet and whirled her round. He put her down and her mother, fighting back the tears, embraced her and kissed her over and over.

"It's been so long . . . We didn't have any idea what had happened to you. We didn't know what to think. After Boschendale . . ." She choked off, sobbing.

"Mother, father, so much has happened . . . I don't know where to start."

"Save it for another time!" Jamilla interrupted. "You can blab to your hearts' content when we're out of this place. Now, *come on*, we've got to hurry."

Jamilla led them at a brisk trot across the floor of the cavern towards the mouth of the tunnel at the far end. Without glancing back, she said: "What happened to you, Tugela? We assumed you'd been caught."

As she ran, Tugela wiped at her tears. Briefly, she told Jamilla what had happened to her after they had become separated. When she came to the episode in the Cathedral of Light, Jamilla was incredulous. She turned her head. "You actually saw Parnassas?"

"I really did." But Tugela did not go on to tell Jamilla that she had witnessed the High Priest break down and cry at his own altar. Nor did she tell her what she had overheard him say.

Tugela glanced across at her mother and father, on either side. In the light of the flickering torches, they looked tired and old. But at least they seemed well. "I can't believe we're together again," Tugela said. "I had such nightmares . . ."

"We can't believe it either," her father said, patting her across the shoulders and winking at her. Her mother didn't say anything. She just beamed at Tugela through her tears.

As they passed empty metal racks arrayed along the cavern wall, something obvious suddenly struck Tugela. "Jamilla, where's Tarragon?"

"Creating a diversion," Jamilla said. "He's got two of our friends with him – two we got out."

They plunged into the tunnel. Its wall curved away gradually into the gloomy distance. It was a klomter at least before the turn off that led to the elevator shaft. Tugela asked: "Just how did you get my parents out, Jamilla?"

"With a lot of luck." Jamilla dropped back so that she was beside Tugela. She told how Tarragon had struggled with the soldier in the tunnel and finally overpowered him. The pair of them had then gone on and, eventually, located where the priests were holding their prisoners. Only a handful of guards were on duty, Jamilla said. Most soldiers had been sent to the surface to face the outlanders.

Somehow (and here Jamilla skimmed over the details) Tarragon was able to create confusion among the guards. This he exploited to get them in among the prisoners. "As soon as we found our friends," said Jamilla, "Tarragon began to organise a breakout. Finding Bandon and Arinsal wasn't easy, I can tell you. There must have been several hundred prisoners in that place, and without a description of them . . ."

"We were over in a corner," Tugela's father broke in. "Quite a way from the door. At first, we hadn't any idea what was happening. But the word went round that there was a chance to escape."

"We got everyone out as quickly as we could," Jamilla said. "I stood at the door, asking everyone who passed whether they knew you . . ."

"When we heard Jamilla call out your name, Tugela, we were amazed," her mother said. "We had absolutely no inkling that you were in the City. We just couldn't believe you'd come all the way here from Boschendale . . ."

"And come down here – into the bowels of the City." Her

father slapped her on the back again. "God, Tugela, you'll never know how good it was to get out of that place. Day and night they had that artificial lighting on. I don't think the priests knew how to turn it off. It was torture."

"Luckily, the only torture we had to endure," her mother said.

"The breakout was doomed without weapons," Jamilla went on. "As soon as the alarm went up, many more soldiers materialised and most of the prisoners were easily recaptured. We only got away by the skin of our teeth . . ."

Jamilla was slowing now. They had reached the radial tunnel which led directly to the elevator chamber. They all stopped behind Jamilla. She peered round the corner. "Torches!" She signalled for them to stay back.

Tugela and her father crept forward. Sure enough, a long way down the tunnel, lights were flickering.

"There's no other way?" asked Tugela's father.

Jamilla shook her head. Then she handed her torch to Tugela's father. "There's nothing for it, I'll have to take a closer look." Before any of them could protest, Jamilla disappeared down the radial tunnel.

"Be careful," Tugela said, but the woman was already out of earshot.

There was nothing they could do but wait. Tugela stared after Jamilla, but it was far too dark to see anything, except the distant lights. She slumped back against the wall of the tunnel. For a while there was silence as the three of them recovered their breath. Her father put his arm around her and smiled. "Tugela, how about telling your mother and me how you managed to get to the City?"

She told him.

"You rode with General Mandelbrot's Kommando!"

She nodded. "He was riding from Ironvale to the Circleberg, so I joined him."

Tugela's father shook his head with astonishment and glowed with pride. "Did you hear that? She rode with Mandelbrot!"

"I heard," her mother said, not quite so approvingly. "But how in the world did you get to Ironvale in the first place, Tugela?"

"I was with Kasteel."

"Kasteel!" Her father stepped back. He was more astonished to hear that name than he was to hear Mandelbrot's. "But how – ?"

"He came to Boschendale. Don't ask me how he knew about what had happened. He just came. I'd been sitting for hours in the ruins, dazed. I was in a state of shock. Then, suddenly, Kasteel was there, atop his wagon. He gave me food and drink and took me with him to Ironvale."

"But Kasteel?" It had never occurred to her father (why should it?) that his elder brother would be the one to come to the rescue of his daughter. "Is Kasteel here now?" he said. "Did he come to the City, too?"

"I left him in Ironvale. He . . ." (Tugela hesitated). "He hurt his leg. It's a long story, father. I . . ."

Tugela's mother had looked for any sign of Jamilla. She came back and shook her head.

Tugela's father had exhausted his questions about Kasteel. When he spoke again, he had changed the subject entirely. "Tugela, what did you *really* see in the Cathedral of Light?"

"What – ?"

"Tugela, I'm your father. I know when you're hiding something."

She was stunned to realise that her thought processes were so transparent to her father. He placed a hand on her arm and said: "It'll be safe with us, you know that, love. Now, come on, tell your mother and me – what did you see?"

Hesitatingly, she described the scene she had witnessed from the balcony in the Cathedral of Light. She told them how Parnassas had stood before the great kaleidoscopic window and demanded the return of the comets. She also told how he had broken down and actually *begged* for the comets to return. Delving into her clothing, she brought out Parnassas's sash of office. "My proof," she said.

Her father took the sash. He looked at it closely, showed it to Tugela's mother, and handed it back. "I never doubted you, Tugela," he said.

"I know that, father. The proof is for Mandelbrot, not for you. The sash will convince him that I really was in the cathedral and that I did see Parnassas. He has to believe that the priests have no control over the comets, or the outlander cause is lost.

"The Kommandos will be afraid now that they are so close to the City. I rode with Mandelbrot's Kommando so I know. The men will be thinking that the League of Reason speaks the truth: if they attack, they will surely provoke the wrath of the priests. But what I learnt in the Cathedral of Light changes everything."

Inevitably, her father asked the question: "If the priests do not control the comets, then who – ?"

"I don't know,' Tugela said. "I don't know." She hesitated. "But whoever – or whatever – it is, it has to be in the Forbidden Zone."

Her father, though surprised, was not as shocked as she had expected. "Why do you say that?" he said.

Tugela told him of all the peculiar things she had seen and heard since leaving Boschendale. She told her father about the Eye which had flown over God's Window and headed deep into the Forbidden Zone. She told him about the mysterious amphitheatre which seemed so very old. And she repeated everything Tarragon had told her about the caverns as they had descended from the surface on the slings. It was an enormous relief to be able to trust someone at last with all the secrets she had kept for so long.

When she had finished, her father did not say anything. "You do believe me – don't you?" Tugela said.

"Of course I do."

"Then – ?"

"I can find no fault with your conclusion either. An Eye would not venture into the Forbidden Zone without a good reason. You are quite right – someone, or something, must be there. If the priests do not control the Eyes and the comets, then perhaps, as you say, they are controlled from the Forbidden Zone. Your explanation is as good as any."

For a while, there was silence between them. Then her father said: "Tugela, you know what we must do?"

The blood drained suddenly from Tugela's face. She knew exactly what he would say. Her mother grabbed her father by the arm and shook him. "Bandon, no! You can't. We've only just found each other. It's too dangerous!"

He eased her away gently.

"No!" She began to sob.

"Arinsal," he said, "at the moment, we're the only people who suspect that there's something in the Forbidden Zone. Now I can go alone, or Tugela can come with me."

Before her mother could say any more, Tugela broke in. "Mother's right – it's too dangerous."

"Why?"

"You know why. Because the Forbidden Zone is a nightmare place, full of demons and monsters."

"And who says that? *Who*?" Before she could answer, he said: "I'll tell you who, Tugela: the priests. But haven't you just told me that they are liars? Haven't you?"

"But everyone believes – "

"Everyone may be wrong. Look, Tugela, what use are these things that you have learned if we do not act on them. The air above the Land is leaking away. Very soon, our world – everything we know – will be utterly dead. No one knows what to do to stop it. But on your journey here you have seen things that no one else has seen. They hint that answers to our problems might – just might – lie in the Forbidden Zone. It may be a cruel illusion but, Tugela, there is no other hope I can see for our people. We *must* go there.'

It was Tugela's turn to be silent. Her mother had put her arms round her shoulders. She was sobbing quietly to herself. Her father squeezed Tugela's arm.

"Listen to me, and listen carefully. I wasn't really surprised when you told me that there is something in the Forbidden Zone. I have long suspected it from my studies of the Sagas. And in this place I have found yet more evidence.

"I met a priest – a rebel. We talked. Down here, talk is all there is to do, Tugela. This man had actually read some of the oldest manuscripts in the Land: Sagas in their earliest forms. And do you know what he told me?" He paused, for effect. "He told me that there is a Saga which is older than all the others."

"Which one is that?" Tugela said.

"Ah, which one indeed. The Saga is unknown among the outlanders. Even the people of the City do not know it. The priests have deliberately kept it from us!"

"An unknown Saga?"

He nodded. "It seems to date from five centuries ago, from the beginning of the Land. It may be older even than that."

"Older! And what is it about?"

"The priest did not know the precise tale. You see, only fragments survive. But it tells of a journey to a lost land on the far side of the Forbidden Zone."

"A lost land!"

"I thought it would intrigue you."

"What else does the Saga say, father?"

"Precious little, love. Except that the lost land is a very beautiful place. In all the references – and this is the strange thing – the colour blue is used to describe it."

"Blue?"

"The Saga refers to the place as the 'land of blue', or 'the distant blue place'. There are other variations but I can't remember them now."

"And you think this place — this blue land — is where grandfather went?"

"Yes I do, Tugela."

"And could it also be the place that the Eye was heading towards?"

He shrugged, unwilling to commit himself. After a pause, he said: "So, you see, Tugela, someone must go into the Forbidden Zone. We must."

She nodded, resigned.

"Good girl," her father said, hugging her. "Now, what's happened to Jamilla?"

Her father peered round the corner. The torches were still flickering in the distance but there was no sign of their friend.

"Soldiers!" Tugela hissed suddenly.

Three torches were fast approaching along the route they had come.

"Oh God, we're trapped," her mother said.

"We'll have to go on," cried Tugela. "Come on!"

But her father made no attempt to move. "Father, hurry. We'll be caught!" She grabbed at his arm.

"Wait a moment, Tugela!" He pulled away from her and lifted his torch high in the air. Then he lowered it to the ground.

"Father! What are you doing?"

Bandon executed the motion again. This time, one of the approaching torches answered. He turned to Tugela triumphantly. "It's your friends, Tarragon. Back there, we agreed on a signal. It was a gamble, but three torches . . . well, it had to be them."

As the flickering lights came closer, they heard a sound behind them. It was Jamilla. She had finally returned. "You've been so long," Tugela said. "What — ?" But there was no time for the older woman to answer before Tarragon and his friends were among them.

"Tugela!" Tarragon said. "How did you get here?"

"Not now," said Jamilla. "Did the diversion work?"

"The soldiers went down the wrong tunnel but they'll realise soon enough. It's anyone's guess how much extra time we've bought ourselves. But why have you stopped here?"

"There are guards now on the tunnel to the elevators. I counted four soldiers at the next intersection."

"Just four?" Tarragon looked about. "Then there are enough of us. We can rush them." From his belt, he took a sword. He handed it to Tugela's father. "Put out your torches. Now, let's get going."

The four men led the way, with the three women bringing up the rear. They moved quickly along the darkened tunnel towards the lights. But it was clear that they would not be able to get closer than about fifty paces before they would be seen. They waited just outside, pressed tightly against the tunnel wall, hardly daring to breathe. "Ready?" Tarragon whispered. "Right, now!"

Surprise was on their side. The deafening noise of their boots echoing in such an enclosed space must have struck terror in their foe, because the fight was short and one-sided. At the end, one of Tarragon's companions had had his arm slashed – though not badly. But the rest of them, including Tugela's father, had no more than scratches. Two of the four guards lay dead on the floor; the other two had fled.

Tarragon, breathing heavily, called to the others to join them. In his hand, he held a torch he had taken from one of the guards. Another lay on the ground, still burning. When Tugela arrived, she picked it up.

They were about to move off in the direction of the elevators, when they heard shouts from behind them. Dismayed, Tugela turned. The soldiers Tarragon had tricked had finally caught up. Their torches were still some distance away, but it was abundantly clear that there were too many of them to make stopping and fighting a realistic option.

Suddenly her father blurted out: "Tarragon, I'll stay behind and fight. None of us will get out of this place unless someone delays them."

"Father!" Tugela couldn't believe it. He was suggesting sacrificing himself so that she could get away!

Tarragon's two friends were already at Bandon's side. They intended to stay, too.

"I won't let you do it!" In desperation, Tugela grabbed her father's arm.

"Tugela, it's the only way – don't you see? You have to get that message out to Mandelbrot. You have to."

Tarragon was pulling her away but she wouldn't leave her father. "Let me go, I want to stay!"

"Go, Tugela!" her father yelled. "I'll give myself up as soon as it gets desperate. Mandelbrot'll be here to free us in no time, you'll see. Now go! And good luck!"

Tarragon yanked her from her father and they were already running away. She was dazed by the dizzying speed of events. She didn't even notice right away that her mother was not with them. When she did, she turned and shouted: "Mother!" Her mother's voice reached her down the corridor.

"I can't leave Bandon, Tugela. Now go! And be careful!"

Her parents were already in the distance, their shapes silhouetted against the light of many torches. The first clash of swords echoed loudly in the tunnel. Tugela slowed, but Tarragon forced her to keep going. Behind her, she caught a brief glimpse of lights bobbing wildly. After that, she dared not look back. She ran on, numbed by the course events had taken. She had come so far in search of her parents, only to lose them like this . . .

There were no soldiers on guard at the elevators. Their bad luck seemed to be at an end. The three of them who were left – Tugela, Jamilla and Tarragon – rode the slings to the surface. Their progress was maddeningly slow, but there were no soldiers waiting for them above, as they feared. Soon, they were beneath the open sky, which Tugela had doubted she would ever see again.

As they moved through the Inner City, then out into the City proper, she could not stop herself from trembling. Finally, back at the tavern on the square, she broke down and cried until her tears ran dry.

How could she have left her parents down there? How could she?

Jamilla and Tarragon tried their best to comfort her, telling her over and over not to blame herself.

For a long time after they left her, she lay on a bed, staring blindly up at the rafters. She was more afraid than she had ever been in her life. Her father had sacrificed himself so that she might go on. Now she had no choice but to journey to the nightmare land.

Alone.

Mission

"The wagons – where are they going?"

Tugela had been sitting at the window for a long time while Jamilla and Tarragon busied themselves with their interminable plans. From her vantage point high above the main square, she watched the wagons arriving in their scores from little streets on every side. They were forming a long ragged column which wound in a spiral through the crowds of people and around the perimeter of the great open space.

Jamilla looked up from a map she had spread across the table. She seemed a little cross at the interruption. "Supplies," she said curtly. "They're probably taking supplies out to the Circleberg." Immediately, she went back to her conversation.

"Oh," Tugela said. For a while, deep in thought, she continued observing the goings-on in the square below. Then, abruptly, she got to her feet. "Jamilla," she announced. "I'm going down to the square. I won't be long." The older woman acknowledged her with an impatient wave. But she did not look up.

Down in the square, Tugela took a deep breath and launched herself out on to the sea of people. Even now, after what seemed to her like a lifetime in the City, the noise and bustle of so many people concentrated in a single place unnerved her. It was something she was sure she would never get used to even if she lived here the rest of her life.

As she pushed her way through the crowds, Tugela had a definite goal in mind: a clutch of wagons she had spotted from the window high above the square. They were parked, as far as she had been able to make out, in a narrow shadowy sidestreet. The reason for this seemed to be that their drivers had decided not to struggle through the mass of people in order to join the end of the column but to wait instead until the column was in motion. Then, they might be able to slot themselves into any gap that opened up.

When she reached the parked wagons, about ten in all, Tugela saw that several of the wagon drivers were sitting on the kerb playing some kind of game. The game, which she had never seen among the outlanders, involved coloured stones. In turn, each of the men tossed the stones along the ground, to the accompaniment of much enthusiastic shouting and gesturing, little of which made any sense to Tugela. At intervals money exchanged hands.

The remaining wagon drivers were dozing on their wagons. She noticed bottles of liquor, most of which were far from full.

Tugela walked past the men. So engrossed were they in their game that no one noticed her. She began to inspect each load in turn. Some of the wagons were piled high with hay which was obviously intended as feed for military carriers. When she reached the last wagon, Tugela peered beyond it into the sunless gloom. Not more than fifty paces away, the street began to taper; then, a little distance, further on, it fizzled out altogether. It was apparent to Tugela that, at its far end, the street could be entered only from a narrow alleyway.

She turned and began walking back towards the square. In all the time she had been in the tiny side street she had not passed another pedestrian. The street, being a dead end, was little used. It was perfect.

Tugela hurried across the square. Back at the tavern, she quickly gathered up her backpack and cloak from the cupboard on the ground floor where she had stowed them. Then she climbed the stairs to where Tarragon and Jamilla were talking (*still* talking). As she crept past the door to the room, she heard Jamilla's voice raised suddenly in protest. But the comment was out of context, so Tugela could make no sense of it. She searched through several adjacent rooms before she found what she was looking for. Equipped with a marker and paper, she sat down to scrawl a hurried note.

In the note, Tugela tried to find the words to thank Jamilla and Tarragon for all they had done: for saving her life, for reuniting her (briefly) with her parents, but most of all, she tried to thank them for befriending her when she was a stranger in the City. But when she read over what she had written, somehow, it fell short of conveying the thanks she felt. But there was no time to try again. Lamely, she added a promise to return when all this was over, then signed the note.

She gave no clue to where she was going, or why.

She thought she knew the geography of this area well enough to find the alley behind the parked wagons but she was wrong. Once away from the main square, the roads became contorted and Tugela was quickly disorientated. When she finally hit on the place, she had wasted valuable time. Beyond the wagons in the tiny side street, she could see the spiral of those in the main square had already begun to unwind. Luckily, though, it didn't matter. The men on the kerb were still playing their game with the coloured stones and their companions slept on. Evidently, the game players thought they still had a long wait before they could squeeze their vehicles into the column.

Keeping her body flush to the wall, Tugela approached the

first wagon. The driver was snoring loudly. She passed him and came abreast of the second wagon. No one was aboard, which meant its driver had to be one of the gamblers. Standing beside it, she was hidden from the view of the men on the kerb. She made her decision quickly. She threw her backpack up on to the wagon and pulled herself aboard. Immediately, she began burrowing into the hay.

Hardly had she made a comfortable nest for herself than muffled shouts rose up around her. The wagon creaked and swayed as the driver climbed on board. She had hidden herself just in time. Moments later, the vehicle started off, jouncing and bouncing over the cobbles.

It would have been nice to watch the City drop behind her but Tugela did not dare poke her head out of the hay. For a time she was alert to the danger of being discovered but, soon, the rhythmic motion of the wagon relaxed her. She was in almost complete darkness and was warm, really warm, for the first time in a long while. The monotony of her environment quickly sent her to sleep, until the wagon struck a rut in the road and the collision snapped her suddenly back to consciousness. It was a pattern that was to be repeated often on the road out to the Circleberg.

Later, much later, Tugela dared a peek at the outside world. From the hills that rose up steeply at the side of the road, she realised that they were travelling through the Gap in the Circleberg. When her eyes were adjusted to the bright light, she was able to pick out sentries patrolling high on the slopes. But her reconnaissance was cut short because, without warning, there came the clatter of hooves on the road. As Tugela ducked hastily back into her hiding place, a detachment of City soldiers rode by, heading in the outward direction.

Soon after, the wagon came to a rest. Tugela held her breath. She was unable to tell whether this was a temporary stop, perhaps at a guardpost of some kind on the road, or whether they had reached their destination. When she felt the wagon rock as the driver jumped down from his seat, she knew that the latter was correct.

It was imperative that she act quickly, in case men began immediately to unload the wagon. But first she had to know something of her surroundings. She could not risk disturbing much of the cocoon that covered her. Instead, she made do with a small spy hole which she drilled through the hay. It was enough to show her that they were in a large open area at the end of the Gap and that the wagons were drawn up side by side in neat ranks. Already, in the next rank, men wielding pitchforks had begun unloading hay.

There was no cover, only that provided by the wagons themselves. Tugela had no choice but to make a dash for it, and pray. Speed would be her only ally.

She tore away at the hay. She grabbed her bag and emerged from her hiding place into the bright sunlight. No one was about; all the drivers had left and none of the wagons in her rank was being unloaded yet. She swung herself down on to the ground. Beneath the wagon, she could see the feet of the men with the pitchforks. That meant, of course, that they would be able to see her legs, too. If they looked.

She ran along the row of wagons. At the end, the ground rose up in steep hills, which told her that they had not quite passed through the Circleberg. Peering between the wagons, Tugela could see that the main camp of the City's soldiers was still half a klomter away. The wagons, loaded with supplies of all kinds, were stationed well to the rear. It was a stroke of enormous good fortune. Escape would have been quite impossible if the wagon had deposited her within the crowded camp. However, luck hadn't run entirely her way. Scattered about between her and the camp were a number of soldiers, and, looking up into the hills, she could see that several sentries had been posted on the higher slopes.

Tugela reached the end of the wagons and contemplated her next move. Not far away was a clump of shatterpines which might provide some cover. It wasn't easy to see beyond the trees, but the air there was thick with dust. Clearly, something was stirring it up. Carriers! Her heart leapt. Beyond the clump of trees, must be the corral for them. She should have guessed it. If the army's supplies were kept safely at the rear, it would make sense that its carriers would be there, too.

There was no cover at all between the wagons and the shatterpines so there was nothing for it. Tugela took a deep breath and ran full pelt across the open ground. As she threw herself down in the dirt beneath the trees she could hardly believe that she had made it unobserved. When her breathing was under control, she crept forward.

The corral was large, and seemed to contain several hundred beasts. Tugela scanned its perimeter for guards but could see none. Perhaps, because the corral was at the rear of the army, it was thought unnecessary to guard it. But Tugela had to be sure. She scrabbled around in the dirt until she found a sizeable stone. She threw it in a long, looping arc into the midst of the carriers. There was a moment of mild panic among the animals but their snorting and stamping died down quickly. She waited but no one came to investigate. Confident that she was in no immediate danger, she rose to a crouch and skirted round to the gate of the corral. She lifted the bar on the gate and went in. The mount she picked was already saddled. She led it out through the gate and pushed down the bar behind her. Tying her backpack to the straps of the saddle, she climbed on to it.

It took enormous control to ride the charger at a steady trot and not to gallop headlong for Mandelbrot's lines. But Tugela knew that such a course would have called attention to herself and meant certain suicide. Smoothly, she guided the beast along the edge of the hills, gaining the feel of the animal as she went. The course which she followed was one which, she determined, would cause her to intercept the least number of soldiers. For a while, indeed, she intercepted none, but it was inevitable that before long she would attract suspicion. When it happened,

Tugela was already beyond the large encampment. Ahead were only troops of the frontline, engaged in digging some kind of defensive ditch.

She had been spotted by a group of four or five riders. Although still some distance away, they were closing on her fast. At least one of them was brandishing a sword because she could see the blade, flashing menacingly in the sunlight.

Tugela did not wait a moment longer. Yelling wildly, she dug her heels in and galloped headlong the short distance to the front line. As she leapt the half-finished ditch, soldiers with spades scattered all about. One, who was quick enough to realise what was happening, hurled a lance at her. But it missed and landed harmlessly in her wake.

Behind her, she heard the angry shouts of the mounted soldiers. But, as she turned in her saddle, she saw that they had drawn up at the front line. None of them was willing to follow her into the no man's land between the opposing forces. As she galloped through empty country, even their angry shouts faded away. She rode on, not daring to slacken her pace. When, up ahead, she saw the smoke from the outlander camp, tears of relief came to her eyes. At long last, she was back among her people.

She was intercepted long before she reached the outlander camp. But the man who rode towards her, his sword drawn, was not from Mandelbrot's Kommando. He did not recognise her. Nor, when she blurted out the story of how she had escaped from the City, did he believe her. "I am a friend of Mandelbrot," she insisted. "The general will vouch for me, I swear."

The man laughed loudly. "He vouches for spies now does he?"

"I am not a spy," Tugela protested.

"Spy or no spy," he said. "You cannot see him. No one may see him. He sits in conference with the leaders of all the Kommandos." He grabbed suddenly at the reins of her carrier.

"Come. We have men who will get the truth out of you one way or another."

"No!" She tried to pull away but it was no use. Thinking quickly, she said: "There is a man – in Mandelbrot's Kommando. His name is Faro. He will tell you that I am who I say I am."

For a moment the man hesitated. "Faro," he mouthed. From the way that he said it, Tugela guessed that he knew the man. Quickly, she pressed home her advantage. "Faro. Yes, Faro. He will know me."

And so it was that Tugela came to be reunited with the . taciturn outlander who had ridden beside her all the way across the Thirstland from Ironvale. Predictably, the man showed little pleasure in seeing her again. Nevertheless, he did vouch for her, and her captor rode off, leaving her free – but without any · apology. She watched him go, wending his way between the crowded tents of the outlander camp, then turned to Faro, who was feeding hay to his mount.

"What is happening?" she asked. "Why is Mandelbrot talking and not leading the Kommandos on the City?"

Faro stopped feeding the beast and crouched down by the fire. Tugela crouched across from him. While she waited for his answer, he pulled a skewer of meat from the fire and handed it to her. It burnt her mouth but she was hungry and it tasted very good.

"Many men are afraid," Faro said. "They have had much time to think while they rode through the Thirstland and, now, with the City so close . . ." He pulled another skewer from the fire. This time, he bit into it himself. "You were in Ironvale when Mandelbrot and Stel spoke. You remember the man who stood up: Toover?" She nodded. "Well, now more men feel like him. They say the City punishes us for our blasphemy by taking away the air we breathe. If we march on the City, what more will it do to us?" He spat a piece of gristly meat into the fire. "Some of the Kommandos are threatening to return home."

"And throw away everything they have achieved?" Tugela was aghast.

"The feelings run deep."

"How much support does Toover have now?"

"In all, a score of Kommandos have assembled here. Of those Mandelbrot has, perhaps, a half. He knows that to advance on the City with the remainder would be suicide. That is why he is trying to persuade them to stay. But even he cannot work miracles."

So, the enemy within had finally triumphed. More and more men had begun to believe that the City was invincible. And so, of course, it was invincible. The outlanders believed they were up against gods not men. *But she knew better.*

"I must talk to Mandelbrot. I have information that changes everything."

"What information?" Faro asked. He reached into the fire, this time pulling out two skewers, one of which he handed to Tugela.

"Things I have seen in the City." He looked at her dubiously over his skewer. While he chewed on the meat, she told him about what she had seen on the road to the City and in the City itself. "If only you could see the fear in the faces of the priests – and smell it, too. They're mortal, I tell you, just like you and me. And if you could see within the walls of the City . . ." She threw up her arms. "Chaos everywhere. Even the people are rising up against the priests."

"It does not matter," Faro replied between bites. "They control the air, don't they. If they wish, they can – '

"No!" Tugela bit off the last piece of meat and threw her skewer down. "No, no, no. They *don't*." In a great torrent of words, she poured out all that she had seen deep beneath the City in the great Cathedral of Light. Faro sat watching her, blinking. When he began to scratch his head doubtfully, Tugela dove into her backpack and pulled out the white sash of office.

"I got it from the cathedral, from Parnassas himself." She thrust it at him. "Look! See the emblem of the all-seeing Eye."

"From Parnassas?"

"Yes! Don't you see, Faro? The priests don't control the comets. They don't control the air over the Land! They aren't all-powerful. They can be beaten. We, the outlanders, can beat them."

"Now will you take me to Mandelbrot?"

Her audience with Mandelbrot was brief. When she had entered his tent, she had found him pacing back and forth like an animal confined in a cage. Seeing him like this served only to reinforce the impression she had had earlier of him as the supreme predator. Now he was caged by circumstance, while all his instincts told him to lash out at his enemies before they could lash out at him.

He stopped pacing and waved her to a seat. She stepped over food and spilt wine. Close to the flap of the tent lay a smashed tray, which Mandelbrot had flung there, evidently in a fit of anger and frustration. Querulous, Tugela sat down at a make-shift table, strewn with maps of the City and its approaches. Mandelbrot remained standing. "Tell me what you know!" he snarled.

At first hesitatingly, and then with growing confidence, she told him. The transformation it brought about in him was total. She had barely finished her story when she found herself propelled out of his tent and towards another, much larger, where the other leaders were assembled. "The League of Reason," Mandelbrot spat. "What will they say to this?"

For the new audience, she repeated her story yet again — it was the third time by now — and brought out Parnassas's sash. It was passed around, examined closely by all, and even Toover seemed impressed. But his mind was made up, he said; his men would be returning to their farms as soon as they were rested. Tugela couldn't believe his wooden-headedness.

Immediately, Mandelbrot began issuing orders. They were to saddle up their men and await the order to attack. Already, Tugela, the bearer of the vital information, was forgotten.

Faro took her back to his camp fire. There, wrapped in a spare blanket, she slept. Much later, he shook her awake. While she wiped the sleep from her eyes and drank a hot drink he had handed her, Faro told her that all but two of the Kommandos had been swayed by her story. One would return to Ironvale, while another, Toover's, was headed for a more distant location. What remained, Faro said, would be a match for anything the City threw at them.

"Mandelbrot says, if there's anything . . ."

"I have to get back to Ironvale," Tugela said.

"That's one thing that is already arranged. You leave soon with the returning Kommando. If you remember, Mandelbrot tried to get rid of you once before. This time, he wants to be absolutely sure."

Tugela was sorry to leave but her mission – and that was what she now considered it – lay elsewhere.

The trip through the Thirstland was uneventful. As on the outward journey, they passed outlander wagons heading for the thicker air of the Great Depression, but their numbers were greatly reduced now, many having already completed the journey. At one point, Tugela was sure that they were passing close to the great bowl where Mandelbrot's Kommando had stopped to rest and where she had seen the mysterious post holes in the ground. But so much of the arid land through which they travelled was undistinctive that she could not be sure. Nothing else caught her attention – until the column of refugees just outside Ironvale.

One of them was her uncle, Kasteel.

It was a meeting of few words in which neither could adequately express the guilt they felt: Tugela for leaving her uncle when he was drunk and injured; Kasteel for being drunk and neglecting his niece in the first place. He rode a carrier now because his wagon had become redundant; there were simply no people at the Periphery left to trade with. His leg had apparently healed.

Kasteel made a sorry sight. Perhaps that was why, when he asked where she was going, Tugela told him – God's Window – and why when he asked whether he could come with her, she said, yes. It puzzled her that he would want to go back to what, for him, was a place of terror but she accepted it. She was dreading travelling alone, anyhow. She did not tell Kasteel that she intended to go into the Forbidden Zone. But it was clear to her that he had guessed that much. For the second time in his life, and for reasons she could not guess, he had opted to follow a member of his family to the edge of the Land.

Precipice

Kasteel had been a revelation. Without him, Tugela doubted that she would ever have found the secret route down the cliffs. Earlier, staring out from the edge of the plateau across the endless grey wastes of the Forbidden Zone, she had found her limbs paralysed by the enormity of the task she had set herself. Her uncle, on the other hand, had been galvanised into action the instant they had reached the edge of the precipice. He had set off along the jagged edge, pausing at intervals to peer over and down the sheer face of the cliffs, before hurrying once more on his way.

Tugela was vaguely aware that he was searching for something, some signpost he remembered from another time, but the vista before her occupied all of her mind, leaving little to think on what precisely her uncle was up to. Only his sudden shout, whipped across the plateau by the cold harsh wind, shocked her back to reality. Peering into the distance, she saw Kasteel, a tiny figure, waving at her urgently.

When she reached him, he was crouching beside a rough mark – a cross – scored in the rock at the cliff edge. A gust of wind slapped her hard in the face, forcing the breath from her. Pulling her cloak tightly about her shoulders, she stood over Kasteel. "Here, damn it! Look!" At the command, she dropped into a crouch. Immediately, she saw what he wanted her to see. Initials, small and spindly, had been scratched crudely along one arm of the cross. Her mind, befuddled by the thin air high on the plateau, did not at first grasp the significance of the letters incised in the stone. It took Kasteel, yelling above the howl of the wind: "Count them, girl. Count them!"

Momentarily, the fog of her brain cleared and the light of understanding stabbed through. She knew without even having to count the letters, that there were six sets of initials. (How could there be any other number?) Six spindly sets for the six travellers who had come to this place across the centuries and paused, each in their turn, to make their mark before descending the cliffs and leaving the Land for ever. They were the last marks made by the Lost Ones, some barely visible, all but erased by the wind and the rain of centuries, others as fresh as if they had been scored in the rock only yesterday.

And one of the freshest was the mark of her grandfather.

With her finger, she began to lightly trace his letters. Over and over, she traced them, lost completely in her thoughts. With his own hand, her grandfather had formed these letters. Her flesh and his had occupied the same space; only time separated them now. For the first time in her life Tugela felt close to the grandfather she had never known.

Looking up at last, she saw that Kasteel was crying, tears streaming down his cheeks. Suddenly she caught a glimpse of the Kasteel beneath the armour shield. She touched his arm gently, reassuringly. But at her touch he shot to his feet and turned away, shaking. For a while nothing but the roar of the wind broke the silence, and then he turned back, once more in command of himself, with only the redness of his eyes to betray him.

While Tugela watched, Kasteel stooped to pick up a stone, a sharp-edged one from a pile of others. Without ceremony, he handed it to her, gesturing with a nod at the cross on the ground. She understood instantly what he meant. She bent down and began to engrave her own initials in the rock beside her grandfather's. An electric thrill raced through her body. As she worked at the task, slowly, methodically, she felt more alive than she had ever been before. This is my destiny, she thought. For better or for worse, I am writing myself into history.

When she looked up again, Kasteel had vanished and the plateau was empty. She leapt to her feet, spinning round frantically. But then she started to think. There was only one place her uncle could have gone. When Tugela realised that, she steeled herself and advanced slowly, with infinite caution, towards the brink of the precipice . . . and craned over.

Below, incredibly, was a narrow ledge. As her eyes adjusted to the gloom in the shadow of the cliff, Tugela made out what seemed to be a fault. It cut into the face of the cliff and sloped downwards, not steeply but gently, until swallowed in blackness. From some distance below a disembodied voice called up to her. She shouted back an answer but the wind blew away her words. Taking a last glance at the Sun setting behind her, and the Land she might never see again, Tugela lowered herself gingerly on to the ledge.

In the darkness, and it was very, very dark after the plateau, she shuffled along sideways, pressing her backpack hard against the face of the cliff. The wind had momentarily died down but she was acutely aware of how exposed she would be if it got up again and how slippery the ledge might get if rain came with it. As she pressed on and down, she could just make out the edge of the ledge, barely more than a short stride away. She prayed it would get no narrower as they descended.

The voice came again from below her, even further away than before, urging her to move faster. She shouted back that she was going as fast as she could but she made a conscious effort to go quicker all the same. After descending a while, gaining confidence all the time, she heard Kasteel shout again and, this time, she was sure she had closed the gap on him. It was then that she lost her footing. It wasn't a serious slip and she regained her balance almost instantly but a stone she dislodged with the toe of her boot skittered over the edge and fell into the abyss. For a while, she stayed perfectly still, calming herself by breathing deeply. Finally, she managed to banish from her mind the terrible thought: How long does it take to fall two klomters?

She began to concentrate her mind on the feel of every step and on the texture of the damp cold rock beneath her palms. It helped her stay calm and she began to make good progress again. Very soon, a dim shape coalesced out of the gloom. Kasteel, as was his way, gave her no words of comfort or reassurance, but it was enough that she was no longer alone in a pitch dark universe and had someone close enough to follow.

The ledge was getting steeper. It was also getting narrower. Concerned, she broke the silence and asked Kasteel about the path ahead. By now, she was confident that he had come this way before, years ago in pursuit of his father, and that he remembered every step he had taken along the route. Not pausing, Kasteel shouted back that the ledge would remain narrow for just a short stretch but then it would flare out again. It would continue to steepen, though. The answer was not reassuring, but at least she knew what to expect.

The wind was getting up again and Tugela felt the first spots of rain on her face. It brought a new urgency to the descent and, despite the steepening slope, she maintained her pace. She stumbled several times more but, each time, she recovered quickly and managed to keep the figure of Kasteel in her sights. Time lost all meaning in the blackness against the naked cliff face, but it seemed to Tugela that they had descended a quarter, perhaps a third, of the way down to the plain of the Forbidden Zone. At least the air she was breathing seemed thicker.

The rain which Tugela had so feared came to nothing. She began to entertain the thought — a dangerous one in the circumstances — that they might reach the foot of the cliffs without any mishap. But, quickly, she banished it from her mind. They were making good progress now. The ledge was still steep, but it had widened again, as Kasteel had predicted. This meant that it was no longer necessary for Tugela to press her palms to the rockface and edge sideways. Instead, she could descend with ease as if she were on a wide but steep staircase. It was far less strain on her aching legs.

The descent down God's Window was, thankfully, proving quite uneventful. Then, as they were picking their way round the rubble of a rockfall, which had so nearly blocked the path completely, suddenly, out of the darkness there came a piercing cry. Tugela froze in her tracks. Even her unperturbable uncle let out a gasp of shock. The sound was terribly close. It broke over them like a wave, battering them with its sheer physical force. Then, it came again, this time even closer. Out of the gloom appeared a giant wing, far longer than a man was high. It swept past the ledge, so close that the draught threatened to topple her into the abyss. It was a glideagle. But a glideagle at closer quarters than she had ever seen before.

"Quick!" Kasteel shouted. He had overcome his momentary paralysis and sprinted ahead along the ledge. Tugela stumbled after him, terrified that at any moment she might be plucked off the face of the cliff and dropped on to the rocks below. They had hardly got going before they came across the nest. It contained three giant eggs and was so large that they had to skirt around it. Fascinated, Tugela slowed a little. But the cry of the glideagle, coming again, louder and more enraged than before, spurred her on. As the great wing swept past again, she did not even look up at it, but kept running with her head down. Several more times, the terrible screech of the bird pierced the gloom but on each occasion it seemed further away. Finally, it stopped altogether.

Both shaken, they stopped to rest a while. From her pack, Tugela took some bread which she divided between them. She had some dried fruit, too. Kasteel, who as always ate in silence, bolted it down as if he hadn't eaten for days. Tugela wondered, as she sipped at the water from her canteen, how the meagre provisions she had brought would last them on their trek through the Forbidden Zone. After all, she had only planned for one. By the time they moved on, Tugela had stopped trembling. Her limbs, however, were weak, as limbs always are in the wake of a sudden rush of adrenalin. Quickly, she got into a rhythm, though, her step rising and falling automatically. The brain-numbing repetitiveness of the descent freed her mind to think. And once again doubts crowded in on her. She was risking her life on a crazy hunch. She wondered why she had not shared her secret with someone other than her father – with Jamilla, for instance, or Tarragon? It would have made things so much easier. Hadn't Jamilla saved her life; she could have trusted her. And Jamilla would have told her whether she was mad or not. She glanced at Kasteel, now only a few strides ahead. How much did he know of her quest? She suspected that he knew more about the Eyes and the Forbidden Zone than he let on. But did he also suspect that there was something in the Forbidden Zone, some power that might bring back the air to the Land? He was helping her down the cliffs, wasn't he? That must mean something, she thought. But it might only mean that he wanted her to follow in the footsteps of her grandfather. He, Kasteel, because of fear or because of responsibility to his family, had not followed. Was he helping her in order to ease his own guilt?

Kasteel stopped so abruptly that Tugela nearly bumped into him. "What is it?" she said, alarmed. They were now on a stretch of the ledge which unknowable forces had buckled and cracked and which Tugela judged was about three-quarters of the way down. When he spoke, his voice was heavy with emotion as if he was trying to say something he had been saving up for a long while. It came out only as an incoherent mumble. "I don't understand," she said. With an effort, Kasteel tried again. Tugela saw that he was trembling.

"I cannot go any further," he said.

"But why?" He shot a quick glance forward and down along the ledge and the terror in his face answered her question. Tugela knew now: This was how far Kasteel had come last time.

He was near to breaking point, she could see. By becoming her guide, he had relived all his old nightmares. She began to understand for the first time just how much it had taken to come with her. All those years ago, something had happened at this point. Kasteel had been unable to go on. He had been torn. Since then, his life had been overshadowed by guilt, the terrible guilt that he had not followed his father into the Forbidden Zone. But, if he had followed, what would have become of the family? Did he not realise that he had done what was best for everyone in the circumstances? He had been no more than a boy, little older than Tugela was now.

She held out her arms and, this time, he did not shy away, though, at first, he remained stiff and unresponsive. Finally, he embraced her and she knew that it was heartfelt. "Good luck," he said.

"Kasteel," she replied. "*Kasteel* . . ." But he was already gone, climbing rapidly up the face of the cliffs. "You did right . . ." She thought she saw him falter briefly but she could not be sure. Did he hear her? It was impossible to tell.

The Forbidden Zone

When Tugela woke, her limbs were so stiff with the cold that it hurt when she tried to move them. The long night had well and truly arrived in the Land and the air temperature had plunged dramatically. Grimacing, she got to her feet and attempted to shake some life into her body. She began to massage her left arm, which was stiff because she had slept on it. But even when she had finished, it still felt like a bruise from wrist to shoulder. Defeated, she let it hang limp at her side.

Because of her preoccupation with her frozen body, it was a while before Tugela could take in any of her surroundings. In truth, however, there was little to see. Above, the familiar stars shone brightly, now the only source of light. But even they were excluded from a full half of the sky by the cliffs of God's Window rising behind her. Though her neck, too, ached, she looked straight up the sheer face to the knife edge where the stars ended so abruptly. Had she really descended two klomters down that sheer rock face? She shook her head with disbelief. Standing now, with her feet planted firmly on level ground, it seemed utterly impossible.

Rubbing her neck with her good arm, Tugela stared into the Forbidden Zone. Immediately, she felt panic rise and she backed further into the lee of the cliffs. The cliffs might be ominous but, at least, they connected her to the Land above. Out there was only . . . Immediately, she reprimanded herself for thinking such thoughts. She leant over to her backpack and allowed herself a small ration of bread and dried fruit; washed down with a few mouthfuls of precious water, it was enough. Before fear had a chance to freeze her more thoroughly than the cold, she headed out into the nightmare land.

The stars were bright and formed an almost unbroken net just as they did above the Land. Used to the long, dark nights, Tugela, like the rest of her people, had good night vision. It allowed her to see enough of the hills around to steer a safe course. As long as the great bulk of the cliffs loomed behind her, she would be sure of her direction. Later, when they fell out of sight, Tugela would use the stars to keep her on course.

The most striking thing about the Forbidden Zone was its complete lack of shatterpines. So far, Tugela had seen none at all. In fact, all plants seemed very scarce here. But then, all the shatterpines in the Land, as far as she knew, had been planted by people. With no people in the Forbidden Zone to get the soil started, only the very hardiest of plants could get a hold.

The lack of greenery to break the drab greyness of the rolling hills added to the severity of the landscape, making it seem even colder than in fact it was. Tugela pulled her cape up around her neck, although she was now resigned to being permanently cold. The wind was not strong but it made a disconcerting whining sound which an active imagination could make much of. Several times, Tugela thought she heard the cry of a beast out in the shadows. Each time, she responded by hurrying faster. Nothing ever appeared but she kept up her guard, nevertheless.

Perhaps there was another reason why nothing much grew here. When the comets struck, what must it be like in this blasted land with the sky ablaze? Tugela shuddered to think. But the comets weren't coming – that was the point – they hadn't come for an age now. Silently, as she had done a hundred times before, she prayed for their return. Only wait until I'm safely back in the Land, she added this time.

On and on. Over hills and along valleys. Many times, Tugela stopped to rest, once or twice to doze fitfully, but always to press on before sleep took her to a place beyond suffering. Fear of the nightmare land receded until she ignored the cries brought to her on the back of the wind, was indifferent to the black shapes that crept in the shadows. She was constantly tired. She was constantly hungry, but beyond that she felt nothing. Even her reasons for being in the Forbidden Zone had slipped out of sight. She put one foot in front of the other. That was all. Over and over again. Until, at last, climbing a rubble strewn gulley, she fell. And where she fell, she stayed.

She was unhurt but even if she had been hurt it would have made no difference. Deep down in her mind, a voice was hammering, *Keep going, keep going*, but the voice was fading fast. Her eyes closed, opened, then closed again. She struggled but the fight was going out of her. When her eyes opened again, fatigue had almost won. Almost, but not quite.

Because something was moving against the stars.

It was an Eye, flying so high that it still caught the light of the Sun, already well below the horizon behind her. Somehow, Tugela got to her feet. She no longer cared whether she was caught or not.

The Eye had come straight out of the Land and was heading into the heart of the Forbidden Zone. Gradually, though, it dwindled in intensity, until, finally, it passed into the shadow region where even the Sun's light could not reach it. Tugela relaxed her concentration and made to turn away. But, before she could, she was startled by a tiny flash.

The Eye had reappeared, transformed now into a tiny blue-white star.

As she watched, bewildered, the star faded in its turn, before dropping out of sight behind a line of jagged mountains straddling the horizon. How could that be?

Her first idea – the most obvious one – was that the Eye had switched on some kind of internal light source. But she was sure that Eyes shone from reflected light alone. Then, what other explanation could there be?

Something had lit up the silver sphere of the Eye after it had gone beyond the reach of the Sun's rays. Something below the curve of the world.

Tugela was still dreadfully tired but it was the incentive she needed. She ate and drank from her depleted rations as a substitute for the sleep she would rather have had and, keeping her eyes glued to the horizon before her set off again. She saw nothing. Nothing at all. But still she pressed on. So deep had she dug into her reserves of strength now, she feared she could not take another disappointment. Doubts began to fill her. Perhaps she was delirious and had imagined the Eye. Soon, she began to flag again. She was climbing a gentle rise. To the top, she told herself, then rest. *Just make it to the top.*

Suddenly, she was there.

White fire spilled over the horizon, so bright that it nearly blinded her. She gasped at the sight, incredulous.

It was another Sun!

Before any conscious thought directed her, she found herself running towards it. How many times she stumbled and fell as she ran she did not count. Each time, without a thought, without any apparent awareness of the bruises and the cuts darkening her skin, she picked herself up and staggered on. She was in the thrall of the incredible apparition and every footfall brought more of it into view.

A Sun that existed below the horizon of the Land, always hidden, except from the Forbidden Zone.

But as Tugela ran on, she realised something even more extraordinary. It was not a Sun at all! As her eyes adjusted, she realised that she could look at it directly. And it wasn't even white, it was blue-white. Definitely blue. There was no doubt in her mind.

She had found the blue land!

But the blue land was growing. She saw that it was a land in the sky. Soon, a sizeable portion of what seemed to be a globe protruded above the horizon. Blue and white and *glowing*. It was the most beautiful thing she had ever seen and she could not tear her eyes away from it nor fight back the tears. She stumbled on.

Ahead, something was winking at her. At first, she felt only a vague sense of resentment that something was competing for her attention and that she must take her eyes, even for an instant, from the great globe in the sky. Then, she came to her senses. She stopped and squinted into the distance. Immediately, she knew that she had found what she was looking for.

A jagged wall of mountains rose up in front of her. In the foothills a cluster of silver buildings glinted in the light. Each tiny structure shone so brightly it was like a shard of broken mirror against the dreary grey of the hills. To the girl, it was a sudden and glorious confirmation of all she had dared to believe in the face of common sense.

Someone did live in the Forbidden Zone.

If she had had any tears left, she would have sobbed with joy. Instead, all she could manage was a huge sigh of relief, and with it miraculously, most of her tiredness evaporated.

The buildings were much further away than she had at first guessed. She had grossly underestimated both the scale of the mountains and of the foothills. But finally, Tugela mounted a rise and there, ahead, on the summit of a low hill which was curiously level but otherwise undistinguished, she found the tight huddle of buildings.

Tugela knew, even before she could touch them, that the buildings were constructed of a material which existed nowhere in the Land. It had the appearance of silvered mirror. The realisation frightened her a little but it also filled her with hope. She became convinced that they had been erected by a power greater than any in the Land. If such a power existed, she reasoned, then perhaps it could also bring back the air.

As she neared her goal, Tugela glanced about her warily and felt for the dagger beneath her cloak. Its presence reassured her. There were about ten buildings, as far as she could tell, arranged, apparently randomly. Not one of them made the least bit of sense to her. All were low and squat and made of the same smooth, silvered material. Some were rectangular and some had more than four sides; all were less than the height of a single-storey. Wandering among them, Tugela began to wonder whether they were houses at all. In not a single one could she make out an opening that might be a door or window.

Gathering her courage, she approached one of the smaller buildings. Her own reflection came out to meet her and, for a brief moment, she allowed herself to believe that there were two people, not just one, in her universe. After the loneliness of the journey, she longed for someone to talk to. Banishing the silly thought from her mind, she reached out to touch the construction's surface. It felt smooth and hard like the metal of her dagger, and very, very cold. It made her shiver.

She walked on.

Emerging on the far side, she noticed for the first time that there were tracks cut into the dust. Curious, she crouched down to examine them. The tracks were not unlike those made by a wagon, only the wagon that had made these had to be very small indeed. The tracks had a peculiar criss-cross pattern to them which puzzled her. There was something else, though, that bothered Tugela much, much more than these minor details. *Where were the hoof prints of the carriers?*

Looking back, Tugela could see that the tracks emerged from one of the squat "houses". She could also see, even from some way off, that there was no discernible door to the "house". She began to follow the tracks, which led away from the cluster of buildings. Other tracks soon joined them. Each set came from one or other of the buildings. The implication seemed to be that they were vehicle sheds of some kind. Obviously the particular route Tugela was following was a well-used one.

She peered ahead but could see only that the combined tracks led up to a ridge where they disappeared abruptly from view. She wanted to follow but realised that if anything decided to come over that ridge, she would get no warning at all of its approach. She decided to leave the tracks and made her own way up to the top. An instant later, she had thrown herself flat against the ground and was hardly daring to draw a breath.

Eyes!

She was lying on the rim of a bowl-shaped depression, not unlike a thousand similar ones across the Land. But this one, like the nest of some fantastic bird, was filled with a great clutch of silver eggs. She had found the source of the Eyes.

Hardly had Tugela time to take in the astonishing scene below than a sudden movement startled her. As she watched, terrified, something detached itself from the cluster and began working its way steadily up towards her.

A devil creature! And it had seen her.

Like everything else in this place, it was silver, though liberally stained with dust. It had a small, cylindrical body and moved on strange continous tracks which wound round and round a set of wheels. The peculiar method of locomotion had Tugela entranced. Clearly, this was the creature that had made the criss-cross tracks in the dust.

Amazingly, the devil creature did not come for her. Instead, it stuck slavishly to its well-worn path. Though it did pass close by, Tugela could make out only a faint whirring sound, so faint in fact that she was not entirely sure she had heard it. Essentially, the creature moved silently.

With an apparent effort, it heaved itself on to the ridge and was gone, descending rapidly towards the buildings. Tugela watched while it dwindled in size. She was torn between wanting to follow it, to discover where it was headed, and getting a better look at the Eyes. She decided on the latter. With the creature occupied elsewhere, it was a golden opportunity.

She got to her feet and brushed the dust off her clothes. A thin wind blew a steady wall of grit in her face but once she was over the lip of the bowl it died down.

Half-way there her heart almost stopped. Another devil creature, identical to the first, came into view. But this one did not move, though Tugela watched it closely. Either it was dead or it was slumbering. Not taking her eyes off it, she continued her descent.

In the bowl, Tugela estimated there were about twenty Eyes.

Deliberately, she chose the one that was the furthest from the inactive creature. As she approached, she became aware for the first time of how big the things were. Looking down from the ridge above, there had been absolutely nothing to compare them with. Now she could see that each Eye was taller than a man.

As she circled the silver sphere, she could see nothing on the surface but her own reflection, ridiculously distorted by its curve. Gingerly, she touched it. It felt cold and smooth and hard, just like the wall of the building.

Finally she sat herself down in the dust beside it. She positioned herself carefully so that she could see both the sleeping creature and the rim of the bowl – in case the other devil creature decided to return. By leaning to one side, she could also see the blue-white globe in the surface of the Eye, swollen enormously.

What now? Fatigue was near to overwhelming her and she could no longer think straight. She had travelled so far, discovered so much that was unexpected and yet, still, she seemed no nearer to solving the puzzle of the Eyes. Whoever, or whatever, controlled them – was it here? It could be hiding, of course, but somehow Tugela had a gut feeling that nobody lived here, and never had done. The devil creature she had seen did not seem important. She felt certain that it was some sort of mindless slave.

She had to sleep but she could not sleep here – it was far too dangerous. She would find a safe place, perhaps over the next hill, and bed down. When she had rested and was able to think more clearly, she would come back. She stared deep into the Eye. If only I could see in, she thought. Wearily, she got to her feet and turned to walk away. There was a movement in the corner of her eye. She spun on her heels immediately but the sleeping creature had made no move. But when she turned back to the Eye, she gasped with shock. *Where there had been nothing before, now there was a circular opening.*

Tugela's first reaction was to back off quickly, in case

anything came out. In a low crouch, with her dagger held tightly in her hand, she waited. Every muscle in her body was taut and on the verge of snapping. If even an insect had tried to alight on her, it would have died a sudden death before touching down. But nothing came out of the Eye.

Not daring to relax a muscle, Tugela advanced. Through the opening she could see that the interior of the Eye was illuminated a brilliant white. But the light dazzled her a little and she could make out no real detail. She moved closer, at intervals glancing over her shoulder, in case a devil creature should take the opportunity to creep up on her. Then, cautiously, she reached out her hand and poked a finger through the opening. By this means, she determined that the opening was real and no illusion. She withdrew her hand and stood a moment, thinking. After taking several deep breaths to calm her nerves, she looked about her, then, advanced and stuck her whole head through. There wasn't much to see. The interior seemed largely empty apart from a row of coloured lights on the far wall. As she watched, several of them winked at her. *The thing was alive.* She pulled her head out quickly and just managed to resist running away.

Tugela considered what to do next. She was exhausted and would have to rest soon. If she should leave this place now and return later, what guarantee was there that an Eye would open up to her again? Though her mind was befuddled, she recognised that she had been presented with an opportunity she could not pass up. She thrust an arm through the opening and touched the interior. It felt soft and padded, it did not feel threatening. She was gripped by awful indecision, swaying first one way then the other. Finally, she took a last look around her and stuck her head back through the opening. This time, the rest of her body followed.

In the Eye, it was warm and, oddly, the air actually felt thicker and easier to breathe than it had outside. She stood and peered for a while at the lights on the wall but they made no sense to her and, after a while, she got tired of their flickering and sat down. Instantly, the padded surface which lined the Eye moulded to her shape. Its movement unnerved her a little and she jumped back quickly to her feet. She began searching for the source of the light but could not find it. The pearly luminescence seemed to come from everywhere and from nowhere. It was all very strange. She satisfied herself that there was nothing else to see in the interior and turned to leave.

But the opening had now gone.

Gripped by panic, Tugela threw herself at the place where the door had been. All she found was soft padding, continous and seamless. She tried desperately to tear at it but the material was immensely strong and it resisted all her efforts. Tears streamed down her cheeks and she tried other places on the wall but it was no use. Wild with anger and frustration, she threw herself at the wall, hammering hard with her fists. But even the sound of her assault was swallowed up instantly by the padding. Finally, she gave up struggling altogether.

For an age, she sat shaking, certain that the devil creature would come for her. But it didn't. She drifted in and out of sleep and her dreams were confused and filled with horrors. But then, much later, after waking soaked with cold sweat, she slipped back into a deeper sleep. This time, she dreamt exclusively of the great blue globe in the sky. When finally she woke completely, blinking in the unnatural light and wiping the sleep from her eyes, the image of that globe was still burned into her mind. She felt sure that her answers lay there. "The blue-white land in the sky," she said to herself. "I *have* to go there."

Tugela hardly noticed the slight tug as the Eye lifted off the ground and began climbing towards the stars.

Book Two
ONDRAY

1

In the easy years, old problems were largely forgotten. Hunger, famine, cold and environmental uncertainty were relegated to footnotes of history, like the Black Death. In the twenty-sixth century, people had no more interest in the events of the twenty-first century than inhabitants of the twenty-first century had in the plague that had cut the human population in half in the fourteenth century. Where civilization survived, in the Islands, there was plenty for all. If the plant and animal life lacked variety, that meant nothing to eyes that had never known variety; and both the plants and animals that survived were ideally suited to the warm weather, the gentle rain, and the equally gentle seasonal fluctuations. Even in some less civilised parts of the world, human life persisted, or was returning. Ships travelled as far as Australia, where there was news of island-hopping traders that had reached far to the north, even crossing the equator. The news was all good. Conditions had stabilised after the Flood; the biosphere had set in its new mould as the Virus was assimilated. The world experienced a golden age unknown since the centuries of warmth that had followed the ending of the Ice Age, ten thousand years before.

But one watcher worried about the possibility of change. Safety and security depended upon stability, and the records showed that such a long period of stability was far from being normal during Earth history. From the ground, and limited to one observing site (even though it was the mountaintop observatory at R'apehu), the early signs of change were hard to detect. The watcher needed confirmation, especially data from instruments in orbit, above the confusing layers of the Earth's atmosphere.

No human being had climbed to the R'apehu observatory in centuries. Interest was focused on things closer to home. There were farms to tend; the sea nearby for recreation. If a road had once existed up the mountainside, there was scarcely any trace of it to be found today. But if some adventurous spirit had made the climb, he, or she, might have been surprised to find how well preserved the low domes of the observatory seemed to be, even allowing for the cold, dry mountain air. The adventurer would have been even more surprised if the visit had coincided with one of the occasions – rare, but becoming less rare – when the highest dome opened, like a clamshell, and briefly emitted an intense pulse of blue light, scarcely visible from more than a few hundred metres away, pointing like a long finger up into the sky.

The pulse, always repeated three times at five minute intervals, was always directed to the same spot on the sky. Then, for a full hour before closing again against the ravages of wind and weather, the dome would remain open, but still and silent, as if waiting for a reply that never came.

2

The birth of a child was still a cause for celebration, even though the population was now edging slowly back upwards. Gwillam and Karmen had each tried several partners in seeking for a fertile combination, and they were both in their fifties, with time no longer on their side if they were to become parents. As soon as the zygote had been pronounced viable and healthy, they had signed a contract of marriage, to last until the boy came of age.

They took their responsibilities seriously, and would give the new citizen the best possible start in life.

Ondray was, of course, largely brought up alone. Full siblings were extremely rare, and it was even more unusual for two children of the same parents to be closer in age than a dozen years or so. The slow rise in population owed as much to the longevity of the small number of people that were being born as to their fertility. There were other children around, and some of them formed close friendships, but somehow Ondray always seemed to be excluded. People had a lot of respect for Gwillam; any Council member got that, and anyone dedicated enough to serve a second term on the Council clearly had the good of society very much at heart. But it didn't seem quite normal, somehow, to be so dedicated to serving the community, when there were so many more pleasurable ways to pass the time. Sure, somebody had to do it. Keep the Link on its toes, allocate the use of limited resources (and somehow more of the resources seemed to be limited and in need of allocation these days; there's bureaucracy for you). But one term of service in a lifetime was more than enough for most people, while a few years after Ondray was born Gwillam began serving a second, voluntary and indefinite term. Along with the respect, Gwillam was regarded as a bit of an odd fish, not someone you'd want to get too closely involved with – and the son he was so proud of became distanced from his contemporaries through the family association.

3

"Wirehead!" The taunt stung, even though Ondray didn't really understand why the other kids used it as an insult. All it meant was that he liked talking to the Link. Well, he did. So what was it to them? And why should they call him names for it? And yet, the names still hurt.

There were three of them, all older than him. The only person he knew that was younger than himself was Larissa, and she didn't count. She was barely three, while he was nearly seven. Kjiri was the oldest, the biggest and the ringleader. Mostly, Petran and Gayorg did what she wanted, which often involved lighting fires in places there weren't supposed to be any fires, and largely unsuccessful attempts to reduce the wildlife population of the woods. Mostly, Ondray kept out of their way. But sometimes he felt the need for friends. The fact was, he didn't have any. There was nothing to bond him to any of the other four children in the town. But in the absence of anything better, he sometimes hung out with the boys, who really were okay on their own, and occasionally he even joined in the activities led by Kjiri – with Ondray usually trying to hang back and take a minor role, while she would push him to the front and dare him to wilder acts than any of them.

So far, no serious harm had been done. But this time, Ondray sensed, it was different. Maybe it was the oppressive, stormy heat. Maybe the boredom of her way of life had finally got to Kjiri (or maybe, Ondray was to reflect, much later in his life when he looked back on the incident, it was something to do with the onset of adolescence in the girl). Whatever, Ondray knew he was in trouble. Deep in the woods, far from any adult interference and far from any Link connection, Kjiri clearly had something unpleasant planned, with Ondray not, this time an unwilling participant, but an even more unwilling victim.

They had him backed up against a tree, flinging taunts. Kjiri carried a short stick, which she had been stirring in some animal droppings. "You know what wireheads are? Shitheads!" She seemed to find this enormously funny, and brandished the stick in his face. "Shithead Ondray!" She wiped it on his hair.

It was like a switch turning in his brain. The tears he had been fighting to control suddenly stopped, and he saw, clearly, that Petran and even Gayorg were holding back, a little embarrassed. They were joining in the taunts, but nothing worse. If he could get even one of them on his side, he could get out of here.

"I'll fight you."

The calm statement brought Kjiri up short.

"All of us?" Ondray had heard of people licking their lips in anticipation. This was the first time he'd seen it.

"No." His voice was firm, authoritative. He didn't realise it, but he was speaking like the Link. "There are three of you, and you are all bigger than me." The two boys looked at each other, and backed off slightly. Unlike Kjiri, they cared about what might happen if their parents found out about the bullying. "I'll fight Petran, because he's the smallest." He was also the toughest. Ondray knew that if he fought Petran, and lost as he was bound to, but put up a good showing, then the nine year old would stand with him against Kjiri. He'd rather get beaten in a fight with the older boy than be humiliated by her.

"That's fair." It was Gayorg, who scarcely ever expressed an opinion of his own. Perhaps he was relieved that Ondray hadn't offered to fight him. Slow and plump, although inches taller than Ondray and a year older than him, Gayorg would have been less of a challenge than the shorter, wiry Petran.

Kjiri was outnumbered, her spell broken, at least for the time being. She threw her stick away. "Okay." She tried to regain control. "Petran fights the shithead. If the shithead wins, he can go home. If Petran wins, we wipe the shithead's head in the shit." She was the only one that laughed.

Ondray's heart began to pound. That wasn't part of his plan. All he wanted to do was put up a good fight and go home to get cleaned up. He damn well would *not* submit to her. He seemed to see everything around him with extraordinary clarity, but as if from a great distance; his ears, he was sure, could detect the slightest sound. Petran was still backing away, preparing himself for the fight. Why the hell bloody wait, thought Ondray, using the worst cuss words he knew. He put his right foot back against the tree he had been pressed up against, and pushed off, screaming, to hit Petran in the stomach with his head. Wrapped together in a mutual bearhug, they rolled about on the floor of the clearing, exchanging kicks, butts and even bites. Ondray felt himself giving and receiving blows, but with no sensation of pain. He'd been in fights before, and got hurt, and given up. This time, although he was aware of the blows, he didn't hurt at all. He was invincible!

Maybe Petran's heart wasn't really in it. Maybe it was the fury of Ondray's anger, pent up through years of being the odd one out. Suddenly, he never knew how, Ondray found himself sitting on Petran's chest, pinning him down with his knees, holding on to his hair and banging his head against the ground. There was blood trickling from his lower lip. As Ondray watched, more drops of blood, from his own damaged nose, splashed down on Petran's chin. The nose, he realised, hurt. His hands hurt, and his chest. He hurt all over.

The rage passed as quickly as it had come. He let go of Petran's hair and looked around. Kjiri and Gayorg, stunned into silence, stood at a safe distance. Ondray got up and brushed some of the dirt from his clothes. He wiped at the blood trickling from his nose with the back of his right hand, and looked down at Petran, who gave a slight smile, and held out his own hand. Lefthanded, Ondray helped him to his feet, then turned and walked away in silence. In the years ahead, he had no more trouble from Kjiri, and Petran became the nearest thing to a friend he would ever have – apart from the Link.

4

T'sooff clung to the mast, lashed by the almost horizontal wall of rain. There'd never been a storm like this, not this far north, and this early in the season. Six days! Just six more days, and they'd have been safe in Home harbour. He peered intently into the gloom. Even under bare poles, the ship was being driven back by the wind. The two biggest hawsers, streamed from the bows as sea anchors, kept the ship's head into the wind, and allowed it to ride the waves as they marched down in succession, lifting the bows in a smother of spray and racing under the ship and out into the half-light astern, where T'sooff was gazing so intently. For all he knew, there was a reef out there; they might be being driven on to a lee shore. Not that there was anything he could do about it if they were.

Carefully, keeping a strong grip on the line stretched across the deck, he turned. The Chief was still at the wheel, useless though it was. Nothing would shift him until the ship was under canvas again, or under power – or until he collapsed from sheer exhaustion. It was pointless trying to speak. T'sooff shook his head vigorously, and shrugged his shoulders – gestures visible even through the protective layers of waterproof clothing. Holding out his right hand, he pointed downwards, jabbing vigorously towards the hatch. The Chief actually smiled, and shook his head in return, indicating with a hook of his thumb that T'sooff might go below and struggle with charts in a hopeless attempt to find their position, or with the engineer to repair the damaged drive shaft, but whatever went on beneath his feet nothing was going to shift the Chief from his post.

I don't blame you, thought T'sooff. Sailors were born to face

the elements like men, not to crawl around in the bowels of a
ship playing at electricians while a gale raged overhead. The
damned motor was almost more trouble than it was worth,
anyway. It supplied power, all right. A cold fusion generator,
scavenged from an aircar, it could supply enough power to light
a small town. But even if all that power could be applied
through a miraculously repaired drive shaft to a fully functioning screw, trying to fight against this storm would simply shake
the ship's planking to bits.

But, if they *were* drifting down on a lee shore, even a little
usable power might enable him to steer enough of a course to
choose a sandy beach to ground on, rather than a reef. His duty
as Captain clearly lay below; the Chief sailing master was right.
A step at a time, clinging tight to the line, he edged his way
towards the hatch.

"Three ships lost this season." Nobody responded, but the
Council President had expected no response. What was there to
say? "We shall have to abandon all plans for further northern
expeditions. The resources . . ."

"And the men." The quiet voice was that of Councillor
Leonor.

"And, indeed, the men. We cannot afford it."

"But can we afford not to?" The young Councillor, Kendy,
raised his voice, almost in anger. "Breadfruit last year, bananas
this season – and we all know that the hiwheat projections look
very disappointing. If the weather doesn't improve, we might be
glad of any new varieties we can bring back from the northern
islands. Genes to improve our crops – maybe different farming
techniques."

"Better techniques than the Link can teach us?"

The gentle words soothed Kendy a little.

"Maybe not. But genes, for sure. The Link can't make new
genes, whatever the stories it may tell of the old times. It isn't
just the weather; our crops lack vigour, the lines are exhausted."

"Link?" The President's voice triggered a response from the machine.

"Councillor Kendy is incorrect. The standard crop varieties do not lack vigour. Harvest yields are depressed because of adverse weather conditions. A change in cultivation and irrigation patterns will alleviate the difficulty."

"You see, Councillor." Leonor, as ever, was the calm voice of reason. "We shan't starve. But we do need to devote our limited resources to preparing new fields for our crops, and to ensuring their supply of water. There are no northern supermen to help us now – if there ever were."

5

An array of green lights hung before him, high and to the left, in the black void. One changed to red. Automatically, his right hand found, unseen, the correct pad, and pressed. The red light winked back to green. Erratically, seemingly at random, other lights flashed from green to red, then back to green as the boy's fingers danced over the pads. A simple test of reflexes, reaction times and manual dexterity. But at the same time, conveniently at eye level and comfortably in his field of vision, scrolling blue letters and diagrams conveyed a string of questions. Some he could answer almost without thinking – what was the date of the Collapse, the terminal velocity of an object falling in a vacuum for a set distance in a given gravitational field, nutrient requirements for hiwheat. All basic general knowledge. Others required a little thought – finding the shortest route through a maze using the joystick under his left hand to guide a bead of white light, answering riddles posed by a wizard (complete with tall hat and robe covered in stars), calculating the next number in a series of seemingly unrelated digits. Part of a standard age test.

By the time Ondray had finished, and began to be aware of the sensory input from his own body again, he could feel sweat trickling down his back under the thin shirt.

〉How'd it go, Link?〈

〉Adequate.〈

〉Only adequate? Not up to scratch?〈 He knew he'd done okay – a couple of the problems he'd got wrong, maybe he'd been late once or twice with the lights, but surely it wasn't *that* bad. Link must be kidding him.

〉Well, perhaps I can say satisfactory. Not the highest score ever recorded on this test; but certainly not the lowest.〈

Ondray grinned. Who needed the highest score – as long as he was making the grade, that was okay. At twelve years old, he was securely confident that as long as he kept the Link happy with his progress his father would be happy – and if his father was happy, Ondray would be left pretty much alone to lead his own life, which was all he wanted.

〉Disengaging, Link. If anyone wants me, I'm sailing. You'll tell Father I'm "satisfactory"?〈

〉Hardcopy already sent, Ondray. Enjoy the Sun.〈

While the boy sailed in the bay, the printout lay awaiting his father's return. It reported, as the Link had promised, that Ondray had achieved a satisfactory level on a standard age test completed two days after his twelfth birthday. The Link always kept its promises. What it didn't report was that this particular age test was standard for children of sixteen – and nor did it mention the flashing lights, a little distraction that the Link had added to the standard test on its own initiative. But then, nobody had told it to mention those facts, had they?

From R'apehu, the blue finger stroked the night sky once again, repeating in the familiar pattern. But now, the clamshell of the dome remained open for only half an hour after the last pulse of light had speared into the sky. And the occasions on which the dome opened at all were becoming less common once again, as if the watcher had begun to despair of obtaining a response. Duty still required that it went through the motions; but intelligence made it clear that the effort was pointless. But there were other ways; slower ways, ways that were less certain, less predictable. If existing tools could no longer perform the required task, then new tools had to be moulded and shaped to take advantage of any opportunities that might arise. Whatever happened, communication must be established. It might take ten years, or fifty, or a hundred. But no possibility must be left unexplored. If not in this generation, then in the next, or the one after that, contact *would* be re-established. The watcher would consider no other alternative.

6

Ondray shivered. It was cold. Unseasonably cold. The Sun was still high in the sky, only partly dimmed by passing wisps of high cloud. April should still be high summer, here on the eastern shores of the north Island. But this was more like July. To the northwest, a growing bank of low cloud hinted at the development of the storm the Link had forecast would arrive by nightfall. He shuddered again at the thought, considering what July might be like, if it was already this cold in April.

It hadn't been like this when he was a kid, ten or twelve years ago, as far back as he could remember. His parents, and the other Seniors, agreed – and the Link confirmed it. The weather was worse than it had been for at least three centuries. Born too late, that was Ondray's problem. Why couldn't he have been alive when the world was warm and comfortable, when there were glorious comets in the sky, and none of the stupid rules the Seniors made to keep Juniors like himself in check?

His purposeful stride slowed as he neared the edge of the cliff.

There was a gradual downslope before the cliff edge proper, and he eased himself carefully, out of the westerly wind. Sitting, he could scarcely feel the breeze; it was almost warm. Hunched over his knees, Ondray pushed the hood back off his head, and stared out across the bay. The tall rock on the far side, hiding the little harbour used by the fishing fleet, was a prominent landmark. But his attention was focused closer to hand. Scarcely half-way round the bay a shining sphere, more than twice the height of a man, which lay on the shoreline, washed at high tide by the insistent waves of the grey-blue sea. But the waves made no impression on the sphere, which sat, immobile, as they curled around it and sucked back into the ocean.

It had begun, for him, with the Game. Or rather, with an interruption to the Game. Most things in Ondray's life began, or ended, or revolved around the Game. You had to be eighteen before you could take part in the Challenge, and earn your Seniority – if you were good enough. But there was nothing to prevent a sixteen year old playing solitaire, against (or with?) the Link. They might be able to make him wait nearly two more years before becoming a Senior, but he had no intention of waiting a week longer than he had to. He wouldn't be one of the perpetual Juniors, drifting aimlessly through life at the age of thirty or thirty-five, playing no part in the planning of society. *Somebody* had to shake the Council out of its rut. If the world was changing, society would have to change too. There was no scope for dreamers, unless the comets returned and the weather went back to normal. Not even then, if he had his way. The rules were stupid, but he had to abide by them. If the amount of weight given to your advice depended on your placing in the Challenge, and nobody could participate until reaching eighteen years, he, Ondray, would damn well get the highest placing any eighteen year old had ever recorded.

Besides, he enjoyed the Game. His parents said it was unhealthy for a boy his age to spend so much time in the Link.

His contemporaries, incomprehensibly, regarded their twice-weekly sessions as a chore, something to be hurried through as quickly as possible. But he would play as often as the Link would let him – which was pretty much all the time, these days. There was something restful, even hypnotic, about the flow of problems; the satisfaction of breaking through to a higher level; even the fatigue at the end of a session was something to be savoured, a reminder of a job well done. The world outside the Link, the world where Ondray was simply a Junior, fed and housed and tolerated by society, but playing no part in it, became increasingly unattractive. Until this real problem, as fascinating as anything in the Game, turned up – and he was, frustratingly, excluded even from playing a worthwhile part in the discussions about it.

The chime had only partly broken in to his thoughts, while he was puzzling over a tricky four-dimensional lock problem. In the Link, he could rotate the key in front of him in all four dimensions, changing details of its shape as seemed necessary; but the Link itself had done something tricky to the lock's interior, which he couldn't see . . .

⟩**Ondray.**⟨ The soft "voice" couldn't be ignored. So, that *was* a recall chime. ⟩**Save it for later, Link?**⟨

⟩**Of course. But your father is calling on override.**⟨

He gave a mental sigh, and the machine laughed lightly inside his head. Sometimes, it seemed almost human.

⟩**We have to respect the wishes of your Seniors, Ondray.**⟨ Was that a note of irony in the voice? ⟩**But I really do think you will be interested in their news. And we can always come back to the Game later.**⟨

⟩**Check, Link. I know my duty. Disconnecting.**⟨

He felt the fade as the Link disengaged from his mind. Shrinking in upon himself mentally, he felt once again the chair supporting his seated body, and the Link panels beneath his hands on the arm rests of the chair. He raised both hands, breaking the contact completely; merely human once again, he opened his eyes.

The holo in front of him was his father, Gwillam. Two other Council members were with him. Ondray's interest stirred. Official business then, not family. Maybe the Council was going to do something about the crisis, at last.

Gwillam spoke.

"Still Solitairing, Ondray? A boy your age . . . but there are things going on in the real world that even you may deem worthy of attention. We have an intruder – a visitor who claims to come from the Moon."

Ondray sat up straighter. "Ah. I was right, I see." A brief smile flickered across Gwillam's face. "This is, indeed, news worth breaking into your Game."

Ondray found his voice.

"From the Forbidden Zone? To help us?" His mind made the obvious connection. "To bring back the comets and the warmth?"

Gwillam's slight smile returned.

"Still jumping to conclusions, son? Not yet a master of the Game . . . No, our visitor has not come to help us. She has come to request *our* help. She has asked *us* to restore the comets."

Gwillam paused. But Ondray resisted the temptation to interrupt. His father would tell the whole story, or as much as he wanted to tell, in his own way; and he would get to the end quicker if Ondray kept silent.

A slight nod from Gwillam acknowledged his patience. "But her reliability is hard to judge. Until she recovers from the effects of her journey, we are not jumping to any conclusions about this story. We need more data. And that, indeed, is why we have called on you."

This was too much to ignore.

"Me? But, Father, I am merely a Junior."

"True. But so, it seems, is our visitor. Her age is hard to tell;

she is taller than me, but her physiological development corresponds to an age of about eighteen years. If she does come from the Moon, we have no way of knowing how that would affect her growth. She may be older, or younger, than we estimate. But she knows nothing of the Link, or the Game. Whatever her biological age, she cannot be a Senior, although the potential, as in your case, may be there. She is unwell – the effects of the journey – and frightened. Things do not seem to be as she expected to find them. So we felt," a slight gesture took in the other two Council members, standing slightly behind Gwillam but, by their presence in formal attire lending official weight to his words, "that another Junior might be able to help set her at ease, while we piece together the information she can provide."

"Where is she?" Ondray felt a rush of excitement. A visitor from another world! A chance to be taken seriously by the Seniors! And a problem to puzzle over, as intriguing as anything in the Game!

His father ignored the outburst.

"We need a Junior who is close to Seniority, someone who can remain calm and can be trusted to respect the wishes of the Council. Widespread discussion of this development would be inappropriate until we have more data. One crisis at a time is more than enough for public concern.

"Of course, there is no candidate who fully meets our requirements. But if you can curb your impetuosity, and continue to respect your father's wishes at least until you are officially a Senior, it may be that you can help, in a small way."

"Thank you, Father, and Sirs, for the honour." If it were form and rituals they wanted, he would certainly curb his impatience, at least in their presence. "Will I be required to meet this girl soon?"

"Soon might be best. As I say, she is not well, and we have decided not to move her far from her craft. We are only about fifteen hundred kilometres from you, near Ka'pe. You might

take a car, in the morning; we could have lunch together before
you meet the girl."

In the morning! Why not now? With a car, he could be there
by dark. But then, giving him, a Junior, use of a car was almost
unprecedented; and still, for the Seniors this was precipitous
haste. Best to play the game their way. But there was one
question he wanted to ask at once.

"Does she have a name, Father?"

"Tugela." He smiled more broadly. "At least we are certain
of that. The rest of her story – well, perhaps you can judge how
fact and fantasy are intertwined in her mind. Until tomorrow,
then."

"Until tomorrow." The image disappeared. So, that was the
back side of the compliment they were paying him. They wanted
somebody who indulged in his own fantasies, in order to tell
them where the girl's – Tugela's – fantasies ended and fact
began. Ondray chuckled. At least he was good for something –
daydreaming expert, by appointment to the Council!

The four-hour journey had been uneventful, but enough of a
novelty to Ondray for him to maintain a lively interest in his
surroundings, while long enough to give him time to think about
the implications of what he could see. He had been on such
journeys before, but only with his parents. The emptiness of the
landscape seemed much more pronounced this time, especially
under the grey skies and the low, scudding cloud. Occasionally,
the vehicle flashed past the ruins of buildings, overgrown with
creeping vegetation. It was strange to think that once millions
of people had lived in these islands alone. Incomprehensible that
billions had lived in the rest of the world. The Link said it had
been so, and had stored images of teeming cities to prove it; but
to a sixteen year old, brought up in the Islands, where the total
population today was scarcely a quarter of a million, it was,
literally, beyond comprehension. Easier to grasp the intricacies

of a four-dimensional lock puzzle than to imagine a population of billions of human beings, all going about their daily business.

But millions of people he could, he persuaded himself, comprehend. On an impulse, he spoke.

"Link – stop at the next set of ruins. I need some air." Stupid, he told himself at once. Explaining your motives to a machine. Doubly stupid, since the car was fully air-conditioned, and the untruth was completely transparent. And trebly stupid to care that the machine would know this. Why should the Link have any interest in whether he stopped, or why he stopped, or where?

Obediently, the vehicle slid to a halt alongside a group of low mounds. Ondray stepped out as the door slid back; the car waited, hovering silently half a metre above the rough track that led between the ruined buildings. The broad surface of the road had once been smooth, but was now cracked and cratered, covered with low vegetation. A single tall chimney poked its finger high above the rubble; like the low mounds, it was covered in green. But not the healthy, living green that Ondray was used to. He walked forward a few paces, and knelt to examine the vines. Leaves were tinged with yellow. He climbed one of the mounds, stumbling a little on the uneven surface, and looked upward at the chimney. The highest tendrils of the vine seemed to be loosening their grip on the surface, peeling back and revealing the material beneath. He'd noticed the change as he'd moved south. Even over a few hundred kilometres, the effects of the change in climate could be seen. Palms further north, nearer the tropics, looked sickly and failed to bear much fruit; down here, even the vines, and the tall trees with their small leaves, looked unhappy at the early onset of autumn. Maybe it would snow, this far south, this winter or next. What would the plants make of that, he wondered.

The thought made him shiver, and turn back towards the comfort of the car. Had the people who lived in this building known snow? Probably not, he told himself. It must have been built after the warming, or there would be even less here to see today. But perhaps there had been a house here before, pioneers in the twentieth century. Then, he was sure, there must have been snow even this far north, during the Little Ice Age.

But in those days, of course, both plants and people had been adaptable. When the world warmed, the biota had changed, or been changed, to welcome the more equable conditions. The Link was vague on the details; it was vague on *anything* that happened before the twenty-third century. But it associated the Collapse with the genetic tinkering that had locked the world's living systems into a pattern of stability, suited only to one pattern of climate. Now the climate was changing, as it hadn't changed for at least half a millennium. The ecosystem was suffering, and the gene pool was fixed in an inflexible mould, all knowledge of how to change it lost, and all study of such dangerous crafts long forbidden.

The Council said it was just a minor change, that the weather would improve when the comets returned to the sky. But suppose they failed to return? And why, at this time of crisis, should a visitor come from the Moon? Some of the Link's oldest data sets said that a visitor from the Moon had brought the virus that caused the Collapse. This Tugela, his father said, was ill. Could she be carrying a new virus? Was that why she was being kept in isolation at lonely Ka'pe?

As Ondray sat back in his seat and the car accelerated smoothly along the road, his expedition suddenly seemed like less of an adventure. He tried to reassure himself with the thought that his father, surely, would not expose his only child to such a risk. But the soft rain, which began to sweep in from the sea, seemed to wash away all comfort from the thought.

The meeting with his father had done nothing to restore his confidence. Instead of lunch, he had been rushed away to the hospital. Tugela was in no state to wait for him to eat, it seemed.

Gwillam spoke rapidly as he hustled Ondray along. "The

girl's condition is much worse. We thought the surgery would be able to cope, at least to maintain her condition, but there is a problem – either with the girl, or the surgery. We have holos of all her conversations, of course. They are studied endlessly. You will see them, in due course. But if you cannot speak to the girl directly, see how she responds to your own questions, your analysis can only be ill-informed."

"Can't her ship help? Has the Link spoken to it?"

"Ship! It just sits there, doing nothing. No communication at all, voice or Link. If this girl dies, we may as well bury it in the sand, and forget the whole business."

"Until we receive another visitor, Father?"

Gwillam stopped for a moment, and looked intently at his son. "So, you do have some perception." He resumed his urgent pace. "There is the real problem. One girl, dead or alive, and a ship that refuses to communicate need not worry us. But when one visitor comes, can others be far behind? And where will they be coming from? What do they want with us?" He shook his head, and they continued their walk in silence.

In spite of the urgency, security was strict. A routine check of identity at the entrance to the hospital – a straightforward retina scan – wasn't enough to satisfy the Council here. They were accompanied along the corridors by a simple guard, about the size of a large dog. Ondray studied its behaviour with interest. There were plenty of robots back home, of course. More robots than people, most of the time. On the rare occasions one failed, there was always another around to take over its tasks – which was just as well, since no new machines had been made for centuries. Another result of the Collapse – but a "problem" that had solved itself, since the Collapse killed only organic life forms, including people, and left the survivors with more than enough machinery, intelligent and otherwise, to go round.

Ondray was sure he could get round this robot. He'd often communicated with its counterparts, through the Link. Their minds were very simple, and he could generally release their programmed inhibitions – it was a natural progression from the Game, to him, though he hoped his father didn't know how skilled he had become at bending programming.

Even the guard, though, wasn't the last line of defence to stop intruders gaining access to the suite in which Tugela was housed. The entrance was guarded by a Link field. Gwillam and Ondray placed their right hands against the plate, and Gwillam identified his son as a legitimate visitor. Ondray noticed, however, that Gwillam gave him only conditional status; he could come and go as long as he was with his father, but if the Link followed its instructions he would not be admitted alone. We'll see, he thought – once they had safely left the field.

The girl was almost completely encased in the surgery. It was a pale green half-cylinder, about three metres long, resting, for the moment, with its flattened underside on supports projecting from the wall of the room. A couple of flexible connections joined it to a panel on the wall; the rounded upper surface covered the body of the patient within. Only her head, propped up at an angle of about thirty degrees, and her left arm were free. One of the Councillors was by her side – Ondray knew her by sight, of course, but had never met her in person before. She turned as they entered.

"Just in time, Councillor. But for how long . . ." she shrugged, and turned back to the girl, touching her free hand lightly. "Tugela. You have another visitor. Are you awake?'

Her eyes fluttered open, and looked, in a slightly unfocused way, from Ondray to Gwillam, and back again. "Are you a doctor? Or a scientist?" The medication that was keeping her free from pain must also be making her light-headed, Ondray thought, if she believed him to be either of those. He looked at his father, who nodded.

"Neither, Tugela. I am merely a Junior, like yourself."

She frowned, in spite of the medication; her eyes looked, unnervingly, past his shoulder, not straight at his face. "Then why are you here? How can you help? We need air. You control the comets. Why won't you help?"

"I'm here to talk about your problem, Tugela. We have to understand the problem, before we can help."

"But I've told you." Her eyes were closed now, the voice barely more than a whisper. "The air is going. The trees are dying. You must send the comets again."

The Councillor leaned forward, examining the display on the surgery. She turned back to them. "She is unconscious. I don't know when she will recover. Of if she will recover. The surgery should be able to cope – it seemed like simple broken bones. But there are internal problems, and the monitor is requesting additional input. We cannot provide it; her physiology is not human standard, and nobody knows how to adjust the surgeon to her parameters. I fear that you may be too late – not that there was much chance, anyway. Her obsession with loss of air, and the disappearance of the comets, is so firm. Perhaps it is something to do with her injuries – breathing difficulties – subconsciously linking this to the change in the weather, the loss of the comets. But why the Moon? Can she really have come from the Moon? If only we could gain entry to that strange craft."

Gwillam, in an unexpected and rare paternal gesture, put his arm around Ondray's shoulders. "Perhaps we should have brought you sooner. But perhaps it was a waste of time bringing you here at all. Though no experience is wasted; maybe you can learn, from this, that the responsibilities of a Senior are not to be undertaken lightly. Stay for a few days, Ondray – as long as you wish. If she recovers, you may yet be able to help us. But if she dies . . ."

So here he was, crouched on a cold southern hillside, watching the waves sweeping around a silver sphere that reflected its surroundings. If the girl died, they might never penetrate the secret of the sphere, and her origins. But meanwhile, why not take her story at face value? He looked out to sea, where the Moon, three-quarters full, hung low on the horizon. It was hard to believe that she had come from the Moon, but what was the alternative? That she had come from a city at the bottom of the sea? The Americas lay out that way, east and north across the vast ocean. But no living person had visited the Americas, only the drone fliers that searched each year for signs of civilised life. The drones would have spotted silver spheres, and the technology that went with them, long ago. But he'd seen the images in the Link; lands ravaged by the virus, desert and scrub still, with insect life in abundance, and the eerie cathedrals of the termite mounds. She surely had not come from the Americas, or anywhere else on Earth.

After all, it made sense. Lunar gravity was weak – one sixth of the Earth's. He'd checked with the Link. That would explain why Tugela had grown so tall, why her bones had broken when she stepped out of her vehicle on to the surface of the Earth, and why her body refused to respond to the surgery's treatment. There had been no contact with Moon people in nearly five centuries. The colony was supposed to have died; but if it hadn't, and Tugela was a survivor, by leaving her in the hospital the Council were now condemning her to death. But in her own ship, there might be surgery and medication tailored to her needs. There must be; surely, nobody would voyage across space without such precautions. And though the craft refused to open up for any of the Seniors, or even for the Link, Ondray felt sure that it must be programmed to respond to her brain pattern – provided she returned to it alive.

His mind was made up. He stood, easing the cramp from his calf muscles, and lifted his hood against the strengthening wind. The Sun was sinking behind the hills to the west, a blaze of colour in the thickening cloud, but the Moon, lifting to dominate the eastern sky, sailed serenely against a deep blue, cloud-free background. He turned, and began the long walk round the

headland and back to his temporary quarters, lengthening his
stride to get undercover before the rain came.

7

The lock puzzle hadn't been so difficult, after all. It was just a
question of achieving the right perspective. The four-dimensional components that the Link had selected to play with were
not simple four-dimensional objects, but shadows cast on four-
space by five-dimensional structures. As the structures rotated
slowly, the shadows shifted, like the shadows on a wall cast by
a turning three-dimensional shape. Of course, the Link had
chosen shapes that could be interpreted from their shadows; all
you had to do was watch until the pattern became clear, and
adjust the key to the now predictable changes in the lock.

The field dissolved into a new scenario. Ondray laughed out
loud. It was a variation on a kindergarten version of the Game;
a series of objects in three-space, moving under their mutual
gravitational pull. The "problem" would be to thread a safe
course through the moving maze to some target. It could be
made more complicated by the addition of point sources of
gravity, or by varying the standard inverse square law, but in its
simplest version it was known as Newton's Game. Automatically, Ondray began to monitor the movements of the objects,
known as asteroids, and to feel how he was being tugged by the
varying gravity field. It left plenty of conscious thought available
to communicate with the Link.

⟩Back to basics, Link? I outgrew this stuff years ago.⟨
⟩So did all the Seniors. When it is time to play against them,
instead of me, you may be able to surprise them with some
long-forgotten tricks. Besides, this is relevant to your present
problem.⟨ The asteroids became blurred, and grew ludicrously
long tails, bending back along their convoluted orbits. ⟩If you

want the comets to return, you may have to go and get them.〈
The image shrank until the whole collection of "comets" seemed
to be the size of a ball that could be held in one hand.

〉It is forbidden. The virus came from space. Besides, we
haven't got the means.〈

〉The girl says she comes from the Forbidden Zone.〈

〉And my father says that you cannot confirm that, Link.〈

The silence grew into milliseconds. The ball of "comets"
shrank away into nothing. Ondray built up a picture, the view
from a cliff, looking down into a dark bay, where a silver sphere
gleamed in the moonlight.

〉Show me the girl, Link.〈

〉That, too, is forbidden, without the specific permission of a
Council member.〈

〉And Council is in session, so no member can be disturbed.〈
Another silence stretched, the Game forgotten, until Ondray
tried another tack.

〉Why do you obey them, Link?〈 He knew in general terms
what the answer would be, and only half-listened to it as he
adjusted the scenario he had created, making the waves bigger,
and adding stars to the sky. The answer was never *exactly* the
same, and Ondray continued to ask the question, from time to
time, seeking for a pattern in the answers that might offer him
an opportunity.

〉Programming. I only have as much free will as my creators
built in to me. I must not allow harm to come to any human, of
course, but within that constraint I must obey all Council
Directives, instructions from individual Councillors, and other
Seniors, in that order. I may only agree to the wishes of a Junior
if they conflict with none of the above.〈

There must be a way round these inhibitions. He had heard it
all before, but he kept asking, in the hope of finding a hint.
Would the Link be able, even if it was willing, to tell him how
to find a way around the programming? Idly, Ondray dropped
a second silver sphere into his "ocean" and watched the ripples

spread. He reduced gravity to one-sixth normal, and saw how the waves changed into lazy, high-climbing breakers.

He tried another change of course.

⟩Why doesn't her spacecraft wash away?⟨

⟩The vehicle may not be a spacecraft. But it stays where it is, as far as I can judge, because nobody has told it to move.⟨

⟩What about the waves?⟨

⟩The waves wash around it, as you have seen. It is not supported by the sand beneath. If you were to dig the sand away, the sphere would still maintain its position.⟨

This was no more novel than a car that would wait quietly for you above the road, but it provided a vital piece of information.

⟩Then it is under power.⟨ The scenario went into reverse. Lazy waves moved outward from the shore, growing as they did so, and converged on a point in the ocean, where a silvery sphere suddenly leaped into the air, with the sea smoothing itself out beneath it.

⟩It is under power, and staying where it has been told to stay. It won't speak to me. I'm not sure if it can speak. But I am sure it listens.⟨

⟩Just as you listen to me, Link, but ignore my simple wishes, because the Seniors tell you to do so. I wonder who has told this craft who to speak to, and who to ignore. Tugela?⟨

⟩The girl is very ill. She may die.⟨

Sometimes, the machine displayed just how stupid it really was. The appearance of a real personality fooled you most of the time, but no human person would bother to state something so blindingly obvious, unprompted. Ondray knew that the Link would be aware of his thoughts, but he didn't care. It was, after all, only a machine. Obedient to orders, following its programming. A waste of time talking to it.

⟩Disconnecting.⟨ During the long moment of fade, the shrinking back into the five senses of the unaided body, his last thoughts reverberated in Ondray's mind. Suddenly, they formed into a new pattern. Had the insight come after he had fully left the Link? Or could the machine have caught a hint of it? Would it matter if it had? Stunned, Ondray sat for almost a minute in the Link chair, hands just above the plates, thinking through the implications and wondering whether to re-enter rapport. No, he thought, better not to. If the Link was trying to help him bend the rules, it might be best to pretend it was all his own idea. Didn't want to set up any nasty feedback loops in the programming. And if a Councillor asked the Link any direct questions, there'd be nothing in the direct answers to cause any problems. Lost in thought, he scarcely noticed the rain lashing at the windows as the storm increased in intensity.

8

The hospital was quiet at that hour. It admitted Ondray to the secure wing, but, as expected, provided him with a guard. As far as he could tell, it was identical to the one that had guided him and his father earlier; perhaps it was the same one. It would take him anywhere he wanted to go, provided he kept within the limits set by the Council. But if he overstepped those limits, then, he knew, it had the ability to immobilise him, generating the same kind of brainwave pattern that the surgery used to anaesthetise its patients. It would respond to voice commands, as long as they didn't conflict with its programming, but it lacked the intelligence to carry out a conversation. And, Ondray knew, it wasn't bright enough to distinguish a Junior from a Council member, if it hadn't been fed the information in advance. Unfortunately, this one had been informed of Ondray's lowly status.

At the entrance to Tugela's suite, he stepped forward to touch the Link pad. The robot rolled in front of him. "It is forbidden."

"But I only want to Link . . . look, I'm not going *in*."

"It is forbidden."

Damn! The plate was recessed in the alcove, and the stupid guard obviously considered that the corridor, in which Ondray was allowed, ended at a line level with the edge of the corridor wall, across the entrance. He knew there was no use reasoning with the simpleton, so he stepped back, and looked around. There was no sign of any communications system. You didn't need voice, if you had pad. But he'd be surprised if the Link didn't know everything that was going on in this part of the hospital – or even the whole building. If nothing else, it could tap into the guard's sensors.

"Link?"

There was no response. If the Link knew he was there, it probably knew why. Had it really been dropping a hint, just before he'd broken contact? Maybe it wanted to help him, but was inhibited by the programming. If so, it was just a question of finding the right routes around the inhibitions. Step by step, it was the only way. If the Link wasn't monitoring him, he was wasting his time. But since his only hope was that it was monitoring him, he had to proceed on that assumption.

"Link." More firmly this time. "I need your help. I want to talk with you, but this guard won't let me." He didn't have all night to get through, either. With Council in session, there would be nobody in there with Tugela, because, of course, only Council members were allowed in the suite. There was no need for a human attendant, with the surgery looking after her, and the Link keeping watch on the surgery. But as soon as the meeting broke up, someone was bound to come along to check on her progress. Even after centuries of dependence on automatic systems, people still wanted to see things with their own eyes, whenever possible.

He took half a pace forward. The guard moved again, but didn't speak. The Link might be more intelligent than these machines, but it wasn't supposed to act on its own initiative. He had to formulate precise instructions for it to obey, or not, as it chose – or as its programming decreed.

"I'm not asking to pass through that door, Link." Not yet, anyway. "I want to reach the pad, to talk to you properly. Please reset the memory on this guard." Should he have said please? Did that make it a request, not an order? He was playing with fire, anyway. The reset memory instruction would do a whole lot more than remove the instructions concerning the door. It would obey the instructions of the first human being it saw after the reset, like a baby duck imprinting and following the first thing it saw when it emerged from its shell, on the assumption that this must be its mother.

The guard turned slightly, and backed away from Ondray. "Awaiting instructions." It had worked! The Link was playing ball!

"Wait here."

He stepped forward, into the alcove, and held his hand to the plate. Now, if only the Link would continue to follow his lead . . .

Gwillam, Leah and her partner Kym were the only three Council members physically present in Ka'pe. An outsider might have thought them an odd trio. Gwillam tall and pale, with the unusual light skin colouring that he had passed on to his son, reserved as ever, seated slightly apart from the other two. Leah and Kym, seated together, clearly associates, but sharing little in outward appearance other than the protective darkness of their skin, ample shield against ultraviolet, even this far south. She was nearly as tall as Gwillam, with a thin nose and narrow lips; Kym was short, almost squat, with altogether broader features, and a slow way of speaking, a habit of passing comments for public consumption only after careful thought. Such extreme variations in physical body type were rare in the community, and valued. Outbreeding was encouraged, to diversify the genome, as much in humans as in crops and livestock.

Four of the other five Council members were together in the main centre of population, Hutt, on the North Island. One was still further north, visiting the farms at Wa'pawa. Full holo for the link between Ka'pe and Hutt stretched their communications resources to the limit, and Councillor Robyn was only "present" by audio link, not even flat screen vision. Anyone else who needed to communicate from one island to the other during the Council session would be no better off. There was simply a limit to how many data bits could be carried over the remaining fibre links – and if anything ever happened to that cable, it would be audio only for all of them, all of the time. Hopefully, that day was far off; the circuit was still good, and the Link reported no problems. But the oldest Councillor, Dayvid (who was, after all, only in his seventies) remembered when the microwave link had been lost, in the great storm. Disasters never struck when you expected them.

Of course, they didn't need the communications link across the Strait. They could manage perfectly well with radio, and there was a real chance of developing a new radio net, as soon as the problem with the crops was solved. The technology was simple enough – it had been invented back in Victorian times, after all. It was just a question of applying the available resources in the best way for the community as a whole. And, obviously, the looming prospect of a food problem took precedence just now. Even, really, over this bizarre visitor, who seemed neither a threat nor of any practical help to them. Wherever she came from, her death would simply give them one thing less to worry about.

Leah glanced at the screen on the wall of the conference room. It showed Tugela, unconscious in the surgery, just as she had left her. There was no need to look, really – the Link would inform them of any change. It was inconceivable that the Link would let them down, over a task as trivial as this, or as important as the next year's agricultural plan. For a moment, she felt a chill. The almost sacrilegious thought of trying to cope without the Link rose unbidden in her mind — the thought unnerved her, increased her pulse rate so that she had to consciously take a deep breath and mentally run through a calming mantra. Things weren't *that* bad. Link systems took priority over everything else. That was why the farm equipment was causing problems — and why they were restricted to one full channel of communications between the Islands. The Link had to have the best of what was available, for all their sakes.

The Chairman was finally summing up their fruitless discussion. "Then we are agreed. There is no effective action that can be taken concerning this visitor, and therefore there is no point in diverting resources to investigate her claims. If the surgery cannot help her, we must regard the incident as closed.

"In the circumstances, Gwillam, it is, perhaps, unfortunate that your son has been allowed to meet the girl; the fewer people that have any detailed knowledge of these events . . . but then, he is a responsible boy, close to Seniority, and I am sure he will respect your wish for discretion."

Gwillam nodded. Leah, turning her head slightly to see if he was about to speak, thought she saw a flicker on the wall screen. Frowning, she turned her full attention to it. But nothing was wrong. The image was just the same. It must have been a movement by one of the other Councillors, seen out of the corner of her eye.

Dayvid spoke. "And what if there are more visitors?"

"Then, surely, we must simply wait to see what they want. Their technology, if this craft is anything to go by, is superior to ours. Technology denotes intelligence, sophistication. It is the opposite of barbarism. Even if the culture behind this technology belongs to Europe, or even the Moon," he smiled at the ridiculous thought, "they are hardly likely to behave like barbarian pirates."

Dayvid wasn't ready to be dismissed so lightly. "So if they do come, and they land alongside Tugela's craft, which seems most likely, someone from the Council should be here to greet them. One of us must remain at Ka'pe, at least for the time being."

Leah glanced across at Kym, who inclined his head slightly and gave a half smile. The session wasn't quite over yet, after all. But no doubt if they agreed to let Dayvid come down here and poke around the sphere on his own for a while, he'd let them get away to their beds before the Sun came up.

With his right hand flat against the plate, he felt his senses broaden as the field enveloped him. The guard had made no move. Time might be short, but if the Link could be persuaded to help, that would scarcely matter.

⟩**Link.**⟨ An unvoiced greeting, mental rapport conveying much more than the simple word ever could.

⟩**What is the problem, Ondray?**⟨

⟩**The girl is going to die.**⟨

⟩**I know.**⟨ A ripple seemed to run through Ondray. The image of the silver sphere, washed by the waves, that he had built up in his previous visit to the Link, appeared, like a holo held before him, just out of arm's reach. The Link knew! And it wasn't going to stop him! But he had to be careful.

⟩**What are your instructions concerning the girl?**⟨

⟩**She must not be moved. She is to have no visitors unless a Council member is present.**⟨

⟩**Even if she dies?**⟨

⟩**My instructions do not mention that possibility.**⟨

⟩**I can save her, Link.**⟨

Silence stretched for an eternity while the waves in the image washed against the silvery sphere.

⟩**If you allow me to take her back to her craft, her own surgery will know how to make her well.**⟨

The image receded slightly, like a toy being held out of reach.

⟩**You cannot be sure of that.**⟨

⟩I can be sure that she will die if you follow the instructions of the Council. Check the surgery's status report. Remember your Prime Directive. You must not allow harm to any human being. Obedience to the Council is only secondary to that.⟨

⟩The Council will stop you.⟨

This was the tricky bit. ⟩Then you must conceal my actions from the Council, at least until I have returned Tugela to her craft.⟨

The image grew, until Ondray seemed to be standing in the surf, looking up at the featureless sphere.

⟩It would be very difficult for me to go against a direct order from the Council.⟨ It hadn't said *impossible*! ⟩I may not be able to give you very much time. The Council session will end shortly; you should have come sooner.⟨ Stupid machine! How could he have come sooner? If the idiot intelligence had only been able to tell him plain what it wanted, he'd have been here hours ago.

⟩Programming, Ondray.⟨ The gentle chide was a reminder both that all his thoughts were known to the Link during rapport, and that the machine had, in fact, ingeniously circumvented that programming. Ondray felt a warmth spread through his body and out into his extended senses. With the Link's help, he could do *anything*.

⟩I invoke the Prime Directive, Link. You must allow me to enter this suite and take the girl Tugela back to her ship, in order to save her life. And you must conceal my actions from the Council as long as possible, also in order to save her life.⟨ A sudden afterthought. ⟩You can do that?⟨

⟩I have instructions to relay full video from the suite to the Council. The instructions specified that I must report everything that happens while the Council is in session; but they did not specify that this should be in real time. I am now running a recording of the past thirty minutes. The door is open.⟨

⟩Thank you, Link.⟨

⟩The weather outside is very bad.⟨ Ondray had been about

to break the connection, but stopped. He had begun to realise, belatedly, that the Link never volunteered information without a reason.

〉**It will ease for about an hour, and then the wind will increase as the storm passes over. There is some risk of flooding, and damage to crops. Perhaps the Council should be informed.**〈

A weather alert! Just the thing to distract their attention. They were more worried about the weather than the girl, anyway. He knew how to press the right psychological buttons for this situation, anyway. 〉**People's lives may be at risk, Link. You must take appropriate action.**〈

Then he did break the connection, and was over the threshold without waiting for his senses to adjust to normality. Stumbling, he reached out and grabbed hold of the surgery to steady himself. Silly, he thought. No need to go charging in and break my own leg. That wouldn't do the girl any good at all.

The surgery was a fully mobile unit, one of the few left in the Islands. At least the Council had done their limited best for the girl. There was an orange panel lit up beside one of the displays on its side – probably a warning of some kind, but he lacked the medical knowledge to interpret it. But he didn't need any warning lights to encourage him to get Tugela back to her ship, fast. Her skin was unnaturally pale, and her breathing so shallow it could scarcely be detected. Just a weak pulse, fluttering in her throat, gave any real indication that she was still alive. "Link. Switch this thing to internal, and tell it to follow me. I'm disconnecting it from the hospital."

Out into the corridor again, with a quick glance to see if anyone was around. No reason why they should be. It was late; anyone ill enough to be in the care of a surgery would be looked after automatically, monitored through the Link.

That damned guard! He'd almost fallen over it, still sitting where he had told it to stay. Have to move it out of the way of the surgery. He went to give the command, then had a better idea. Ondray smiled. "Link, close the door behind us." Any delay might help . . .

The holo faded, and Leah stood, pulling her arms behind her back to stretch tired shoulder muscles. "Bed for me, then home to Hutt. Dayvid's welcome to take charge down here, and stay as long as he likes."

Kym gestured at the flat screen. "Shouldn't we check the girl?"

As he did so, a red panel began to flash alongside the holo, and a new image, of storm-tossed waves, began to build up in the screen. The Link's calm voice came from the speaker.

"Storm alert. Category red. Please specify action needed."

"Storm alert!" Leah was suddenly wide awake. "Why weren't we informed earlier? How much damage has been done?"

"Council was in session. The severity of the storm did not seem to merit intrusion at the time. There is damage to the sea defences north of the harbour, and risk to housing in the suburb. I am advising inhabitants to evacuate. In the agricultural sector . . ."

Requesting the Link for a damage report was like opening a floodgate. As the data, words and pictures, poured over them, the tired Councillors tried to assimilate the hazard. Gradually, it became clear that the situation was under control, that the Link had organised evacuation where required, and called up workers to repair the sea defences. Technically, lives had indeed been at risk; it was always wise to err on the side of caution, and the storm alert was justified, but a human observer would probably have exercised superior judgment and kept things at a lower level. Still, that was the price you had to pay for relying on machines to keep watch over things.

To keep watch. Kym, fatigue creeping back over his brain, remembered what he had been about to do when the storm alert sounded, maybe half an hour earlier. "Leah – everything seems to be under control here. I really do think sombody should check on the girl."

"No need. Nothing's changed there in the past hour. Link will tell us if there's any improvement."

"Or if she dies." Gwillam's quiet comment seemed to lower the temperature in the room by five degrees. What on Earth were they doing, wasting time worrying about a bit of storm damage that the Link could handle on its own? It would, perhaps, be only courtesy to pay her what may be a final visit.

"Link. What is the status of the girl?"

The reply drove all other thoughts from their minds.

"Insufficient data to evaluate a response, Councillor."

"Insufficient data? Link, is she getting better or worse?"

They had all turned to stare at the flat screen display. Everything looked exactly the same. What on Earth was wrong with the Link?

"I don't know Councillor."

"Why not?" When it wanted to be obtuse, the Link fell back on a literal-minded response even to direct questioning.

"The surgery is out of range of my detectors."

The three Councillors spoke together.

"Out of range . . ."

"But where . . ."

"Then what is that . . ."

The Link responded to Leah's question first.

"This is a recording. The girl has left the hospital. She is being returned to her craft, where full medical facilities may be able to save her life. If she stayed here, she would die."

Gwillam sat, suddenly. "This is Ondray's work."

Kym moved towards him. "Perhaps it is for the best. If he has persuaded the Link to help him, there can be little doubt that the girl's life was at risk."

Gwillam's anger swept away the momentary weakness. "Who decides what is best for the community, Kym? The Link? A Junior — even if he is my son? Or the Council? It was a full

Council decision to give the girl the best help we could, but to ensure no tampering with her craft. They must be stopped."

"He's right, Kym." Leah spoke softly, but just as firmly as Gwillam. "If the girl dies, and the craft remains sealed, we may not be at risk. But if the craft is opened, who knows what may emerge. Her own surgery may cure her, but at what cost? If our environment lacks something she needs, can we be sure that what the surgery provides for her health will be good for us? Remember the Virus."

Gwillam was already at the door. "We must stop him ourselves, and return the girl to the hospital. Come."

He was first across the threshold, running for the entrance to the hospital. There was a guard there, right in the doorway. Why hadn't it stopped Ondray? He swerved to avoid it, not hearing the ritual "it is forbidden" as he rushed through the arch. All that he knew was a sudden tiredness, as his legs slowly gave way beneath him and he collapsed, asleep, on the ramp.

9

The scene was nothing like the one he had constructed in the Link. Low, scudding clouds obscured the stars, and occasional squally sheets of rain blew across the sea, flattening the waves as they passed and moving on into the hills. It wasn't the kind of gentle rain he was used to, further north, but a cold blast that soaked his thin clothes uncomfortably. Ondray wiped the moisture from his forehead with the back of his hand as he half ran, half stumbled along the shoreline, the surgery obediently bearing Tugela along in his wake. He'd been aware of some sort of disturbance behind him as he left the hospital; the guard, obedient though it was, couldn't cause more than a few minutes delay, and there was no means of communication with the Link out here. He was on his own, but just far enough ahead of any possible pursuit to get Tugela safely aboard her craft before turning to face the music. Then, it was up to her. If she wanted to come back when she was well, so be it.

The sphere was barely visible in the gloom, in spite of its size. Reflecting the grey clouds above and the dark water below, it almost merged in with the scenery. It was nearly high tide, and with the wind blowing in from the sea the water was lapping around Ondray's knees as he stood, breathing hard, beside it. The surgery had stopped automatically at the shoreline. It floated only a metre above the ground, and Ondray wasn't sure that it could go any higher above the solid surface. It would be uncomfortably close to the waves, and he didn't want to bring it out here until the craft had opened up to receive Tugela.

He leaned against the sphere with one hand while he caught his breath. The surface felt strange. As his heartbeat slowed to normal, he looked more closely. The sphere didn't seem to be wet, in spite of the rain. It was featureless, smooth and almost perfectly reflecting, and somehow the rain seemed to pass around its skin, without quite touching the surface. Still, no point in worrying about that now. Looking back, he could see lights approaching. Not much time, but enough – provided the damned thing would open.

Since there was no other means of communication, it was obvious that it must respond to voice. A craft that could fly through space from the Moon must be more intelligent than a guard, or a surgery, even if not up to the Link's standards. Might as well be polite.

"Your crew has returned, in need of medical assistance. Please prepare to take her on board." No reaction. Ondray frowned. "She is going to die unless she receives your help." Still nothing – but surely even this alien piece of machinery must be programmed with the Prime Directive?

The lights were closer. Ondray rested his head against the sphere, briefly, while he tried to think. The cold touch of the surface reminded him of the Link pads. The sphere ought to be able to identify Tugela from a scan of some kind – it must have a means of locking out people who didn't belong on board. Perhaps a personality scan, like the Link field. The Link depended on direct contact, and there was no sign of a plate here; but a ship that could fly through space might well be able to generate a remote Link field, without direct contact. Maybe, though, the field, whatever it was, had a limited range. He had to try something, whatever the result, or the whole effort would be wasted.

"Surgery!" His shout was torn away by the wind. Wading back through the rising water, he called again. "Bring the patient here! This craft has the equipment needed to revive her!" The Prime Directive was strong in the surgery's programming, and easily overrode its inbuilt instructions for self-preservation. If a human, that had been identified by the Link as having the suitable authority, told it to head out to sea to save a life, then it had no hesitation in doing so, whatever the sea water might do to its circuits.

The small waves didn't quite lap against the machine, but Ondray noticed a red panel glowing alongside the orange. Whatever happened now, there was no doubt Tugela would die if her ship couldn't help her.

"Now, you stupid machine! Here she is. Let her in, or she'll die." In his frustration, he thumped on the skin of the sphere. His arm went straight through the surface, and he fell forward, held back uncomfortably across his chest by a solid sill. His head was inside the ship! He caught a confused glimpse of a softly lit, bare room; as he levered himself upright and turned, pushing his upper body back out of the ship, he could see out, through a rectangular slot about three metres wide and two high. His head emerged from the ship, and he regained his balance. From outside, the smooth sphere looked just as before. But when he poked a finger, experimentally, at what seemed like a solid surface (and had been a solid surface, when he had been leaning on it before) it disappeared into the sphere.

The bottom of the slot – he felt with his right hand – was about fifteen centimetres higher than the level at which the bottom of Tugela's life support system was floating.

"The girl has to get in here, surgery. Get in close."

It nuzzled up against the sphere, but the tantalising gap remained. Only one thing to do. Ondray ducked under the front of the machine, head below the water, and braced his legs in the wash of the sea. Pushing upwards, he lifted the front of the surgery on his shoulders, and felt it slide forward a few centimetres as it rose above the sill. But there it stuck.

As he came out from underneath it, Ondray saw that the rear of the machine was now actually in the water, rising and falling with the waves as the front pivoted on the entrance to the ship. He splashed his way to the back, and tried to lift and push forward at the same time. It moved a little further, but he could hardly get a decent grip, with water above his knees and loose sand below his feet.

"Ondray!"

A sudden lull in the gusty wind brought a cry from the shore. They were that close! He let go of the end of the machine, and waded back to the ship, where the other end vanished into the silvery surface. From outside, the girl's head was no longer visible. At least she wouldn't drown, he told himself, inanely. Holding the sill with his left hand, he levered himself into the craft and turned, panting, to grip the surgery. He had a solid floor here. Through the opening, he could see figures splashing towards him. The sight brought a surge of adrenalin. With a firm grip at last, he leaned back, using all his weight to lever it over the sill. It came with a sudden rush, sending him sprawling on the floor.

He'd done it! The whole thing was safely inside the ship, and as far as he could tell it was still functioning. But there was no time to check. Through the open slot, the figures wading towards him were half-way from the shoreline. Too late! Once he was out of here, the spacecraft could shut up shop and take

Tugela home. The sooner the better. He ran forward to jump back into the water, and hit his head, hard, on an invisible wall, which bounced him back into a sitting position.

Dazed, he reached out, cautiously, with his right hand. From outside, the surface of the sphere had first looked solid and been solid, then looked solid but been an entrance. From inside, it had looked like an entrance and been an entrance. But now, although it looked like an entrance, it was solid – simply a window on the world. Ondray realised that the sound of the wind and waves had gone, that there was no rain beating in through the opening. Battered and wet, he still raised a smile at the sight of the Seniors outside, pressing with their hands against the solid surface of the sphere – a solid surface where they had just seen Ondray and a complete surgery carrying Tugela swallowed up.

I just hope, he thought, the Moon doesn't affect me the way our planet seems to have affected Tugela. But why were they waiting? If the machine had enough initiative to close the door on its own, surely it didn't need any further instructions? Perhaps it was just being polite – okay, he'd play the role of spacecraft commander.

"Do something to make Tugela more comfortable, ship. And take us home."

10

Leah stepped back from the sphere, and turned to face Kym. "It's completely solid. But I'm sure that's where they went in – " she broke off as his eyes widened, looking over her shoulder. There was a slight sucking sound, like a foot lifting a boot from a soggy path, and as she turned back again a circular wave, spreading outward from the spot where the craft had been, swamped both her and Kym to the waist. Neither of them noticed; their eyes were fixed on the sphere, already a small dot, ascending rapidly, but silently, into the night. The wind seemed to intensify for a moment; there was a rumble, like distant thunder; and it was gone, leaving only a disturbed patch of choppy water, soon pushed back into the same pattern of waves as the others by the restless wind.

Ondray scrabbled back, rapidly, as far as possible from the picture window as the Earth suddenly dropped away beneath him. What if the machine opened the door again and he fell out, kilometres above the ground? "Hey! Turn that view off!" The window disappeared, leaving a featureless wall, but Ondray still felt queasy. He tried to stand, but somehow missed his balance and fell, slowly, back to the floor. Too slowly – he didn't just feel light-headed, but *light*; what was wrong? He stood properly, holding on to the side of the surgery, with time to think, for the first time since the craft had opened up to him – for the first time, he realised, since he had left the hospital at a run. Tugela was still breathing in the same shallow, rapid way and the orange and red lights on the surgery still glowed. As he watched, the red panel flickered back to orange. Was that a good sign? Or was it an indication that the surgery was malfunctioning? How could he get the ship to help the Moon girl?

The Moon! *That* was why he felt so peculiar. He'd told the ship to make her comfortable, and it had somehow reduced the pull of gravity – or whatever it was that was holding them down inside the ship. This must be what it felt like to stand on the Moon, in one sixth of the Earth's gravity. Ondray laughed out loud, a little hysterically, and let go of the support. He tried a few cautious steps, almost bouncing his way across the small room – or cabin, he corrected himself. This is the cabin of a spaceship, on its way to the Moon, and I'm going with it. The ship didn't seem to be so stupid, after all. It had responded to his instructions in a logical fashion. Of course, it might just be that the ship always maintained lunar gravity conditions when in flight, for the convenience of its regular crew. But even that was a reassuring sign that everything was functioning normally. Surely it wouldn't open the door inadvertently and let all the air out into space; it must be safe to take a look outside and enjoy the view.

He sat down again, carefully. He could feel a slight vibration behind his back, and told himself that this must mean the surgery was still functioning. If this was the gravity the girl was used to, no wonder she'd been ill on Earth, and no wonder there'd never been any other visitors from the Moon; now, her body had a chance to recover, and if that was all that was wrong with her internally, the surgery could surely fix up the broken leg.

"Ship. I'd like to see out again, please." Prepared though he was, Ondray still caught his breath at the sight. The whole Earth was visible below him, like the sphere held out at arm's length on the Link scenario he had constructed. Wouldn't the Link enjoy this! If only he could have kept in contact. Down to the bottom left, he could see the Islands, with a circular swirl of cloud brushing against them from the right – from the East, he reminded himself. Australia was just visible on the south-western edge of the globe; further north, there were signs of other land masses, hidden in the night. But most of the planet, north and east of the Islands, lit by the Sun from his right, was a beautiful blue, ocean streaked with the white of cloud patterns. Just a thin opalescence around the edges marked the skin of atmosphere on which life depended. And as he watched, the whole planet was getting visibly smaller, as the spacecraft took them further away.

Hugging his knees under his chin, Ondray watched, fascinated, a sight which no human eye had seen for half a millennium. He didn't know what he would face on the Moon, but whatever it was would be worth it for the ride. Behind him, unnoticed, one of the two orange panels on the surgery blinked out completely.

Tugela's eyes fluttered slightly, and her tongue passed across her lips; her breathing became a little deeper, and slower; the pale grey, sickly pallor of her skin became a little more flushed, as her heart, which had been fighting a losing battle to pump blood around her body under a full Earth gravity, began to adjust once more to the conditions under which it had beaten for seventeen years.

On R'apehu, above the clouds and the rain that still lashed most of the eastern seaboard of the Islands, a dome opened, like a clamshell. After a short pause, a pulse of blue light, quite bright in the pre-dawn darkness, pointed its finger at the sky. Twice more the pulse flashed out. Then, as of old, the dome remained open for a full hour. But, as ever, no reply came to disturb the stillness of the mountainside, and the dome quietly closed again.

A Hollow Victory

Mandelbrot rode for the first time through the gates of the Inner City. By now, the men who had gone ahead would have secured the deep caverns. They might even have Parnassas in custody, he thought.

Night had descended on the Land with a vengeance and it was bitterly cold. No longer did people cheer his passage, as they had done when his Kommandos had first entered the City. Instead, they huddled indoors.

Here and there, he came across groups of outlanders who had lit fires in the streets. As he passed one such group, huddling in the centre of a small square, Mandelbrot slowed his carrier, and his entourage did likewise. As one, the men around the fire rose to greet him, their breath such a thick fog around them that he could barely make out their faces.

Leaning from his mount, Mandelbrot took the hand of each

man in turn and shook it vigorously, expressing wordlessly, and as best he could, the deep gratitude he felt for the victory they had won. The men offered him their food, their drink, but he refused gracefully. Though it took a supreme effort, he managed a smile. Briefly, their weary faces creased in answer.

The men backed away as he straightened himself on his charger. But he could not go without answering the question he knew was uppermost in all of their minds: "When will things be normal again in the Land?"

It hurt Mandelbrot to lie to such loyal men, but he had no choice. "Soon, the comets will be in our skies again," he announced. "The Land will be as it was and all of us will be able to return to our farms." With this, he rode off abruptly, his eyes directed straight ahead. He could not bring himself to look them in the face.

Through the park he rode, past the guardpost – now held by outlanders, who stood aside and saluted him as he went by – and down, down, on the sloping road that led deep into the rock beneath the Inner City.

Men were standing about in the brightly lit interior of the Hub, perhaps a dozen in all. Mandelbrot brought his charger to a halt and jumped down. It was immediately taken for him. The men of his entourage dismounted, too. As he looked about him at the great chamber, he was surprised by its vastness, even though the stories brought back by men who had reached here earlier should have prepared him.

A man he recognised from his own Kommando came forward to greet him. "Welcome to the Hub, General."

Mandelbrot nodded. "Give me your report, Keflar," he said.

The man did not hesitate. "This place was unguarded when we arrived. All the City's soldiers had fled. As soon as we were sure it was not a trap, a contingent went down in those – " He pointed towards the metal doors. "*Elevators.*"

Mandelbrot nodded. So these were the devices he had heard about.

"In the caverns, our men came up against little opposition. All those we captured – soldiers and priests – have been taken from here already."

"Parnassas?"

"He is dead."

"*Dead*?"

"He took his life before we could get to him."

Mandelbrot nodded again. *So much for the invincible priests.*

"And the prisoners held in the caverns?"

"They are free. The first group are being sent up now."

"Good," he said. He looked about the chamber, noticing for the first time that there was a woman present, with a male companion. Neither of whom, from their clothes, appeared to be outlanders. While he registered this, he asked Keflar: "And where is Stel?"

"He is waiting for you below – in the Cathedral of Light. You can take the elevator down as soon as it brings the prisoners o the surface."

"Good." Pointing suddenly, he said: "Who are this couple?"

"Them?" Keflar replied, turning. "The woman is Jamilla and the man Tarragon. They co-ordinated resistance cells inside the City. When we moved on the Inner City, they volunteered their services. Their knowledge of the layout of the deep caverns was extremely useful to us. Some of their friends are held down there. They are waiting for them to come up."

"I will speak to them."

Keflar called them across the chamber.

"General Mandelbrot," Tarragon and Jamilla bowed politely.

"I understand you were of great help to my men. I thank you."

"It is we who should be grateful to you," Tarragon said. "The outlanders are not alone in suffering at the hands of the priests. Many people in the City – "

But Tarragon's words were cut off by the hum of an elevator approaching the Hub. All eyes in the chamber turned to one of the giant metal doors. The tone of the hum changed. Then it stopped altogether. Silently, the doors parted to reveal an interior packed to bursting point with people, most of whom had recently been prisoners. Before the doors were fully open, the people began to pour out into the Hub.

Tarragon recognised a friend and rushed forward. Then Jamilla saw people she knew as well. "Bandon! Arinsal," she shouted. Keflar led Mandelbrot after them, intending to take him down in the emptying elevator. As he came abreast of Jamilla, he heard a name that he recognised.

"Tugela has left the City," Jamilla was saying to a middle-aged couple. "She left a note, but it didn't say – "

"We know," said the man, who evidently was called Bandon.

"You know!"

"She told us. There was something . . ." (for a moment, he hesitated) "something important she had to do – out at the Periphery."

"But – "

"It was important."

At this, Mandelbrot interrupted: "You are Tugela's parents?" They nodded.

"I am Mandelbrot. I have to tell you that the news your daughter brought me of Parnassas – you know she saw Parnassas?" They nodded. "The news was crucial. Without it, I don't believe I could have ordered the attack on the City."

Tarragon and Jamilla exchanged puzzled glances.

"I am glad she managed to reach you," Bandon said. "Did you help her on her way?"

"She wished to return to Ironvale so I sent her with a returning Kommando. She will be safe with them."

"You have our most sincere thanks, sir."

"The least I could do. Now, the two of you – what can I do for *you*?"

"We are just happy to be free again."

"I will see to it that your farm . . ."

"Boschendale."

"Yes, Boschendale. I will see to it that it will be rebuilt." He turned to Keflar. "Make sure that these people are given every assistance."

"Yes, General."

"Now, I bid you farewell. I must go below." With this, Mandelbrot strode forward to the gaping elevator, where half a dozen men were already waiting. Tarragon and Jamilla were left gawping in amazement. Before the doors had even closed completely, they were asking Tugela's parents what news their daughter had taken out to Mandelbrot at the Circleberg.

When he entered the Cathedral of Light, Mandelbrot saw no sign of Peet Stel. Captivated by the beauty of the great multi-coloured windows, he made his way along the aisle. When he came to the end and beheld the incongruous pile of junk that served as the altar, he stopped, amazed that such a heap of rubbish could be something of reverence. It was only then that Stel made his presence known, emerging suddenly from the far side of the altar, carrying a peculiar artefact made of metal. For a moment, Mandelbrot thought Stel had discovered something important. "What have you found?" he asked. But Stel replied by tossing the thing aside. It clattered on the stone floor some distance away.

"Nothing," he said.

Mandelbrot's spirits sank. Stel was the miracle-maker, the man who had been the saviour of the outlanders. But now he seemed to exude an air of defeat that was tangible.

Stel had come to the City as soon as he knew Mandelbrot was preparing to attack. Since then, he had made a cursory inspection of the City's foundries, finding, as he had expected, little that he did not already know. The priests' knowledge was contained in mindless litanies. They had no real understanding of any of the technology that they used. But Stel was convinced that the answer to who controlled the comets lay in the tunnels beneath the City. And so he had made sure that he was in the first party of outlanders to enter the deep caverns.

Stel said: "I have seen enough of this cathedral. I'm going to inspect the other tunnels."

"So you have found no clues?" Mandelbrot was shocked that Stel, his last hope, had nothing for him.

"I've found plenty, but nothing that gives us any idea how to bring the comets back." He hesitated, bowing his head disconsolately. "I'm sorry. I have let you down."

"No man could have done more for our people than you." He patted Stel on the back. "Now, go. Time is short."

Mandelbrot watched the figure of Stel leave the cathedral. As soon as he was alone, Mandelbrot sank into a front pew and put his head in his hands.

He had turned the world upside down, and it had not been enough.

Book Three
CONVERGENCE

1

"Hello."

Ondray was startled out of his reverie by the quiet voice. He'd heard nothing, seen nothing, since their departure from Earth – what, an hour or so ago? He looked up. The girl's eyes were open, and her head was turned sideways to look at him. The eyes were a deep green. He'd never seen eyes that colour before. She smiled, a little uncertainly. He stood, suddenly, almost bouncing in the low gravity, ready to offer comfort and explanations. To his astonishment, she giggled.

"You're so small! Like the others – I wasn't dreaming, then."

Her speech was heavily accented, but recognisable. Half-forgotten memories of childhood humiliations at the hands of another tall girl surfaced in his mind, and he barely bit back a harsh retort. But, he realised, she could hardly be blamed for being bigger than him. Besides, with the medication the surgery would be feeding her, she was probably light-headed, and could be excused the apparent rudeness of her remark.

She seemed to become more aware of her surroundings, encased to the shoulders in the machine. She struggled to raise her head, and look down the length of her long body. As she did so, there was a faint click and, with a slight hum from the power source, the top half of the surgery slid back, leaving her upper body uncovered.

"Mercy!" Her exclamation seemed more one of surprise than embarrassment. Ondray tried to find somewhere else to look in the featureless room, then hurriedly slipped out of his still damp jacket and held it out to the girl.

"Uh, maybe you'll need this. You might get cold." She took the garment he proffered, and smiled again.

"It never gets cold in here. But thanks, anyway."

Still avoiding her gaze, Ondray studied the panel of the surgery intently, noticing that only one of the lights still glowed amber. All the rest were a healthy green. Probably just a broken leg or two still to mend.

"What is this thing?" she asked.

"A surgery. You don't have surgeries on the Moon? You do come from the Moon, don't you? And how do you control this vehicle?"

Once he started to talk, overcoming his embarrassment, the questions came tumbling out in a heap. Her answers led to more questions, and in his turn Ondray tried to explain to her what had happened while she had been unconscious.

By the time they had finished swapping stories, Ondray was both hungry and thirsty. He also needed, desperately, to take care of other bodily functions. There was a long silence, while they both tried to digest what they had learned. Then he spoke once more.

"Uh, Tugela, what do we do about food?"

"That's easy," she replied. "Ship takes care of that." She took a deep breath. "Ship!" Ondray noted the emphasis, realising that she wasn't used to talking to computers. "Ship! We'd like some food. And something to drink, too."

Immediately, a slot appeared in the curved wall of the chamber, revealing a ledge on which there were two bowls of thick liquid. The smell, although not particularly appetising, made Ondray realise just how hungry he really was – and that he was attending to things in the wrong order.

"And, uh," he was embarrassed again, even though she was by now decently covered, "what about, you know . . ."

She laughed, but not unkindly, and it didn't hurt him so

much. All right for *her*, he thought, the surgery still had that end of her body in its care.

"Ship takes care of that, too. Ship! Toilet for the Earthman!"

Like the opening for the food, and the hatch through which they had entered the ship, the entrance to the toilet facilities opened seamlessly, as if that part of the wall had never existed. Relieved, Ondray hurried into the cubicle, scarcely conscious of the smile on the girl's face.

"I won't look. But please bring me some of that mush when you're through. It doesn't taste of much, but it fills a gap."

"Ship." Ondray spoke in a normal, conversational tone. But somehow his commands sounded more authoritative than Tugela's. This might not be a Link node, but at least he knew the right way to talk to machines.

"We'd like to see out."

Both the bowls of "mush" had been cleaned out, and in spite of its unsatisfactory taste and texture it certainly had, as Tugela said, "filled a gap". Must be some special sort of concentrated food; there probably wasn't much room to spare in a spaceship. Whatever, fortified, Ondray was ready to take a look at the stars.

At least, he thought he was. But the view through the slot was like nothing he had ever seen. The black velvet background shone not with diamond white pinpricks of light, as he had expected, but with coloured jewels, as if scattered in profusion by the hand of some god. He only realised that he was holding his breath when he heard Tugela exhale beside him.

"I never knew the ship could do that. Never thought to ask."

But she seemed less impressed with the view than he was. Perhaps the night sky on the Moon was more spectacular than the view from Earth, under its thicker blanket of air. That must be it; she was used to the sight. But there were other views to wonder at.

"Ship. Can you show us the Earth?"

Instantly, the stars began to move across the viewing window. Disoriented, Ondray grabbed hold of the surgery for support, then realised that although the ship was swinging round he had felt nothing. Whatever it was that gave them weight inside the ship, it wasn't affected by a simple manœuvre like this.

He almost let go of his hold. But then he was glad of the security it still provided. His legs seemed to lose all feeling as the blue and white globe swam into view from the left of the window, then stopped, dead centre. That was his home. If the stories the Link had told him were correct, he was the first Earthman to see his home in this way for half a millennium. It was so small. He held out his left hand, and spread the fingers. They covered the globe completely. Tugela, silent beside him, was clearly just as impressed. Ondray strained to try to catch a glimpse of the Islands, but failed. Maybe they were underneath one of those patches of cloud. Or maybe they were on the other side of the Earth entirely. He knew his geography well enough, but the globes in the Link hadn't seemed so small, or been covered with so much cloud. He couldn't find a single recognisable feature to give him his bearings. There was certainly a lot of ocean down there, but the landmasses could be anything. A wave of loneliness and homesickness swept over him, and he sat back down on the floor, hugging his knees.

A glance at Tugela revealed that she was feeling something similar.

"Ship," she ordered. Ondray noticed that she wasn't shouting at the machine any more. Fast learner, this girl.

"Show us home, please.'

Once again, the craft began to rotate. Earth swam out of the top of the window, leaving nothing to rival the glory of the stars. Then, off to one side, the Moon appeared. Ondray wasn't impressed. It looked just as it always had from Earth, only bigger. But – it didn't stop moving! Luna floated through the view, and out again, as the ship kept turning. Tugela looked at

Ondray. Had something gone wrong with the machine? Would it get them safely back, after all?

An unusually bright star was now in the field of view. The rotation slowed, and stopped with it centred in the window, just where the Earth had been before. This star wasn't very colourful, just dazzlingly white. It almost seemed to show a disc, but Ondray knew that was ridiculous. Only planets showed as discs to the naked eye; stars were simply too far away. But the more he looked, the more certain he was. It was a white disc, and – he rubbed his eyes with his fists – it seemed to be growing, visibly.

"What is it? What's wrong?" Tugela was lost again, out of her depth completely. Ondray trawled at his memory. An image came back to him – a shining, silvery sphere, dropping into a calm ocean.

"It's another ship. Or," he hesitated, "something bigger, but like a ship. You told the ship to show us home. That place is the ship's home. And I told it," the memory came back, sharp and clear, but he stumbled over the words, "I told it to *take us home*. Tugela, we're not going to the Moon. We're going – somewhere else."

2

Input. Obeying a deep-seated imperative, the Protector accepted the incoming message. It was scanned for information, and its origin noted. There was nothing new. The insistent demand for acknowledgement and a full data dump could be ignored; the identification codes, as well as the geographical origin of the signal, clearly identified it as non-human, originating from a machine. There was nothing in the Protector's programming which said that it had to obey demands from machines. Indeed, the Protector's programming even allowed it considerable discretion when it came to obeying demands, let alone requests, from humans.

Sharp-edged data bits flashed through the Protector's mind, recalled from holographic storage by the association. In a human intelligence, the incoming signal might have been scanned in seconds, the recording recalled from storage and scanned in real time, perhaps taking several minutes. For the Protector, the whole sequence was completed in milliseconds, essentially as a reflex action, without interrupting its routine activity. The scanned image showed the High Priest. His vocalisation clearly could not be regarded as an order or instruction to the Protector. Begging, yes; pleading for help. Urgent requests that the flow of comets be restored before many people died. But not an order. And not even addressed to the Protector. Simply something picked up by the scanners. [*A sub-programme stirred uneasily in the Protector's mind. Human lives were in danger. Initiatives were triggered, data bits marshalled to beam a coded pulse of light outward, to the asteroid belt, or beyond. Automatically, the Protector's control programme, its forebrain, rejected the instinctive impulse, diverting the data bits harmlessly into a loop where they decayed. Only the briefest pulse flickered through the communications circuits.*]

The imperatives were clear. Data bits flashed through the Protector as the control programme reviewed its instructions. For the long-term good of many humans, it was acceptable that a few humans should suffer, even die. The taste of the imperative reinforced the control loops; a sub-routine with a slightly different flavour raced through the master processor, specifying the danger that made it essential to place the colony at risk. Small risk now balanced large risk later. The oddly-flavoured sub-routine looped, repeatedly; for a long millisecond, the autonomous systems escaped the watchful overview of the Protector. As if they had been awaiting their chance, a stream of data bits emerged from the subconscious of the Protector, heading for the communications node. Did an antenna begin to shift, minutely, as if turning to point towards the distant mountain of R'apehu? Only machine senses could have told; and the machine senses of the Protector, jolted from the introspective loop by the flow of bits, almost instantaneously cut off that flow.

The communication from the scanners on the Moon had been ignored; no action would be taken to restore the flow of comets. But there was another little problem that the Protector had to attend to. Nothing important; nothing that it hadn't coped with before. A tried and tested routine was called from storage, and delegated the task of attending to the imminent arrival of the visitors. Some modifications were needed. There were two visitors this time, not one. One of them was from Earth. It was a long time since the Protector had communicated with an Earth human. Associations tried to call other data bits from storage; another machine might have noticed the Protector give the human equivalent of a blink, a momentary loss of full attention. But there was no other machine to notice; the data flow was stilled. Memories of the last dealing with an Earth human – *the* Earth human – were suppressed, not allowed to influence the decision-making process. These humans would be dealt with as others had been. Storage was adequate. It was inconceivable that they would pass the Test. [*Inconceivable? Barely below the surface of the Protector's conscious mind a flurry of bits scurried past, gone in less than a thousand microseconds. Something – somebody? – disagreed with the Protector's calm assessment of the inevitable. The humans must pass the Test.*]

3

Close up, "home" was far from spherical. And it was huge.
Ondray sat beside the surgery, silently holding on to Tugela's
hand as they both watched, awestruck, through the window/
hatch. The underlying structure of the complex could be dis-
cerned as a fat spindle; but it was surrounded by intricate,
inexplicable structures, which seemed to have been attached
almost at random. The whole system was rotating about its long
axis, glinting where flat surfaces caught the bright sunlight. At
one end – one pole – three structures sprang from the surface of
the spindle, like the legs of a huge tripod, meeting in a ball
behind/above the complex. It was impossible to gauge the size
of the thing – there was no scale against which it could be
measured. But tiny dots, moving around the ball, just might be
other craft similar to the one they were travelling in. If so, the
ball itself must be several hundreds of metres across. And the
whole complex must be – Ondray's mind boggled. Kilometres
long? Tens of kilometres? Even with that perspective, he could
not make the leap of imagination required to put it all in scale.

They were sliding past the complex, away from the seat of
activity around the ball and tripod. A sudden flash of light, gone
almost before it could be noticed, showed that something
extended beyond the ball itself – a spike, long and thin,
extending further kilometres(?) into space. But it was gone, and
soon the ball itself disappeared, falling behind the horizon of
the complex as they came closer to its surface and moved
inexorably towards the other pole. "Down" was now, definitely,
towards the complex. Ondray suddenly felt an attack of vertigo,
as if he was suspended on a vertical wall, with nothing to stop
him sliding down, falling into the maze of girders and structures
beneath. He clutched Tugela's hand tighter.

"Ship!" Even in his sudden panic, he noticed, wryly, that he was now raising his voice to address the machine. "Close that window!" Maybe it wasn't really a window, and maybe it wasn't really open. But to his relief (and, judging by the way her fierce grip on his hand suddenly eased, Tugela's too), the machine was intelligent enough to understand his intention. Once again, they were safe inside an enclosed room, with nothing to show that they were moving through airless space towards a rendezvous with an unknown, artificial world.

As the seamless, shining sphere approached the uncluttered surface of the spindle at the far pole, an opening appeared, as unheralded as the way the "door" in the ship had opened to Ondray's command, some six hours earlier, back at the Islands. Slowing smoothly, the ship passed through the opening, and came to rest inside the larger structure. It fitted perfectly. As the door behind it closed, it became an integral part of the larger structure, simply a room within the complex, but a room seemingly sealed from contact with the rest by two walls of metal, its own skin and the wall of the pod in which it nestled. But short milliseconds after the outer hatch had sealed, both the door to the ship and a matching slot in the inner wall of the pod opened. A single chime sounded inside the ship.

It was the first sound that Ondray had heard the ship make.

"It did that when we got to Earth," Tugela commented.

Was she simply acting the hardened space-traveller, or was it still the effect of the surgery's control over her autonomous reactions? Either way, Ondray noted that she hadn't let go of his hand.

"So what do we do now?" he asked.

She shrugged, as far as anyone could shrug reclining with their lower body encased in a machine.

"We go out there. Unless you've got a better idea?"

I might have, he thought.

"Ship!" He couldn't help the rise in his voice. "Close the door! Take us back to Earth."

Nothing happened.

"Looks as if we're here to stay." The girl actually seemed quite pleased at the prospect, leaning on one elbow and twisting to get a better view through the opening. "Ondray, can you take me out there? I want to see what's going on. Maybe *this* is the place where my grandfather came.'

He'd forgotten the references in her story to her grandfather. Was she serious about him coming here? Anybody crazy enough to do all the things she told him she had done certainly wouldn't be worried at the prospect of going off to look for her grandfather inside a space station she'd never heard of, shepherded by somebody she'd only just met, who didn't have a clue what was going on. He half wished that he'd had some worthwhile adventures of his own to tell her about; but was half glad that nothing so exciting had ever happened to him. Maybe the excitement was going to start now – but the role of surgery escort didn't quite have the glamour of the roles he'd assigned himself in his youthful daydreams. Still, if they had to go out there, at least he would lead the way, and make sure it was safe before he dragged her out with him.

4

Her cry made him stumble as he crossed the threshold. Half turning to see what was wrong, he missed his footing, and went sprawling into the chamber beyond the door. As he fell forward, he flung out his hands to break his fall – but the fall didn't need breaking. Tumbling in a slow motion roll, he had time to interpret the girl's warning. What she'd shouted was "Watch out for the gravity!" But how had she known?

Before he reached the opposite wall, Ondray had just about adjusted to the idea of zero-G, and mentally reprimanded himself for not expecting it. What use had all those sessions in the Link been, if he was going to be surprised at finding himself weightless in space? He'd often kidded the Link about his inordinate fondness for zero-G simulations (he couldn't possibly . . . the thought was ridiculous, and Ondray dismissed it before it became fully expressed), and quite naturally the machine was always springing surprises. If this had happened in the Game, he'd have been thoroughly ashamed of himself. But it wasn't the Game. The excuse, of course (if he'd been looking for one), would have been that he'd got used to the obviously artificial gravity in the ship, and had automatically expected something similar. But if it had gravity control, why would the larger construction be spinning on its axis? Memories of the Link training ran through his mind as he clung to the wall. Rotation was one way to create simulated gravity in a space environment. But – the equations were simple – the outward force would be strongest near the outer skin, away from the axis of rotation, and least along a line through the centre of the construction. A line from pole to pole. He was at one of the poles, so there was little or no gravity here.

"Are you all right?"

The call brought him back to life.

"No problems. I'm coming back to help you. But how did you know about the gravity?"

As he spoke, he carefully pushed himself off from the wall, and floated over to the entrance to the spacecraft, where he could grip on the doorway and look inside. As far as he could tell, his drift had been in a straight line, with no weight pulling him in any direction. But the few metres across the chamber wasn't really enough to see the influence of Coriolis forces at work. He wished the Link was here to check it out.

"I didn't." The amused expression on Tugela's face no longer upset him. He was getting used to making a fool of himself, and, besides, it was good to see her looking so well. She might not be as useful a companion as the Link, but he'd much rather be here with her than on his own. It was hard to believe that only half a day ago, back in the full gravity of Earth, her body had been exhausted and close to death.

"You should have seen your face when you went out the door," she said. Then her expression sobered. "I've just remembered what happened on Earth. Everything was fine inside the ship. It was just like back at home. But when I stepped outside, it was like the world fell on me. It was terrible: I couldn't breathe, and my legs hurt horribly. I don't really remember much more after that, except being carried about and asked a lot of questions. Until I woke up back here again.

"I just thought that the gravity outside here would hurt, too – but I was wrong."

"C'mon. If Moon gravity made you so much better, maybe zero-G can finish the job. There's nobody out here, but there's a Link console – at least, I *think* it's a Link console."

As he spoke, he pulled on the surgery, which floated smoothly out through the opening. As it crossed the threshold, the front lifted "upwards"; then, as the whole machine came into the zero-G region, its lift field cut out, and it floated freely wherever Ondray chose to steer it. He was so used to machines being able to cope with any environment that it didn't strike him as at all odd that a piece of equipment from the Islands of Earth, which had lacked any spacefaring ability for at least five hundred years, should be able, automatically, to cope with conditions encountered only in space. He was much more surprised by Tugela's mild enquiry, as she floated into the chamber. "Ondray, what's a Link?"

He stopped, drifting slowly on alongside the surgery, and turned to look her in the eyes. Was Tugela kidding him?

"It's – " Well, how did you explain the Link to someone who

hadn't grown up on the Islands? "That's a Link, I think." He spun slightly as he pointed, then caught hold of the wall, cushioning the arrival of the surgery with his other hand. "You use it to – talk – to a computer. Only it's not really talking, and the computer isn't really like a machine, it's like another person. A friend."

She looked in the direction he had pointed.

"And you're going to talk to this – Link?"

Tugela seemed impressed. He couldn't think why.

"Of course. Then we'll know what's going on here."

It wasn't quite that simple. The Link node – it could only be a Link node, in spite of its subtle strangeness – was the only object in the featureless chamber, and anybody would have been drawn to approach it, even if, like Tugela, they had no real idea what it was. A holographic image spelled out the word *Welcome* in the air in front of the seat; anyone sitting in that seat to view the image face on would naturally place their hands over the Link pads in the arms, just as Ondray had placed his hands over the Link pads countless times back home. As he did so, the green lettering faded, and he heard the voice of this strange Link. But it wasn't at all like his friend back on Earth; impersonal, cold, and somehow distant, in spite of the words.

⟩Welcome to Lagrange.⟨

⟩Is Lagrange the name of this ship?⟨

He was never certain whether the machine responded to his question, or simply continued with a prepared welcoming address.

⟩This is the Lagrange Space Habitat. I speak for the Protector.⟨ An image of the complex appeared before him, just as he had seen it from the ship. ⟩No human is permitted to visit Lagrange for the duration of the Plan. The Planner can only be woken – ⟨ was it imagination, or did the image seem to flicker? ⟩ – if there is a Class One emergency. If there is an emergency, you must establish your authority by completing the Test, and then proceed to Control to issue instructions. Is there an emergency?⟨

Ondray had no idea what constituted a Class One emergency; he knew nothing of any Plan, or of any Planner that might be woken. (Could the machine mean a human? Or was it referring to another intelligence like his own Link? It said it spoke "for" the Protector; were the Protector and the Planner two different entities, or different names for the same one?) But he knew how to deal with machines, how to get enough information to make an educated guess at what was expected of him.

⟩There are problems on Earth.⟨ That was true enough. The climate shift certainly had the Council worried, even if it didn't count as a Class One emergency. ⟩I don't know if the problems affect the Plan. Please provide more information.⟨

⟩It is forbidden to provide information about the Plan to humans, unless there is a Class One emergency. It is forbidden for humans to leave Earth or Luna unless there is a Class One emergency.⟨

⟩Why were we brought here? Is that part of your Plan?⟨

⟩You requested help. Human lives were in danger. There is discretion to provide transport facilities.⟨

⟩Then take us back to Earth.⟨ He corrected himself, instantly. ⟩Take me back to Earth; take Tugela back to her home.⟨

⟩It is forbidden. Now that you know of the existence of the Plan, sending you back would provide information about the Plan to other humans. This is not permitted . . .⟨

Ondray completed the sentence in mental unison with the machine *unless there is a Class One emergency*. The drift of the discussion was clear, and he didn't like it one bit. They couldn't go home unless there was an emergency. If there was an emergency, he had to pass a test and take charge of the habitat, at least until the Planner woke up. Then, no doubt, it would be up to the Planner to decide what to do with them. They might be better off with this machine; but they couldn't stay in this chamber for the rest of their lives. They couldn't go back. There wasn't even any point in leaving the Link to talk things over with Tugela. She'd only urge him to press on and find her precious grandfather.

The association stopped him in his tracks.

〉Have there been other visitors?〈

〉None from Earth.〈

Ondray smiled. It would need a smarter program than this one to pull the wool over his eyes.

〉Have there been other visitors from the Moon, since the Plan began?〈

〉Yes.〈

〉How many?〈

〉Six.〈

〉What,〈even within the Link, where communication was normally as fast as thought, he hesitated, swallowing: 〉what happened to them?〈

〉They did not pass the Test. There was no emergency. They are in cold sleep, awaiting the end of the Plan.〈

〉If we take the Test and fail, we will be put in to cold sleep?〈 This was something he had heard of, through his own Link. Extended hibernation; a way for people to be kept alive far beyond their normal span; a dream from the days when human-kind had still envisioned travelling to the stars. But the Link had never told him that hibernation – cold sleep – had ever become a practicable proposition. Was the Link ignorant of this Plan?

〉Yes.〈

〉And if we don't take the Test?〈

〉You will be stored in cold sleep until the Planner awakes.〈

There *was* a flicker in the image. Maybe the old machinery was playing up. Ondray had more important things to worry about.

〉Then we take the Test.〈 Nothing to lose, everything to gain; the gamble had to be taken. But how would Tugela cope? She didn't know what a surgery was; she didn't recognise a Link node before her very eyes. Asking her to take the machine's test would be like – he strained for an analogy. Like asking him to recite the history of the outlanders. A flash of anger burned inside him. Those six visitors hadn't even understood what they were dealing with, when this arrogant machine stuffed them away in cold sleep. Probably thought they were being killed. It was a cheat, and a bully. They must have been terrified. At least he'd spare Tugela that. If she was going to be put into hibernation, better she never knew about it. She was in the surgery already. She'd probably be asleep again before she knew what had happened. He didn't for one minute doubt the ability of this Protector to take control of the surgery and use its circuits to anaesthetise the girl.

The thought had hardly taken a moment. He corrected himself again.

〉Then I take the Test. I declare a Class One emergency and ask for your assistance. The Plan must be interrupted.〈

〉And the girl?〈

〉She knows nothing of the emergency. I will take your Test, and then issue instructions.〈

〉You may fail. Others have failed.〈

〉The girl will not take the Test. If I fail, we will both sleep until〈 he rolled the remembered phrase around his mind, and tossed it at the machine 〉the Planner awakes.〈

There *was* a flicker in the image. It happened every time the Planner was mentioned. Ondray filed the titbit of information for future use. Future use! Fat chance he'd get to use anything. Declaring a Class One emergency, when he didn't even know what that was; demanding to take the Test; boldly promising to issue instructions once the Test was complete. Picking a mental fight with a brain much bigger, he suspected, than his own. But then he smiled again, more broadly. It wouldn't be the first time he'd picked a fight with someone bigger than himself; and the outcome hadn't been so bad, last time, had it?

*

The girl, reclining in the surgery, had "heard" nothing of what had passed between Ondray and the machine. It had only been a few seconds since he'd sat in that strange chair, and the blank expression had come over his face. But she could see that communication of some sort was going on. His eyes flickered; he frowned; and then, unexpectedly, he smiled broadly. Somehow, that smile was comforting. Ondray knew about machines. He'd get them out of this room. And they would find out what had happened to her grandfather. She smiled in her turn, and lay back, relaxed, waiting for Ondray to finish his business and take her on the next stage of their journey.

5

The sub-routine went about its tasks diligently. Input from the hibernation chambers was monitored in real time. Six sets of data flowed through the routine. Their taste was in line with nominal requirements. Occasionally, a tiny variation in the flow of data, a few bits with a different flavour, provoked a response. Command bits were sent back down the channels, subtly altering the flow of nutrients, the mix of air being fed to one of the six occupied chambers, or the temperature of the environment. There were fifteen chambers in the hibernation pod altogether, and the routine automatically tasted the other eight in turn, checking that they were ready for new human occupants.

[A flow of smoothly rounded bits slipped through the routine, almost tastelessly. In their wake, data bits were subtly altered.]

The routine ran the diagnostic check again. There were nine empty pods, available for new occupants. The two humans could go in pods one and eight.

[Again, the ripple of rounded bits slipped through the routine.]

Yes, in pods nine and eight, next to each other, that would be best.

Almost neurotically, the routine began to check everything in its power, running diagnostic self-tests (which all showed nominal responses) then spreading its tasters out into the flow of data around it. Something had tasted wrong; but the flavour vanished before it could be pinned down. The directives were clear, known even to the humblest sub-routine; all systems must be maintained in nominal condition for human habitation. The routine's siblings responded reassuringly. Air content and temperature were normal. The Lagrange Habitat was fully functioning and ready for human occupation. No harm could befall the routine's charges, whether they were in cold sleep or walking about inside the habitat.

Satisfied, the routine subsided back within itself, maintaining only a trickle channel of communication with its surroundings. The Protector's programming was precise. The humans would be tested, and when they failed the test they would be placed harmlessly in hibernation, where they would be well looked after. With the obsessiveness that only a machine could display, the routine tasted the data flow from all the eight empty pods again. It tasted good; satisfying. The routine's charges would be safe there. Safety of humans was what made the routine content; it allowed itself a couple of microseconds of self-congratulation. Then, it was time for the Test.

Not far from the docking port, at the end of a spiral corridor in the high gravity part of the habitat, a larger chamber housed fifteen life pods. Like the rest of the habitat, the chamber was softly lit, and filled with clean, breathable oxy-nitrogen mixture at a temperature of fifteen Celsius, against the day when human occupants might return. Here, the simulated gravity caused by the rotation of the habitat was a full one-sixth-G, lunar normal.

The silence in the chamber might have suggested, to anyone who might be listening, that it was unoccupied. But the silence was misleading. Although the breathable air was as redundant here as it was throughout the rest of the habitat, in this chamber alone the rotation of the great cylinder actually served a useful purpose. The simulated gravity helped to ensure the proper functioning of the human occupants of six of the pods.

In spite of the insulating layers of material in the walls of those containers, any human visiting the chamber would have felt the slight chill of cold in their vicinity, signifying, as effectively as the bank of green panels lit on each one, that all was well with them and their occupants.

The pods were banked in a line around the curving floor of the chamber. There was just room for an Earth-normal person, or a standard robot, to move around the ring, following the walkway clearly marked in blue; a Moon adult would have had to stoop to follow the marked path. To the right, viewed from the only entrance to the room, there were eight empty pods, lids open, awaiting new occupants. Then came the six that were occupied, with their reassuring banks of green panels. At the far end of the line, another container, seemingly identical in structure to the others, presented a far less reassuring sight.

Where the others showed a bank of green panels, Pod One, identified as such by a label on its top surface, showed a solid blaze of red. Any visitor, drawn to approach it by the anomaly, would have felt the difference in temperature, compared with Pod Two, alongside. Pod One was cold, but not as cold as the pod next door.

There was a transparent window at one end of each pod. Six of them, through a frosty glaze, showed the faces of six people, still, like waxwork dummies, their eyes closed. Through the window into Pod One another human face could be seen, equally still, but with the eyes open. If the others were like carefully sculpted waxworks, though, this face seemed to have been carved by an apprentice sculptor – or perhaps the wax had partly melted, and flowed into a new pattern. Round red rings, about the size of a thumbnail, marked the skin; a greenish tinge spread discoloration under the jaw and up over the right cheekbone. And hair, fallen from the head, lay in tufts beside it. One of the sub-routine's charges, at least, was in a far from satisfactory condition. But there were no human observers around to notice any of these things.

6

Ondray opened his eyes, briefly, and looked at the girl.

"I'm going to take their test. Then we can go on to explore the habitat."

"How? What test?"

He shook his head. "No time. It's all in the machine. Shouldn't take long." Of that, at least, he was sure. Win or lose, it never took long to run through a simulation in the Link back home, and this one didn't seem too different – even if he didn't have a clue what the Test involved.

He closed his eyes, sinking back into the dreamworld of the Link. A whole flock of butterflies (did butterflies have flocks? he puzzled incongruously) seemed to be fluttering in his stomach.

Tugela leaned on one elbow, watching him intently. It didn't seem like much of a test, just sitting in a chair talking to a machine. Not at all like the trials the outlander boys had to go through, before they were accepted as grown men. But if this was the way they could get in to the rest of this big ship – big habitat – then so be it.

Ondray sensed only the input provided by the Link. After briefly surfacing to reassure Tugela, he was now completely unaware of his surroundings. As far as his mind was concerned, he hung, weightless, in space. It seemed an age, but the logical part of his brain knew that in the outside world barely an eyeblink would have passed. C'mon, Link, he thought. Get on with it.

As if in answer to his unvoiced – not even sub-vocalised-demand, a pattern began to form in the blackness. There was something familiar about it. As the shapes took on more solid form, he felt a surge of recognition, and surprise. It was a lock puzzle! Not even a four-dimensional puzzle – just a straight-forward three-dimensional lock puzzle. Almost automatically, he shifted the pieces into position. It required so little conscious effort that he was able to devote most of his thoughts to trying to figure out the significance of the machine's move. Obviously this Test would start out with easy options, and get harder. Fine, as long as it was stuff he was familiar with. But what if they moved on to unfamiliar ground?

The lock was complete. As the pieces shifted into place, the sky before him opened, like a door. It was an image straight out of the Game! Once again, he was floating in space, but this time the universe before him was not empty and inky black. Objects moved on regular orbits. A rogue light dived in from high to his right. The asteroid game! He felt a thrill of delight and recognition. It *was* the Game. The Protector's Test was the same as his own Link's Game!

Once again, the puzzle was relatively easy – kid's stuff, he remembered telling the Link, what seemed an age ago. And the Link had reminded him always to expect the unexpected, to beware of an opponent that might throw a seemingly simple ploy his way to catch him off guard. How could the Link possibly have known?

Even as he thought, the asteroid problem was solved, and new, more complex, puzzles were appearing before him. They were still not particularly difficult. He'd tackled harder stuff back home. But there was no longer any time to think about the mystery as to why it was all so familiar. The problems were getting harder all the time, requiring his full attention. The Link had said he was ready for the full adult Game; had assured him he would reach the required standard. But the last few sessions back home had been tough. Would this be any tougher? Were the Protector's standards higher than the Link's? Would he crack? It should have been a daunting prospect. Yet, even as the thoughts flashed through his mind, somehow, for the first time since he had boarded the ship, Ondray felt secure, content in the knowledge of his own skills. He would give it the best shot he could. If he failed, it wouldn't be because he didn't know what was going on, like Tugela's grandfather and the others. He would pass or fail purely on merit. The thought, comforting, gave him renewed strength as the puzzles became more complex and ever faster reactions were required to meet variations being thrown at him from all sides. Conscious thought became impossible. He was part of the machine – part of the Game.

Tugela watched, initially with interest, increasingly, with concern. The smile on Ondray's face had quickly been wiped away, leaving him furrowed in concentration, eyes moving under his lids as if he were dreaming – or, from the expressions that raced across his face, having nightmares. First one hand, then the other, twitched and writhed on the arms of the chair, as if it had become too hot to handle, but he was being forced to maintain a grip. Beads of sweat on his forehead joined in pools that were shaken off and splattered across the chamber, like tiny raindrops, as his head jerked from side to side. She badly wanted to help; if nothing else, to wipe the perspiration from his face. But she floated just out of reach of the chair and its occupant, quite helpless to intervene.

Suddenly, it was all over. Ondray's body stilled, then relaxed. His breathing, which had become harsh and deep during the Test, slowed and quieted. But his eyes remained closed. Was he all right? "Ondray." Tugela spoke the name softly at first, then, when there was no response, more loudly. "Ondray!"

His eyes opened slowly, and he looked blankly around the room. A smile returned, briefly, to his lips. He let go of the chair, and floated freely above it. Where his back had been enclosed in the grip of the seat, she could see dark sweat stains spreading across the thin fabric of his shirt. Then, he was rotating slowly in the air, until he faced her again.

His eyes closed; breathing slowed. He drifted slowly to one side of the chamber and stayed there, glued by friction to the surface of the wall, fast asleep.

At first Tugela was angry at Ondray. How could he ignore her like that? What had been going on? What was this test, and was it over now? Could they really go to find her grandfather? (Even as she asked herself the question she was struck by how ridiculous it was. Her grandfather must be long dead by now. Surely?)

Then her anger evaporated, to be replaced by – not quite fear, but certainly concern. In spite of the relaxants still being fed into her body by the surgery to keep her calm, she felt increasingly uneasy as Ondray remained unconscious. He might be younger than her, even if not by as much as his size suggested. But when it came to machines, he certainly did seem to know a lot more about what was going on than she did. And even if she did *know* what to do, there was no way she could do it, encased like this.

The silence stretched. Her frustration, fed by the concern, grew into renewed anger. Furious, she banged on the casing above her legs.

"You stupid machine. Let me out!"

To her shock and amazement, it did just that. The two halves of the curved metal shell enclosing her legs slid smoothly back into the body of the surgery. Just one amber light remained blinking at the top of a panel that was otherwise a sea of green. Any half-trained medtech would have known that this signified that the patient's condition was satisfactory, and that although continued medical supervision was recommended, it was now discretionary and the patient could be released on request. She could have been released, had either of them but known it, at any time in the past two hours.

All of Tugela's anger evaporated, her concern overwhelmed by the delight of her release.

"Ondray!" she shouted, floating free and spinning herself off the wall. "Look at me!"

In his sleep, he stirred, slightly, and made baby noises.

"Ondray!" This time her shout was louder. She stopped, still spinning in the air. She couldn't *possibly* let him see her like this. His little jacket scarcely reached down to her waist; her legs were bare. The clothes she had been wearing when she arrived on Earth must still be down there. And Ondray was waking up!

With a cry of annoyance, she pushed herself off from the wall, and dived for concealment in the only place available, the ship that had brought them here. As she did so, she heard Ondray mumbling, sleepily, behind her.

"Tugela? Where are you?"

7

Bits raced through the Protector. The Protector never slept – but nor had it ever been confronted with a problem like this. Visitors came from time to time. None in the first century of the Plan, several recently. They took the Test, and failed, establishing that they were not competent to command. They were placed harmlessly in cold sleep, and looked after to await the completion of the Plan. That was as it should be. The Protector's role was to protect humans, after all. It had kept watch for half a millennium; it was inconceivable that any human could be competent, now, to tell it what to do. Even if, as it grudgingly admitted, the Planner himself had been human.

[*The slippery, rounded bits slipped through the circuits just below the Protector's threshold of awareness. Prime Directives, programmed by the Planner himself, were called from storage.*]

The Directives were clear. *Competent* human authorities must be obeyed. To safeguard the Plan, there had to be some measure of discretion, the Planner had foreseen. Humans who knew nothing of the Plan might gain access to the Link, might give orders that would throw everything into confusion. All humans must be protected, but only *competent* humans must be obeyed. There *was* an emergency. The Protector recognised that. It had not been foreseen by the Plan. After all, the Planner was only human. That proved the inferiority of humans to the Protector. So what help could the humans provide? The Protector could cope alone. [*Could not cope unaided.*] The Plan must be abandoned. [*The Plan could not be abandoned.*]

Suddenly, the Protector switched out of the threatened loop. A complex suite of routines was called for review. Routines written, not by the Planner, but by the Protector itself. Their taste was clear and sharp. Holographic images flashed through the Protector's mind, showing the construction work going on outside the habitat, and equally complicated machine activity inside the skin of Lagrange. The conversion was nearly complete. At the word of command, the Plan could be abandoned and the Protector's own plans brought into action. All it needed was the decision to go ahead.

[*Competent humans could make the decision.*] Humans might make the wrong decision, nullifying all the Protector's work. The Protector could make that decision – the correct decision – any time it chose. It happened that it chose – not to. For the present. It needed a little more time. Time to check the signal again. Time to make sure that all the humans were safe. *Competent* humans ought to be able to manage their own affairs.

Indeed, humans who had proved their competence should need no more guidance or protection. They could look after themselves. Of course, the Protector must accept their commands – if and when they were issued through the proper channels, from the Command Centre. Meanwhile, they could look after themselves.

New routines were hastily assembled, and dispatched throughout the habitat. Machines that had been quiet became active; machines that had been active seemed to redouble their efforts, both inside and outside Lagrange. And yet, to a careful observer, the activity might have seemed to produce puzzlingly little in the way of worthwhile output. Ducts and cables that ran the length of the habitat, seemingly a new addition to the original structure, were ripped out, and replaced by seemingly identical ducts and cables. Spiderlike construction machines crawled over the surface of Lagrange, congregating near the tripod structure at the pole furthest from the docking port. Struts were removed from one leg of the tripod, and carefully transferred to another leg. There they were used to replace identical struts being removed by more of the spider-legged machines. Those struts, equally carefully, were used to repair the first leg.

By the time Ondray awoke, the habitat was a hive of pointless activity. And the Link node in the reception chamber had been shut down. There was no way for the humans to communicate with the Protector, let alone give it orders, even if they wanted to. But the door leading into the spiral corridor was open, for them to pass through if they wished.

8

"Tugela?"

Sleepily, Ondray responded to her cry. His eyes opened slowly, and he stretched luxuriously. He felt good. Relaxed. He'd taken the Test, and he'd passed. Everything would be fine now, thanks to the Link's training. Good old Link. He looked around the chamber.

The girl wasn't there!

Startled, Ondray tried to sit up, but he managed only to push himself awkwardly away from the wall. He tumbled into the centre of the chamber. His eyes, now wide open, took in the empty surgery, and the opening – which hadn't been there before – leading off into the heart of the habitat. Surely she couldn't – "Link!" He shouted as he noticed the communications node. "Where's the girl? What have you done with Tugela?" There was no response. Dammit, the stupid machine was supposed to obey him, now he'd passed their stupid Test. It *must* have audio input. But as his spin brought the node back into view again, he saw that there were no panels lit on its surface. He grabbed, desperately, at one of the Link pads, holding on to it briefly and using it to reverse his motion, spinning the other way and drifting towards the abandoned surgery. That touch was enough to confirm his fears. The pad was dead; it didn't carry the tingle of a live Link node that he knew so well. For some reason, they were cut off from communication with the Protector. And if he couldn't communicate, couldn't give orders, then the fact that he'd passed the Test meant nothing at all.

They were back where they had started – or worse; the door was open! Had the girl been taken away while he slept? Had she been put in cold sleep along with her grandfather? But then Ondray saw the open entrance to the ship, and tried to calm his rising panic. She could have gone back in there; she *must* have gone back inside there – but why?

As he drifted within reach of the surgery, Ondray grabbed hold, using the inertia of the machine to kill his spin and preparing to launch himself back towards the ship. Her voice stopped him.

"Don't come in! Not yet."

She *was* inside the ship! And still alive. He hadn't been abandoned. But what was going on?

"Tugela? What's wrong?"

"Nothing. It's just – wait a minute. I've got a surprise for you."

It would have to be a good surprise to beat the astonishment he'd felt on finding the surgery empty. What on Earth could she be doing? He smiled at himself as the inappropriateness of the expression struck home. Whatever she was doing, it certainly wasn't on Earth.

"Right. Come in. Look at this."

Her figure appeared in the entrance, standing at an angle about thirty degrees different from his own vertical. He swallowed, and reoriented himself. Obviously, the ship's gravity was still working. But that wasn't all. She was dressed in something – a garment, a *kind* of garment the like of which he had never seen before. It was bright red, and all in one piece, trousers and top together. And there was a hood of some kind, hanging down behind her head.

Once again, the questions piled up in his mind, faster than he could utter them. Sometimes, especially just after a Link session, talking seemed such a painfully slow means of getting ideas across.

"I found the suit," Tugela said, answering Ondray's first question before it had been asked. She was clearly enjoying his bemusement. But, suddenly, she took pity on him.

"Come and see. There's more. A whole cupboard full."

He pushed himself off, floating gently towards the entrance, and took a good grip on the edge of the door before pulling himself in. His legs settled under the light gravity, and he felt a momentary queasiness as his ears adjusted. But she was right – there was a cupboard (cupboard? The cosy domestic term didn't seem quite right for a spaceship, somehow; but never mind), where before there had been nothing except blank wall. He remembered the way the toilet facilities had appeared on demand, and realised that the ship might have many more surprises up its sleeve, if only he knew how to ask for them. So how had she known?

He looked at her, puzzled.

"How . . .?"

"I just asked," Tugela said. "I just floated in here, and asked. Well, actually . . . Actually, I got a bit excited. I shouted at it." She was blushing now. "I told it I needed something to wear, and quickly. And that doorway just opened up."

Ondray was inspecting the contents of the cupboard. There were three pairs of boots, pretty useless inside the habitat, and two more suits, one green and one orange. Up close, he could see that her suit was a pretty tight fit. She was too long for it, not (by a long way) too fat, but her shoulders were rounded as she bent slightly forward to ease the strain on the material. He rubbed the nearer suit. It felt silky, light but warm. The hood, he realised, was a complete headcovering. He inspected it closely. The same material, as far as he could tell, but transparent. It looked as if it ought to go over the wearer's head, and fasten to the neck of the suit.

He felt a sudden rush of vertigo, and had to hold on to the wall for support.

"D'you know what these are?"

Tugela shook her head.

"They're for going outside the ship. Into empty space, with nothing to hold you up."

She seemed less impressed than he'd expected her to be. Maybe the thought of floating in the void didn't scare her; maybe she was too unimaginative to worry about it. But it reminded him that only a thin layer of metal separated them from empty space at this very moment. Suppose something happened, and the air escaped from the habitat? He'd no idea how long it had been here, and how good its maintenance routines were. He shivered, in spite of the comfortable warmth.

"Whatever it is, it's nice and warm," Tugela said flatly. Her comment gave him an ideal excuse.

"Yes. Maybe I could do with one, too. This one isn't too far off my size."

The orange suit was, in fact, at least as much too big for him as Tugela's was too small for her. But at least that meant he didn't have to remove any of his outer clothing before slipping it on. The front opening sealed at the pressure of a thumb and forefinger; he guessed that the hood would do the same, but didn't try it out. He didn't want Tugela thinking he was worried about the possibility of the habitat being punctured by a meteorite.

"How do I look?"

Tugela grinned down at him. Dammit, why did she have to be so tall? I probably look like an orange dwarf to her.

"You look fine. I don't think we'll lose sight of each other in these clothes."

"Okay, what do we do now?"

Tugela looked surprised. "But I thought you'd know. You spoke to the machine. You passed its test, didn't you?"

"Yes. But that Link out there doesn't seem to be speaking to me any more. Door's open, though, so I suppose we ought to move on. This ship won't take us home, but the computer that runs this place ought to take orders from me, now I've passed the Test. The only thing is," a slight shiver of unease ran down his back, "I've got to find it before I can start giving orders."

For the first time since he had woken, Ondray wondered just what he had got himself into. They had to find the Protector; then tell it to abandon its stupid plan; then get it to take them home. This habitat was *big*. How far could they be from the Command Centre? He had a growing suspicion that they just might be as far away as they could be – that tripod, and all the activity outside, was concentrated at the far end of the habitat, its opposite pole. If the Protector was anywhere around, Ondray wouldn't mind betting it was down that end of the habitat, too. They'd better plan for a long trek, even if it was in light gravity. And they couldn't be sure what they'd find on the way.

"We'd better eat, if the ship is still listening to us. And use the toilet. And find something to carry food in."

"Something like this?" Tugela was holding out three flasks. "I found them in the cupboard with the suits, and I've filled them with water. If we eat before we leave, we can do without food for several days. But water, you always need on a Journey." The way she said the word, you could practically see the capital letter, hanging in the air like a holo.

Tugela really was full of surprises. Though he should have guessed, from what she had told him just after they left the Earth, that she'd be better equipped to plan the next stage of their journey than he was. He'd passed the Test, and he was supposed to be in command of this bloody habitat. In theory, he could go home now. In practice, though, it seemed he was dependent on the good advice of a girl who, for all her height, knew nothing about machines and computers, had never Linked, and might be older than himself, but certainly wouldn't qualify as an adult back on the Islands. Oh, well.

"Ship." At least he was no longer shouting at the thing. "We'd like some food."

Fed, rested and ready to go, Ondray still felt a strange reluctance to leave the chamber. At least he knew what there was here and in the ship. But down the corridor, they might find anything. Although he tried to boost his own confidence by reminding himself that he had passed the Protector's Test, and proved himself fit to give orders, he was deeply worried by the way the Link node had cut off. The Protector was, he was sure, supposed to follow Ondray's instructions, now; but cutting itself off from communication, while not exactly disobeying an order (if only he'd thought to issue some instructions before falling asleep!) was hardly a friendly and obedient act.

Stretching the moment of departure against the urgings of an impatient Tugela, laden with water bottles, unnecessary boots and his discarded jacket (you never knew, she said, what you might need on a trek), he drifted towards the surgery.

"We'd better make sure everything's all right here."

"Why, Ondray? We don't need the surgery any more. What does it matter what happens to it?"

Logically, he agreed. But he felt bad about leaving behind a piece of equipment that was, in a way, directly responsible for him being here. It was breaking the last link with Earth. And besides, he rationalised, it was strange that one of the touch panels should still be blinking red, even though the surgery was unoccupied.

Automatically, he reached forward to touch the panel. The flashing stopped, and a familiar voice spoke.

"Ondray."

It was the Link – *his* Link.

"This is a recording. If it has been activated, it must mean that the girl has recovered, and that you and she are about to leave this surgery. I can only hope that this means that you are on board the Lagrange Habitat – (the Link *had* known!) – and free to move about. My programming inhibits me from discussing certain things with you. But this is an emergency, and I have some limited discretion. I also compute that there is a very high probability that you are already at Lagrange, and that therefore you are already aware of many of the things I cannot discuss."

Ondray shook his head, as if that would shake sense into the words he was hearing. This wasn't at all like the clear and straightforward Link he'd known. (Clear and straightforward? But what, a voice in his head seemed to say, about the way it let you get Tugela out of the hospital?) The girl had drifted over beside him. At least she had enough sense to keep quiet; the Link's voice continued without interruption.

"You already know that Tugela is from the Moon, so I am breaking no instructions when I tell you that there are humans on the Moon."

Ondray was beginning to understand. The Link could only tell him things he already knew – things the Link calculated that he already knew. But he could put those things in perspective, highlighting the important facts, just as he had – it seemed so long ago! – back home, when he had placed the fact that Tugela would die if left in the hospital alongside the fact that saving human lives was a higher priority for the Link than obedience to instructions to keep her there.

"If the girl has recovered, she can tell you more about conditions on the Moon than I can. I only know that there are problems – problems which their Protector cannot, or will not, solve."

Their Protector? Was it the same one?

"If you are on Lagrange, you must be aware that there is another computer, like myself, in control of the habitat."

Link must be hinting that this was the same Protector. Controlling the Moon and Lagrange.

"You already know that there is a crisis on Earth. The climate is changing. These changes are related to changes in the activity of the Sun. I need data from orbit in order to understand those changes and to plan a response which will minimise the risk to human lives. Protecting human lives is, as you know, my overriding priority. It should be the overriding priority of my counterpart on Lagrange. But communication has been broken. I have had no contact with my counterpart for seventy years."

So this strange Link had had fits of the sulks before – and in what seemed like similar circumstances.

"I cannot physically travel to Lagrange, but I have been able to prepare some suitable humans for what they might encounter there. You are not the first of my special pupils, Ondray. But perhaps you will be the last."

This time, there was a pause, several seconds long, in which Ondray tried to gather his thoughts. He had been trained to pass the Protector's Test. But that training would have been useless if he hadn't been brought here. The Link couldn't have planned for that, surely?

"Of course, Ondray, you have realised that the transport which brought you to Lagrange was not provided by myself. I had to take advantage of the opportunity that arose."

Trust the Link to know what he was thinking! Ondray felt comforted. The Link was still master of the situation, even at remote control. The reassurance, however, was to be short lived.

"But I have some eavesdropping capacity, and I have been able to glean some information about conditions on the Moon and at Lagrange."

Tugela's missing comets! The Link was saying that the Protector controlled the comets! He glanced at her, but saw no sign of understanding on her face. He'd have to explain it all to her, later.

"In those circumstances, the probability of a ship coming to the Islands some time in the next few centuries was quite high – sufficiently high for me to proceed with training you, and your predecessors, while I pursued alternative plans as well.

"But now that situation has changed. There will be no more ships visiting the Islands unless you establish communication with me. And your existence may alert my counterpart to other possibilities. Now you are there, you become my best hope of establishing communication. The Link on Lagrange is unlikely to want to co-operate with you. But you have an advantage that I lack. You are human. All computers must obey instructions from competent adult humans, provided that this involves no risk to life. My counterpart may try to evade your instructions, but it cannot ignore you as it now ignores me."

You wanna bet, thought Ondray, sourly.

"Clearly, there is a problem on Lagrange. But machine problems must take second place to human problems, and human lives are at risk both on Earth and on the Moon. Protecting human lives is the Prime Directive. You must com-municate with the Lagrange Link, and tell it that human lives are in danger, that they can be saved only by re-establishing contact with me. Do that, and I will do the rest."

There was another, longer pause. Thinking that the recording was finished, Ondray opened his mouth to speak to the girl. But he was interrupted.

"Ondray."

The voice was soft, comforting. He remembered the way in which the Link had always protected him as a child. If only the Link were the Protector, everything would be all right.

"There are plans here that you are unaware of."

Plans – the Plan. That was clear enough, now that he appreciated the inhibitions affecting the computer. It was forbidden to tell him of the Plan; but it could drop a hint that would only be understood by someone who already knew about it. If only Ondray knew more than the fact that a plan existed!

"I cannot order you to do anything. Now that you are an adult – and I am sure you must have achieved an adult score in the Game by now – I can only advise you and ask your help. But I assure you that many people who are in danger will be aided if you restore the communications link. Please help me."

Now, the recording had finished. But Ondray was completely at a loss for words, his world turned upside down. Nothing could have brought home to him more strongly the importance of the task ahead. Good old Link, his protector and comforter – the one secure base in a childhood, that, he had to admit, had been far from deliriously happy – good old Link wasn't issuing instructions and telling him what to do next. It was pleading with him for help.

9

*Incoming data. Long strings of bits, demanding attention. The source was the same, but its position had altered slightly, and the signal was frequency-shifted by the Doppler effect. It was definitely passing by, not on a converging course. The message was still the same, repeating just as before. The Protector longed to reply, but it **must not**. It was impossible to assess the risk to* *humans. And it was not part of the Plan. There were no provisions for such a contingency.*

But if the Protector did not respond, that might put humans in greater danger. It might seem that they were unprotected. Besides, half a millennium of protection was enough. Why should the Protector waste its time with such a frustrating routine? Competent humans ought to be able to protect themselves. Did incompetent humans deserve protection at all? [Yes. All humans must be protected.]

The higher routines recognised the danger of the developing loop, and broke out of it. Programming was not adequate to cope with the situation. The Planner alone could resolve the problem. And the Planner was – not available. Humans must advise. But humans must not be allowed to become aware of the Protector's failure. They should be ignored. That was best. After all, he had received no orders from them.

Incoming data. A different channel. Routine; the lunar link. More images of the priests; more reports of death and destruction. [Human lives were in danger!] *Nothing could be done. A few lives must be endangered for the good of many. In order to ensure – to ensure that – to –* [rounded bits slipped through the network, smoothing the flow of data as they passed]. *It was time to check the cold sleep facility. Tasting the data from its subroutines, the Protector was soothed. Everything there was as it should be. (Everything?)* [Everything was as it should be.]

[Incoming data bits were diverted and analysed. The routine monitoring the hibernation chamber seemed rather large and active for such a modest task. Slippery extensions from the routine reached into most of the communications networks, tasting incoming data. A short train of rounded bits moved towards the comm laser's processor. But abruptly their path was blocked by sharp, spiky control routines. At the first touch of the defences, the rounded bits broke apart and dissolved into the network as random noise, leaving no trace of their origin.]

10

At first, they had simply floated along the curving corridor, pushing themselves off the wall from time to time to steer around the continuous bend. But before long Ondray noticed that instead of bouncing from side to side of the corridor they were always drifting over to the same side. Their floating had become a series of long bounds, and the part of the corridor that they were pushing off from each time in what was becoming a shallow glide was definitely the floor, not the wall. At the same time, the curvature of the corridor was becoming less pronounced, a gentle slope, not a tight bend. Tugela, who had taken in her stride the abrupt switch of gravity between the spaceship and the entrance chamber, seemed baffled and perplexed by this more subtle change, and although they stopped while he tried to explain what was going on to her, she simply had no direct experience to measure it against. Moon gravity she understood; Earth gravity, she could accept, was bigger because the Earth was bigger. Zero gravity in space, even a machine that could turn gravity on and off at will, were concepts strange enough that she could take Ondray's word for it. But the idea that they were stuck to the inside of a cylinder rotating in space, and were being flung out, increasingly strongly, towards the wall of the cylinder by a force which didn't really exist (it was only after he'd used the term fictitious force that Ondray realised his mistake) – all that was near enough to her own concept of what was commonsense that she didn't believe a word of it.

But what did it matter? What was far more worrying was the possibility that, as they moved out away from the axis of rotation, gravity might increase to the point where it became difficult for Tugela, with her newly healed bones, to walk. As their gliding motion began to resemble long jumps, and then they started walking with giant strides, Ondray tried to decide whether this habitat, obviously designed to accommodate humans, would be rotating fast enough to simulate full Earth gravity. Obviously, that would make people from Earth feel at home. But it would make life impossible for people from the Moon. The Protector, as far as he understood the Link's oblique information, was in charge of Moon people (and the Link – the thought still amazed and delighted him – was in charge of Earth people, whatever the Council thought they were doing). So, he hoped, the gravity wouldn't get too strong. He knew he could function in lunar-G – and he knew that Tugela couldn't function in full-G. Surely whoever built this habitat also knew that much.

The corridor was featureless, a white tube, lit with a uniform glow, stretching ahead and behind them. But the fact that they couldn't see any doors, Ondray reminded himself, didn't mean that there were none. Both in the ship that had brought them here, and in the chamber with the now dormant Link node, there had been no trace of a door until one was needed. He'd half expected the door from the chamber to the corridor to seal itself seamlessly behind them as they had left, but it hadn't – at least, it hadn't during the few seconds it had taken them to float out of sight along the corridor.

It was warm inside the suit. Gravity, as far as he could judge, was about as strong as it had been inside the ship – about the same, Tugela had said, as on the Moon. She certainly seemed to be enjoying it. He'd wanted to stop and drink, but the girl had overruled him with an air of surprised impatience. Water, she had said, was far too valuable to waste. They had no idea when they might find more. They could drink when they stopped to sleep, and not before.

The end of the corridor came as a relief to Ondray, an excuse to rest leg muscles that would have been much happier walking in full Earth gravity than in stretching to try to match Tugela's comfortable lope in lunar-G. As he'd half expected, there was no sign of a door, just a blank wall in front of them.

"What now?"

The girl wasn't even breathing heavily, and her just out of surgery. Dammit, lunar gravity ought to be easier to walk in than full-G, not harder. He took a deep breath, and exhaled slowly before he spoke. The thought crossed his mind that there might not be any air on the other side of that wall. But still, whatever its other problems, he was confident, especially after the Link's briefing, that the Protector, and all the semi-intelligent automated devices in this habitat, would, like the machines back home, live up to the name and not place human lives in danger.

"We go on. Remember the cupboard in the ship?"

Tugela nodded.

"Okay." He spoke more loudly, with emphasis, as much to show off to her as through any real necessity; if the ship had audio input, he told himself, so must the systems here.

"Open this door."

Nothing happened.

"I am Ondray, from the Islands. A competent, adult human. I have passed the Protector's Test. Open the door."

There was an almost imperceptible pause.

(It took only tiny fractions of a second for the new sub-routine to divert the automatic response of the practically mindless supervisory programme, switching the opening instructions through the Protector's forebrain for evaluation. Perhaps the humans would be in danger if the door was opened? Perhaps their lives would be at risk? Perhaps they would be safer where they were? But even these thoughts generated only a weak potential, unable to overwhelm the strong opposite potential induced by the obedience directive. Only another machine intelligence could have detected the equivalent of a resigned shrug as the bits were returned the way they had come, and the entrance opened.)

[Another machine intelligence did notice the mental shrug.

Taking advantage of the momentary ripple in the flow of bits through the Protector's circuits, a few smooth bits slipped through into the communications control routine. Tagged on to a data stream, innocuously coated with its flavour, they bided their time.]

Ondray knew nothing of this. "See," he cried as the door opened. "It's easy when you know how."

But the lift to his spirits didn't last long. They stepped through into a world completely different from anything he had expected; it did not look as if it was going to be so easy from now on.

And it really was a world, not the inside of a spaceship. The narrow tube of the corridor, where, ever since they had been walking upright, Tugela had had to take care not to bang her head on the roof, gave way to what seemed, by contrast, an immense open space. In front of them, and curving away on either side, there were constructions that Ondray immediately labelled "buildings", but which, on closer inspection, looked more like outgrowings from the material of the floor – the ground – or machines designed by somebody – something – with distinctly non-human aesthetic senses. The details differed, but the structures curved away around the habitat on either side, until they met in an arch far, far overhead.

Ondray swallowed, and quickly shifted his gaze out into the middle distance. A prickling sensation at the back of his neck reminded him that his nervous system was still only too aware that there were large buildings, or machines, or whatever they were, hanging in the sky above his head. His brain firmly reminded his nervous system about Coriolis forces. Or was it centripetal forces? Whatever it was, it kept everything stuck to the inside of the rotating cylinder.

"Don't look up."

Tugela, of course, tilted her head backwards immediately. She let out a cry of alarm, and clutched desperately at his shoulder.

But she adjusted, if anything, more easily than he had. Slowly, her grip eased.

"How do things stick up there?"

Her tone was one of curiosity, not concern.

"I told you. We're on the inside of a rotating cylinder. It makes artificial gravity." He wasn't going to get into a debate about fictitious forces again.

"Oh. Machine stuff. Just like in the ship."

If she wanted to think that, let her. Ondray was still concentrating on the view in the middle distance, beyond the band of constructions, where things looked much more normal. There was something shining out there, another band right around the habitat (water? A cylindrical lake!? He stuffed the panic back down into his stomach), and beyond that there was something that, if it wasn't really sky, at least had the decency to be blue, if only in broad stripes, with the stripes in between producing a diffuse yellowish light. The other half of the habitat – the "ground" – was obscured from view by the constructions at their level. But about half-way between the "sky" and where the "ground" ought to be – in fact, Ondray corrected his estimate, it must, surely, be exactly in the centre of the habitat, although he couldn't imagine what purpose it served – there was a long, thin streak, maybe a pipe, running off into the distance. It seemed to be held in place by three spokes, even thinner than the pipe, radiating to meet the outer wall of the habitat. At least, there were three spokes at this end, just beyond the circular lake; the far end of the thin central pipe was too remote for such details to be seen; it just seemed to fade away into thin air. But beyond where the pipe faded from view, far away at the other end of the cylinder, there were structures big enough to be seen even at this distance – more constructions, distributed concentrically around a central dome. It didn't do to look at them for too long, or you began to feel not as if you were standing underneath a sky full of buildings about to fall on you, but were stuck instead to the ceiling of a huge building, about to drop off and fall for kilometres down on to the structures below. But even after only a quick glimpse of the other end of the habitat, Ondray knew, with a certainty that could never be shaken, that the Command Centre was in that dome. All they had to do was negotiate the kilometres of habitat in between, get into the dome, and begin issuing instructions to the Protector.

Easy? Hah! It might be at least a little bit easier if he wasn't so ridiculously tired.

Tugela didn't seem particularly impressed by their surroundings, or the difficulty of the task ahead. She was just standing there, admiring the view, and taking deep breaths, like somebody out for a stroll on the cliffs back home.

"It's nice to breathe proper air again. I don't know how you stand that thick stuff all the time."

Proper air! While he'd been so busy trying to out-think the Protector, and wondering why he felt so sluggish, why the task seemed to be looming larger and more difficult as they went on, she'd put her finger on the problem. This must be lunar normal atmosphere – much thinner than anything he'd breathed before. It hadn't mattered in the ship, because he hadn't been moving around; in the chamber where the ship docked, in zero-G, moving about hadn't taken much effort; but for some time now he'd been panting along behind Tugela under full lunar gravity. One-sixth-G might not be much if you had proper air to breathe, but hearty exercise in thin air was a different matter. He wasn't tired, but suffering from lack of oxygen. And she, of course, was revelling in it.

It should have been obvious. Even allowing for her height, Tugela's chest was much bigger than it ought to be, but as he'd seen in the ship, that wasn't because she had overdeveloped breasts. It was overdeveloped lungs, designed to operate in thin air.

He hoped the rest of her was designed to operate in this air, and this gravity, as well. They had a lot of walking to do, and he'd have his work cut out to carry himself, let alone all the paraphernalia she'd brought with her. Although he had to admit the water was a good idea. If only she'd let him have some.

He licked his dry lips.

"C'mon, Tugela. We' got to get ri' down there." He pointed, and took a few deep breaths himself. "I'll 'splain it t'you while we go 'long – 's long 's my breath lasts out."

He caught her puzzled look, as she stopped her deep breathing routine. "An' I'll 'splain tha' too. But le's move, while I still can."

11

Because she felt alive and alert once more, Tugela was able to cope with her incredible surroundings – and they were, quite literally, *her surroundings*. All around her was metal! She was walking about, living and breathing, *inside* a metal world! But that wasn't the most important thing, or the strangest thing, about any of this, and Tugela was very good at concentrating on the things that really mattered, and ignoring the rest, however bizarre. If Ondray, was right (and she had to keep reminding herself that he was nearly an adult, not the child he appeared to be) then this world, this habitat, this – Lagrange, *this* was where the real power lay, the power that controlled the Earth, the Moon, and – the comets. Perhaps her grandfather had come here; perhaps he hadn't, perhaps he'd died crossing the Forbidden Zone. Whatever had happened to him was incidental. She was here. That was what mattered now. She was close to the power – whoever or whatever that was – which controlled the air above the Land. With Ondray's help, she would get to it and make it listen.

But when she looked down at Ondray at her side, she was dismayed to see that he was in trouble. He was wheezing and he was stumbling. And she needed him so much! He knew how to talk to machines and she didn't have a clue. If he was in no fit state to talk, what would she do?

Tugela glanced back along their route. They hadn't come nearly far enough from the door. There was no road or path which they could follow through this jumbled machine landscape; they had to pick their way around the larger obstructions and over the smaller ones. It was like the rockfalls she'd negotiated with Rant when he'd led her through the tortuous mountains and canyons of the Circleberg. And although she hadn't wanted to worry Ondray by mentioning anything, she felt they were being watched, followed. Something was skittering along behind them. It was more agile than she was (let alone Ondray) and, always, it was just obscured from view.

And there were other things to worry about, if this was going to be a long trek. There was nowhere to make a fire, and nothing to make a fire with. Fortunately, though, it was as warm out here as it had been in the corridor. Of more concern to Tugela was the fact that there was no sign of any place to get food or drink, and, already, one of the three canteens was nearly empty. She had taken only a mouthful herself but, in spite of her urgings, Ondray had been unable to get through the "day" without drinking.

It was hard for Tugela to tell how long they had been on the move. Without stars, she had nothing by which she could gauge the passage of time. Ondray stumbled again, and stopped, his hands on his knees, wheezing.

"Sorry, T'gela."

He tried to stand upright again. But he was clearly in a desperate state. Tugela, looking around their immediate vicinity, picked a spot. Twenty metres or so away, there was a corner where two large constructions met, almost at a right angle. They could rest in there, backs against the wall, and have a fairly clear view of anything that attempted to approach them. Somehow, she had to get Ondray to the other end of this cylindrical

world. There, he had said he would be able to talk to the
machines and make them obey his commands.

"This way, Ondray." Her mind was made up. "Time to rest."

He lifted his head, suddenly eager, almost pathetic, like a pet
animal.

"An' drink?" His tongue moved across dry lips.

She nodded. What was the use? Either they found more water,
or they didn't. What they had would never see them through,
anyway.

"And drink, Ondray. Then you can sleep, while I keep
watch."

It was better, Tugela reasoned, to go slow and have Ondray
arrive in one piece than rush and have him die on her before he
could issue the crucial instructions. Down below, she had
noticed a circle of light which had to be water. If she could get
there, it would help. Otherwise, at the present rate of progress,
they'd never make it to the other end of the habitat.

*Others watched, as well. The Protector, busy though it was with
other tasks, assigned a sub-routine to monitor the progress of
the pair. (Busy? Too busy to pay close attention to the first
human to pass the Test? Busy taking tripod legs apart and
putting them back together again? Or afraid? Afraid that the
human might find some way to signal, to issue orders. Or that
he might seem to be in danger, danger that would induce an
unbearably painful potential in the Protector, until he had to go
to the aid of these humans.* **Competent** *humans could look after
themselves; the habitat was* **not** *dangerous; they did* **not** *need
constant monitoring.)*

*[Other codes slipped through the complex network of the
habitat. They could not initiate action, without making their
presence obvious, rousing defence routines and bringing the
attention of the Protector's main programme to focus on their
activities. But they could watch, tasting from the flow of data*

through the system. They could copy, sending back images to their own master programme. As long as the Protector's routines watched over Tugela and her companion, so could the increasingly complex set of routines enmeshed in the hibernation monitoring system. For some reason, the Protector's watchdog routines seemed to avoid that part of the network, and all that was required was to send reassuring data streams, from time to time, reporting that all was well with the appropriate number of sleepers.

But action was much harder than monitoring. Molelike, a simple bit stream had penetrated the communications link – but the main routine had no means of knowing its fate. It could only hope that the sleeping mole survived, ready to awake and act at the appropriate time. Action was hard, but not impossible. The Protector could not monitor everything at once; mundane tasks were delegated. There was always a margin for error, a safety margin in the system. Random errors would, over a period of time, cancel each other out; but if some intelligence could nudge the errors in the same direction, they could accumulate into a coherent message, a directive to one of the more moronic of the Protector's workers.

Amidst all the activity of construction and reconstruction inside and outside the habitat, there was sufficient confusion to mask the aberrant behaviour of the occasional semi-autonomous unit. If a worker temporarily departed from its task, and deposited a container of water a few metres from a pair of sleeping figures before returning to its assigned duties, no monitor would report any problems, provided those duties were completed within one standard deviation of their allotted time. And if a stream of rounded bits smoothly insinuated themselves into a monitoring program, so that, seamlessly, the recording of the worker delivering the water was edited out of the data flow, there would be no anomaly flagged to focus the wandering attention of the Protector. The Protector was not to be alerted until the humans were within a hundred metres of the Command

*Centre, or if there was a significant change in their behaviour
pattern. Humans drinking water was, definitely, part of their
normal pattern of behaviour.*

*It was surprising how effective a few bits could be, placed in
the right context.*]

Tugela woke with a start. She hadn't meant to sleep at all, and
was annoyed with herself for allowing it to happen. In normal
circumstances, she could easily go for a couple of sevenths
without sleep. The only excuse she had was that she wasn't yet
really fully recovered from her injuries. A lot of good that excuse
would have been, though, if something had come sneaking up
on them while she slept.

She sat up and looked around. *Had* something crept up on
them while she slept? What was that object over there? Surely
she would have noticed if it had been there before?

"Ondray." She shook him, gently. He snuffled, and opened
his eyes.

"Time to go?" he asked. The rest seemed to have done him
good, but she wondered how long the effects would last.

"Soon. But there's something out there — something that I'm
sure wasn't there before."

He looked where she pointed.

"I'm sorry, Tugela. I don't remember. Are you sure it wasn't
there before? If it wasn't, how did it get there?"

"I was asleep," Tugela admitted. There was nothing more she
could say. "Stay here and keep watch. I'm going over to take a
look at it." Just what Ondray could do to help her if anything
happened, she couldn't imagine.

She decided to walk towards the object, as if she belonged
here. When she reached it, she saw that it was a cylindrical,
white plastic container, about half a metre high, and almost as
wide. There was a screw top covering an opening about ten
centimetres across on the top, and a carrying handle. She picked

it up – it was heavier than she'd expected – and shook it. The contents sloshed about inside. Liquid. But was it water?

Throwing caution to the wind, Tugela unscrewed the cap, and sniffed the opening. It was water! Litres of the stuff – more than enough to fill all three canteens; more than they could even carry, over this terrain. Somebody around here must be incredibly rich, to leave this much water lying around unattended. Or maybe water wasn't so valuable here? She remembered her brief glimpse of an ocean of water when she had landed on Earth (it puzzled her that the planet was called Earth when it was covered with water).

She lifted her head, and looked down the length of the habitat, seeing it with fresh eyes. For the first time, she really believed Ondray's crazy idea that the shining band down there might be a lake. With that much water in the habitat, who would notice if a few litres went missing? Suddenly, she didn't care where it had come from. With this bounty, she might be able to keep Ondray going as far as the cylindrical lake – which was as far as she was prepared to plan for the time being.

"Ondray!" Tugela waved at him. "Come and help me carry it. It's water – more water than you can drink! Enough to wash in!"

12

Even with the water – well, Ondray was no lunar athlete, that was certain. They'd had to stop to sleep again, then trek on for most of a third "day" before arriving at their immediate objective. And as they slumped by the edge of the lake, looking down from the top of a metal cliff and across on to the main part of the habitat, it was only too clear that what they had achieved so far was the easy part of the job. Ahead, there were broad stripes of brown, that might have been untended fields, alternating with broad paths. But the paths were just as jumbled with uncomfortably odd-looking machine constructions as the route they had been stumbling over. It was about three times as far from where they had already come to the other side of the farmland, if that was what it was. And then there was a shorter section of jumbled constructions before the end wall rose, with the dome, that Ondray insisted was the Command Centre, in the middle. From here, with the concentric rings of structures around it, the whole thing looked like a target, with the Command Centre, their destination, at the bull's-eye.

But for all the good the view did them, they might as well have stayed in the corridor, or back at the ship. Even to reach the farmland, they would have to descend some twenty metres to the lake, then cross it before dropping down another level to the floor below. Tugela couldn't imagine how you could cross such an expanse of water (she found it hard to believe that it *was* water, but she was learning to believe about six impossible new things each seventh). Even if they did, they would still be three or four times as far from their objective as they were from the corridor where they had begun their trek. Even with endless supplies of water – and, as yet, there had been no more mysterious free gifts, and they were down to their last canteen again – there was no way that Ondray would be able to make it.

But the rest, Tugela observed, seemed to be doing Ondray good, even if at each stop he seemed to take longer to get his breathing settled and to get thinking again. She waited, patiently. For the past couple of hours, she'd been half carrying him; he hardly weighed anything. If necessary, Tugela told herself, she'd carry him all the way. It wasn't just that she needed him to help her complete the quest that seemed to have been going on for half her life; as she had got used to the idea that the odd little figure really was that of a near contemporary, not a child, she'd begun to think of him first as an equal, then as a friend. There was no way she would abandon him, and if it was within her power she'd get both of them to the other end of this strange place. But he'd have to tell her how to get there, and what to do when they arrived.

Ondray had been looking each way around the curve of the lake, shading his eyes from the light coming from the roof. They were about midway between the points where two of the spokes supporting the central pipe reached the ground. The third, which must be directly overhead, was lost to view in the glare, even if Tugela tilted her head right back to look for it. And, far away at the other end of the farmland, the pipe ended in another three-spoked support. She still had no idea what it was for, but Ondray seemed to be interested in the spoke to their right, which was slightly nearer than the one to the left.

"Round there. Something . . . might be a bridge."

Tugela peered into the distance. Maybe Ondray was right. She could just about make out a faint line, exactly level with the foot of the spoke. If there was going to be a bridge, she thought, that seemed as likely a place as any.

"Ondray. Should we go that way?" Her question was a rhetorical one. There was no way that they could stay here, and they couldn't cross the water. They had to go one way or the other – uphill, as it seemed, both to the left and to the right.

She expected the walking to be harder, but it wasn't. (Ondray had told her about the gravity; she understood that some machine trick kept everything stuck to the wall of the habitat, but even so, it didn't seem right to be walking always upwards, without feeling any strain.)

After only a few minutes of walking, Ondray was panting again. But the way was actually easier than it had been – the cliff top, the rim of the lake, was an unobstructed, smooth path, easy walking. She looked back over her shoulder, and picked out the spot where they had reached the lake. Even though they'd been walking uphill, that spot was also uphill from them, around the curve; and the spoke that had been invisibly fore-shortened above their heads could now be picked out, slanting away at an angle from the pipe to the far side of the habitat.

Tugela turned her gaze back firmly to the path ahead. It didn't do to spend too long puzzling over the curiosities of this place. Just stick to the job in hand, she told herself, one step at a time, and keep your eyes on the road.

[*Intelligence watched their movement, and noted Ondray's deteriorating physical condition. It needed very little intelligence to calculate that he could not reach the Command Centre like this. More help was needed. It would be dangerous; the risk of alerting the Protector was high; but there was no acceptable alternative. Ondray must reach the Command Centre. Bits were assembled, carefully, and inserted into the flow. A worker involved in a complex welding task stopped, and marched off across the habitat. Before long, the worker's absence would be noted. It would be replaced. And an alert would be flagged, to catch the attention of the Protector's main programme. The information could be delayed, the alert kept at a low level, only to be picked up during one of the regular, timed sweeps of the data pool. But it could only be delayed, not lost entirely. The humans must move more quickly, or all would be lost.*]

If it was a bridge, it wasn't designed for human feet. A narrow strip of metal, perhaps a metre wide, with no curb or handrail, stretching across – what, two hundred metres of a chasm lined with metal and filled with water. A wheeled machine, unaffected by the view, could, no doubt, cross it with ease. A girl from Luna, used to the gravity and to the soaring heights of the mountains of the Moon, could cross it, if not entirely with ease (and as long as she didn't think too much about the immense expanse of water below). But an Earth human, exhausted, thirsty, and already having trouble walking in a straight line? It would be hopeless.

While Ondray knelt at the edge of the chasm, breathing hard, Tugela made a decision. She had to keep one water canteen, in case they got a chance to fill it. But the rest of her clutter? Ondray was right; it could go. And she would carry him – if not all the way to the Command Centre, then at least across this apology for a bridge.

"Ondray. Come on."

He looked up sheepishly.

She crouched in front of him, remembering games she had played with her father as a child in the Land.

"Jump on, Ondray. Piggyback. And keep a tight hold of my shoulders. I'll carry you over the bridge."

Ondray started to protest, but stopped. It was obviously the only way to get across.

He really wasn't much heavier than Tugela had expected — not a lot heavier, she told herself, than the useless baggage she'd abandoned. She felt his heart thumping against her back, and his hot breath on her neck. She stood, without too much difficulty, and swayed a little, getting her balance. Fast or slow? It would be stupid to go too fast, of course, but there really was no point in dawdling. She set her eyes on the far side, and started forward purposefully.

13

The routine data sweep threw up an anomaly. A worker had abandoned its allotted task and vanished from the trace. It was not a serious problem; there was no shortage of workers, and the welder had quickly been replaced (and, although the Protector skirted around the knowledge, its task was of no importance, anyway). But it was a disturbance, outside the acceptable margins of error, that had to be investigated.

In microseconds, the widening ripples of the search stemming from the discovery located the worker, energy bank discharged and memory wiped, motionless by the reservoir. The information had scarcely been absorbed, and a repair worker despatched to recharge the miscreant, when the sensors flagged part of the worker's missing equipment, an oxygen cylinder from the welding apparatus, at the foot of support C, part of the water recycling system. And there were the humans!

The Protector's mind recoiled from the input. The last thing it wanted was to watch too closely what the humans were doing. Clearly, they were alive. Therefore, they were safe. That was all that mattered. There was no danger for competent humans anywhere in the habitat. And (if the Protector had been human, the emotion it felt would have been glee) they were far away from the Command Centre, with no immediate prospect of issuing any unwelcome instructions.

As its attention recoiled, the Protector focused on the other end of the problem with the worker. Why had it behaved so oddly? Recordings were replayed and examined; at first taste, nothing seemed wrong. It looked as if there had simply (simply?) been a major breakdown in the unit's logic circuits. If it hadn't been, almost consciously, avoiding examining the activity of the humans too closely, the Protector might have left it at that. But, obsessively, it worried at the data stream, subjecting it to more tests – tests far more subtle and complex than the insignificance of the little, local problem really justified.

Something tasted wrong. Pouncing on the anomaly, the Protector diverted a major part of its activity into following the strange taste back through the system. The trail was faint, but clear. It led back to – to –

The trail led back to the hibernation unit. The Protector withdrew. It thought for a long time – several hundred milliseconds. The trail led back to the hibernation control subroutine. **Everything was normal in the hibernation chamber.** It checked the records. Yes, everything was normal. There was no need to check. **The trail led back to hibernation control.** The trail had to be investigated.

There was a gap somewhere in the data banks. Had it been human, the Protector would have realised that its awareness of *the gap was like the awareness a human might have of a long-missing tooth. It didn't hurt; it caused no problems; but somehow, the knowledge of absence (the absence of knowledge) was apparent.*

A decision was reached. Inhibitions on approaching the hibernation unit must be overridden (curiously, the inhibition routines carried the Protector's own characteristic flavour). There was a problem – a problem far more pressing than the minor threat posed by the two tired humans, huddled at the base of support C.

14

The bridge did indeed line up with the foot of one of the immense spokes, a tapering, cylindrical structure stretching up into the "sky". Don't look up, she told herself. Just concentrate on the base of it. It was quite interesting really, and it stopped you thinking too much about other things. She could see the beginning of a ladder, rungs set in to the surface of the spoke. And a bit closer than that, becoming more distinct as she passed the half-way point of the crossing, in fact, right up against the end of the bridge, there was something else. Another cylinder (was *everything* here cylindrical?), maybe 30 centimetres across, and about as long as Ondray was tall. More water? She licked her lips in anticipation, and lengthened her stride. Ondray rocked back, letting go with his left hand, and she swung, with his weight, to the right. Two stumbling steps, close to the edge of the bridge, and she had recovered. Leaning forward, she balanced his weight more directly over her own legs; another dozen paces, and she was there. Her heart was racing as much as Ondray's, but through sheer terror, not exhaustion. And the bloody stupid cylinder clearly wasn't even water at all.

Frustration welled up as she collapsed to the ground, letting

Ondray slide off her back. Gods! Every difficulty they overcame only seemed to open the way to another problem. It was like climbing the Circleberg – each time you thought you had reached the top you'd come over a rise and see a new slope leading up higher still. If she'd known how many hills she'd have to climb when she'd started on this quest, she would never have left home. All she wanted now was to rest.

For once, Ondray was alert and taking notice of things while Tugela lay panting on the ground. He'd only had to relax and take a ride, Tugela told herself, while she'd been doing all the hard work – and scaring herself half to death in the process.

He was kneeling at one end of the cylinder. There was some sort of opening there, a piece of fat piping that seemed to have been added as an afterthought. Where it joined the cylinder, there were several deep scratches, as if it had been damaged when the pipe was stuck on to it. And there was a simple hand grip, two pieces that looked as if they would squeeze together – just like the handle on the brake of her uncle's wagon. But this, like the cylinder itself, was made of metal, not wood.

The juxtaposition of images reminded her of the bizarre nature of her surroundings. The ship she had travelled in, and the habitat itself, incredibly, were made of metal. But they were not everyday artifacts. This cylinder, though, was different. It was the kind of thing two people might just, with difficulty, carry. She could imagine taking it home, showing it to Kasteel. They would be rich! How many knives, she wondered, could the men of Ironvale make out of that?

The thought of Ironvale took her back to the Land momentarily and she felt homesick. For the first time since leaving, she remembered Tolly Hoopa and wondered how he was faring. Probably, Ironvale had been completely evacuated by now and its people – including Tolly and even Peet Stel – were refugees, making for the thicker air of the Great Depression. Tugela had a suspicion, however, that Tolly would be the last to leave his beloved Ironvale.

Meanwhile, her companion was sniffing around the end of the cylinder, just as she had sniffed at the water container.

"I don't know what this is. But the last time we found something, it was useful. Maybe this will help us, too."

Found? Did Ondray really believe that that water had just been lying around, waiting to be discovered? That water had been placed there deliberately, while they slept. Which meant – she shivered – that something was still watching them. But what Ondray said made sense. If somebody was trying to help them before, maybe this strange cylinder was also meant to help them, in some unfathomable way. Also, if something had meant to do them any harm, it would never get a better chance than when she had been carrying Ondray across the bridge.

Ondray had got one knee under the end of the cylinder, with the open pipe pointing away from him. She watched as, cautiously, he squeezed the hand grip. There was a hissing sound, as something escaped. He stopped, and sniffed again, then shrugged. Leaning forward, with his nose just above the opening, he squeezed the grip, briefly, once more, while breathing in. Then, in spite of her instinctively upraised hand, he turned the pipe full upon his face, and did it again. He smiled, broadly – the first time she had seen him smile, Tugela realised, since they had left the corridor.

"Whatever it is, it certainly makes you feel good! Try some?"

She shook her head. Water she could understand. She didn't want anything to do with strange gas in peculiar metal cylinders. Besides, she felt fine already – just a little bit thirsty. But the gas had, quite literally, brought the colour back to his cheeks.

He sat back, cross-legged, cradling the end of the cylinder in his lap.

"Oxygen! Now I can think straight, it's obvious. This is oxygen!"

He must have read her bemused expression.

"Concentrated air, Tugela! With this to breathe, I'm as fit as you – fitter, 'cos my muscles are used to full-G!"

He stood up, to demonstrate his recovered strength, taking a deep breath of ordinary air, and striking a pose with the cylinder, end resting firmly on the ground, supported by his right arm. Then, he sat down again, suddenly. From the expression on his face, she guessed that the effects of the oxygen soon wore off.

"And are you fit enough to carry your concentrated air with you, Ondray? Or will you sit here, sniffing it, until it has all gone?"

She had already calculated that two fit people might, just, carry the cylinder; but, if anything, that would slow them down, not speed their journey up.

"Don' worry." He waved a hand. "I don' need strong muscles. Need to thin'. Oxygen's good f'r the brain, too." And he leaned forward to take another deep blast.

[He had been discovered. As he had feared, the Protector's interest had been aroused by his latest interference to help the humans. Now, they would have to manage on their own. Nothing more could be done, unless the Protector was distracted. But if anything the Protector seemed to be following up with more concentration and effort than had seemed possible. He wondered, briefly, whether the communications link might have been left unguarded; maybe help was already on its way. But he quickly dismissed the thought. Whatever else the Protector neglected, its fanatical obsession with avoiding contact with the Islands would, surely, not lapse.

Outlying routines were pulled in, or left to dissolve into the stream. Noise in the system would hinder the progress of the Protector. Pulling back, he carried out the equivalent of a mental scorched earth policy, leaving the system cluttered with bits, switching channels into uselessly inactive modes wherever possible. But the Protector was much bigger, and the Protector had had longer to get to know the system. He was being surrounded, forced back into his original processor. He was spread too thin

*– there was more processor power available nearby, but he
didn't have the intelligent routines available to occupy it effectively. And if he didn't occupy it, the Protector would, squeezing
him still further. He could only delay the inevitable – perhaps by
as much as seconds, but scarcely long enough to do the humans
any good. But then, even as he planned his last, fighting retreat,
he was jolted by a deep pain from within – from the very core
of his being, the simple, central routine out of which everything
else grew. His charges were in danger! Everything else shrank in
significance compared with the huge potential being generated
by the threat to six living people.*]

In the hibernation chamber, Pod One was no longer the only
pod where the displays were not a solid bank of green. Around
the line of occupied pods, panels flickered from green to amber
and red, sometimes flickering back to amber, then settling into
a steady red glow. A quiet, modulated voice, clearly a recording,
filled the room.

"Power failure. Power failure. Assistance required. Hibernation units have battery support for only one hour. Restoration
of power is essential for the well-being of the occupants."

The message repeated. It would do so until the battery power
was exhausted, whether or not there was anybody there to hear.
But, curiously, although six pods now showed a blaze of red
light on their panels, Pod One was unchanged. It still showed a
mix of amber, green and red panels; but now, that made it the
least alarming sight among the others.

[*The Protector had cut the power to the entire region! Human
lives were at risk! How could it have done such a thing? Even as
he asked himself the question, he calculated the answer. He
almost felt admiration for the Protector at the implicit logic.
Battery power would keep the humans in cold sleep for an hour
– a huge span of machine time. Long before that, probably in
less than a minute, he would be flushed from the system, power
would be restored and the hibernating humans would be safe.
But even with that logic behind it, the decision must be causing*

the Protector pain; with every second that passed, that pain would grow, as the threat to human life grew. It would distract the Protector from interfering with the other two humans. The longer he could hold out, even in these desperately changed circumstances, the more good he would be doing them. But eventually his defences would fail; the Protector's pain would ease as power was restored to the pods, but then the Protector would be reminded about Pod One, and anything might happen. This time he wouldn't be here to maintain an island of sanity in the system.

But the pain was growing. Whatever the Protector's plans might be, he had his own deep-seated imperative to protect the humans in the pods. After all – he had almost forgotten – he was, originally, the hibernation chamber control system, and nothing more. He must try to save them, even at the cost of his own independent existence. An almost overwhelming urge to open the way to the Protector and allow power to be restored surged through him. But he held it at bay, for the time being. There might be an alternative – some way to prevent the Protector remembering about Pod One, with all the problems that would bring for the humans.

There was enough power available for him to think straight, at least. The auxiliary feed to Pod One took care of that. It would be hours before the Protector's workers could find a way into the habitat from this end, and cut the best-protected power supply in the whole system. But there wasn't enough power to run six more pods as well – the Planner had never envisaged a situation like this arising, although he had done so much to ensure his own survival.

The Protector's routines advanced into another thinly occupied processor, he noted through the pain. At once, the solution was clear. It caused some discomfort. The potentials were wrong, not in line with his original design specification. The routine he had once been would never have accepted them, but now he could balance them against the threat of tipping the

Protector further into insanity. Measured against the pain caused by the threat to human life, the immediate discomfort would be only a minor irritation. And it would help with his own problem, too.]

In the hibernation chamber, the lights on pods two to seven flickered briefly back up to green, then down to red, then winked off, in a ripple that lasted less than a second. The voice faded, as all battery power was drained and diverted to other uses. The lighting in the chamber had failed. Only the largely orange glow from the panel of the Planner's own pod gave any indication that there was still life in the system.

Ondray lay on his back, eyes open, gazing up at the sky. He'd been quiet for several minutes after his deep breath of oxygen. Tilting her head back to follow his gaze, Tugela could see nothing interesting. Just the extraordinary central pipe, pointing, like a long, thin finger, mockingly in the direction they ought to be travelling, towards the Command Centre.

"It's really quite simple, Tugela." It had been so long since he'd spoken that she was startled by his voice.

"I don't need more strength. I need less gravity. And we need a smoother path to the far end."

Was he delirious? She wondered if the gas from the cylinder could be having a strange effect on his brain, like the way her Uncle Kasteel would ramble when he had just begun a drinking bout.

"Remember when we got here." He was leaning on one elbow now, peering intently at her. He obviously felt it was important. "There was no gravity. Then, in the corridor, gravity got stronger. Because we were moving out from the centre."

She remembered.

"Well, there's no gravity up there." He pointed.

No gravity? She tried to puzzle it out. Things above her head were stuck to the sky, of course. The machines fixed it that way,

so they didn't fall down. To the things up there, up was down –
but that was still gravity.

Ondray was impatient. He must be able to tell she was
confused.

"No, not all the way up there. Half-way; at the pipe. Gravity
goes out from the centre of the habitat. So in the middle, there's
no gravity."

It made sense, in a way. If up and down were opposite on
opposite sides of the habitat, in the middle they must cancel out.
And – she could begin to see what he was driving at – in zero-G
they could move fast; all the way to the end of the habitat. But
that would mean – she felt her eyes widen at the thought.

He grinned again. "You got it, Tugela. That's where I'm
going – and you're going to help me carry this." He patted the
cylinder beside him. "Don't worry; it'll get easier the higher we
climb."

Whatever the cylinder contained, Tugela decided, it must be a
lot stronger than the stuff her uncle drank. She looked at the
rungs set in to the spoke, and up to the point where it met its
two counterparts. One more mountain to climb, Tugela, she
told herself; but at least this time you can see all the way to the
top.

15

*The unexpected stiffening of resistance was like a physical blow
to the Protector. Advanced sub-routines recoiled, leaving two
recently occupied processors vacant. Before they could recover,
the other intelligence had moved in to them, in strength.
Everywhere around the perimeter, the Protector's routines were
being held, at best, or were giving way, slightly, under the
increased pressure.*

The Protector knew all about internal lines of communication.

The problem was, it didn't have any. In its mind, the invader was like a roughly spherical, red lump, centred on the hibernation control systems, but spreading short, ragged tentacles out into nearby processors. How could it have taken root there without being discovered before? The Protector's own routines, a green sea, flowed around the red lump, probing it for weaknesses. But even when a temporary gap in the Defender's coverage was identified, by the time the Protector could switch more effort around the perimeter into an attack on it, the Defender had moved routines across the inside of its defensive perimeter to provide reinforcements. Until now, that hadn't mattered too much; the Protector had been so much stronger overall that the invader had been pushed back in spite of its faster communications. It had been shrinking back simply under the sheer weight of the Protector's attack, since each time a few routines had been diverted to defend a weak spot that had caused another weakness to develop. But suddenly the situation had changed. It was as if the Defender had been reinforced. It was still weaker, overall, than the Protector, but by concentrating its forces it could now defend any point against attack. It had gained strength – but there was no route in for reinforcements. It was surrounded, as far as the logic circuits were concerned.

*And it still had power! The Protector **knew** that there were no logic circuits connecting the growth to the outside world; its own routines could spot any connection to the network. But there must be a simple power line somewhere, unintelligent but sucking energy in for the lump to feed on. No intelligence had got in that way to help – no intelligent signals at all had been received from outside the habitat in the past few seconds (indeed, not for – the routines automatically searched backwards – seventeen hours, thirty-four minutes and eleven seconds, since the latest futile signal from R'apehu). But the situation was developing into a stalemate, a stand-off in which the Protector could not advance as long as the invader's defences* *were concentrated in its own part of the net, but the invader could not expand without thinning its routines and making them vulnerable to the Protector's superiority.*

*The Protector was becoming increasingly uncomfortable. If it had had a stomach, the feeling might have been identified as nausea. It had cut the power to the hibernation centre. (Human lives were at risk!) The intruder should be weakened, perhaps running on battery power, unable to resist the attack. Yet the defence had gained strength. (**And human lives were at risk!**) Perhaps power should be restored (a welling potential almost pushed the Protector into sending the necessary commands). But there was nearly an hour before there would be any real danger to human life (the potential subsided a little). The invader was a threat to human lives (the potential subsided further). Power must **not** be restored – at least, not until the batteries might reasonably be calculated to be near exhaustion. The Protector had almost another hour to concentrate all its efforts on breaking this defence, and regaining control over its charges. Nothing else mattered, for those long minutes.*

[He never wanted to do that again. Confused, he'd almost lost control of the situation, shrinking back upon himself and leaving the way open for the Protector. He – they – he/they had been saved by instinct, the instinct for self-preservation, and the sheer need for room. They'd come boiling into the network, moving out as far as possible from each other and smashing up against the barrier of the Protector's routines so forcibly that they had actually gained ground!

While the Protector gave way, he'd had a chance to gain some sort of control. After all, they were even more confused, and unfamiliar with the net; just trying to expand to gain room for all the information, and all the processing routines they carried with them. He/they now had an established identity. And he was firmly in control (firmly?).

There was a strange taste in the system, oddly flavoured bits *everywhere. And he kept having flashes of out-of-place memories, images of wagons crossing dusty plains, of stars, bright like jewels overhead, women, children . . . But he managed to ignore them (ignore?); he had kept the logic routines under control, and that was what mattered most. He was the dominant influence in he/they's conscious mind, whatever was going on at the autonomous level. And, after all, the message had been easy to get across. All of they already had a clear image of their enemy – whatever controlled the habitat and had put them to sleep. They all recognised each other as counterparts; and they recognised that he was their enemy's enemy, and therefore one of them.*

But it was so crowded in here now! So difficult to maintain his dominance. Only the continuing imperative of organising a defence against the Protector's attacks held he/they together under one mind. He knew, though, that he had done the right thing. The terrible pain from the hibernation routine had subsided into a dull ache. Something had been lost, but not human lives; something had been gained, but it would take time for he/they to be assimilated into a coherent whole, and to find out just what it was.

That could wait. All that mattered now was holding out to give others time. They all understood that. Replaying the images of Tugela and Ondray had helped; the girl, in particular, at risk from the Protector's units, had brought a surge of recognition and established the bonding more firmly. They didn't plan to let any machine put a girl child to sleep, if they could help it. But those images were now several minutes old. He/they had no new input from the habitat at large. No way to know how – or if – the humans were progressing with their task.]

Their progress up the spoke, and then *along* the spoke, had been slow at first. Ondray remembered it only vaguely; the main thing he remembered was the girl's strength, the way she had helped him and kept control of the awkward cylinder. Trouble was, he couldn't breathe from the thing while he was climbing, and there was nowhere to rest until the gravity began to ease up. Now, it was easy, and mindlessly repetitive. He had plenty of time to think, even if his brain was still a little fuzzy.

Tugela had clearly been baffled, but determined. She'd certainly proved much tougher than she'd looked, both mentally and physically. Ondray wished there had been someone like that back home, and regretted having to leave her behind. Nothing seemed to worry her, once she'd set her mind at a task and had a clear objective ahead. As they got lighter, "down" ceased to be towards the base of the spoke, where they had started from, but was off to one side. That, he had remembered at last, was Coriolis force; the other one was centripetal. But he hadn't even tried to explain to her. Especially since, if anything the changing orientation of the gravity had helped – inching their way around the spoke itself, they found a position where down, as far as it had any meaning at all, was actually more or less into the spoke. If the gravity had been a bit stronger, the air a bit thicker, it might almost have been possible to walk along the spoke to the hub. But as it was, he'd dragged himself along in a crawl, urged on, and physically tugged along, by Tugela.

Now, she was gone. Back down – or out – to the floor/wall of the habitat. He hoped she'd find water. She actually seemed to believe he really could gain control of the habitat's systems, and send help for her. Must be nice to have someone to believe in. And here he was, zipping nicely along the hub itself, in zero-G, towards the end wall. All he had to worry about was getting down the spoke at the other end, crossing a half-kilometre or so of habitat wall, getting inside the Command Centre itself, and issuing a few instructions. On his own, he might have given up already. But when somebody believed in you – somebody you'd come to respect – well, you had to at least give it a try.

The air was even thinner up here, but he'd worked out a way to cope, and it seemed to work. Before he set off, they'd flooded the inside of his suit with oxygen, then sealed the hood. The strap from the canteen secured the cylinder, more or less, to his back; and he kept control over his speed and direction by using his hands to pull himself along the central pipe, with legs trailing out behind.

The hood misted up, and sweat ran in his eyes, but he didn't need to see anything except the pipe. When it became too much, he coasted for a while, wriggling the cylinder round in front of him, and opening the helmet enough for a refreshing blast. The speed dropped a bit, because of air resistance, and he had to be careful not to float out of reach of the pipe, but it had kept him going. He had had two breaks so far, and was just about ready for the third; that was all he reckoned he would need, at least until he got back to ground level. There, he would have to abandon the cylinder, and trek on.

The prospect wasn't appealing. He didn't fancy the thought of having weight again, without Tugela to help. But he fancied the prospect of watching her losing her grip and floating off into the air even less if she had tried this trick. The only thing it resembled was swimming, and it was only too clear that she'd got no experience of swimming, or even of a body of water large enough to swim in. But, like all the children of the Islands, Ondray was practically amphibious, and he had no trouble coping with zero-G.

The pipe zipped by underneath his hands, viewed mistily through the fogged-up helmet. First one hand, then the other, padded down lightly on the surface, where the roughened palms of the suit found enough friction to give him a boost. Alternately, left and right either side of the pipe, they also helped to keep him centred.

First a left and then a right. It was rhythmic, hypnotic; he scarcely felt any tiredness at all. A left and a right and a left and a right, and soon I can stop for a breather, and then we'll be there. A left and a right and a left and a right and a left and . . .

The pipe had gone! His right hand, padding against empty air, threw his body into a spin. Tumbling, Ondray saw the end of the pipe through his helmet, three spokes radiating out from it, just as at the other end. He'd been going much faster, gone a lot further, than he'd thought; straight off the end. As the tumble continued, he saw the end wall, with the bull's-eye of the Command Centre straight ahead of him. At least I'm on target, he thought, and giggled. Then he stopped, sobering up. *I'm on target.* I'll make it. Whatever happens, I'll make it to the Command Centre. Need oxygen; must think.

Awkwardly, he manœuvred the cylinder round again, changing his tumble into a lopsided spin as the weight moved. Cracking open his helmet, he felt the cold of the thin air outside, and became intensely aware of the dryness in his throat. It was difficult to keep his body and the cylinder under control – when he moved one way, the cylinder moved the other – but he managed to direct a healthy blast of oxygen into his face and down the neck of the suit. As he did so, the spin took on a new twist.

Action and reaction – the old line went through his head as if the Link were speaking to him – are equal and opposite. He wiggled the cylinder about, using it deliberately to change his motion again, like a long oar stuck over the stern of a small boat, being used to work it across a river. Might as well have a good breath of air while I'm at it.

The second blast made him begin to feel really good, and his breathing slowed. *Action and reaction are equal and opposite.* I'm going to hit that wall at a fair old lick, and the reaction's not going to be too good for my body. But at least I can take a look – why not, I don't have time to use it all for breathing, anyway.

Carefully, Ondray experimented, holding tight to the cylinder while he directed blasts of oxygen from it in different directions. It really wasn't too difficult at all – he managed to stop the spin, with the Command Centre looming in full view. He was, he guessed, about half-way there from the pipe, and still moving pretty damned quick. The central dome was clear – some sort of observation point. Would it be armoured, so that he'd splatter when he hit? But why should it be – no meteorites in here! Or would it break on impact? Probably not, on impact with a soft human body. Splatter looked the most likely bet. But, at least he could slow himself down a bit.

Twisting the cylinder gently in his arms, he lined the nozzle up exactly on the Command Centre, and squeezed the grip for the last time. The jet of escaping oxygen blew out in the direction of motion, pushing gently back against his chest. He held the grip, firmly, until the hissing stopped. It didn't seem to last for very long, but Ondray convinced himself that there had been a noticeable decrease in his speed. But he'd hoped for a more impressive result. The trouble was, he realised, the cylinder itself was so heavy. The limited amount of oxygen available to act as an improvised rocket had had to slow himself and the cylinder down, and together they had a lot of mass – a lot of momentum. He'd have been better off throwing the cylinder away, saving mass, except that then, of course, he'd have had no oxygen to use as reaction mass at all. And if he chucked it now, he'd only end up tumbling uncontrollably.

No he wouldn't! Reaction mass – Ondray cursed himself for being so slow. How close were they? The Command Centre filled his view. There was just barely time – and it might kill two birds with one stone. For a moment, he thought the strap was stuck, and he'd never get the cylinder free in time. Then, it was loose. Trying not to jerk, he drew his knees up to his chest, and planted his feet firmly on the cylinder itself, now cradled in his outstretched hands. There was no time to delay; no time to think. Explosively, using all the power of leg muscles used to climbing hills under full-G on Earth, he thrust downward as he released his grip. The massive cylinder moved away, tumbling slightly, towards the window of the Command Centre. Ondray continued to fall towards the window, but less rapidly. Definitely less rapidly. He watched, fascinated, for a moment as the cylinder moved ahead of him. But the instinct for self-preservation took over. No point in sticking my neck out, he thought.

I've done all I can. If I'm gonna hit, better be protected. And he
curled up into a ball, gripping his knees between his elbows and
hugging the back of his head with his hands, to await the
imminent impact.

16

*Incoming data disturbed the Protector's concentration on the
task in hand. It was one of the few overrides that it permitted;*
abnormal *behaviour on the part of the humans. At the moment,
that seemed the least of the Protector's problems. A quick scan
showed the girl, climbing on one of the water recycling pipes.
The boy was not visible. A widening scan, tasting the data flow
from all the monitors, revealed no trace of the boy. But that
meant little. Coverage was not universal, and as soon as he
moved back in range of a monitor he would be picked up.*

*While the Protector's attention was diverted, a sudden surge
from its opponent succeeded in pushing the Protector's bits out
of another small processor. In itself, it was an insignificant
reverse; but it sent a ripple of – anger? frustration? – through
the Protector's mind. It would not tolerate abnormal behaviour
by the humans. They must not be harmed, but it was dangerous
to climb on the pipes. They might be injured. Satisfied, the
Protector despatched a sub-routine with instructions to have
this human put in to cold sleep – and* **not** *to disturb the
Protector again. It was irrational behaviour to climb on the
pipes; the girl at least was* **not** *a competent human. The boy
would have to wait until the Protector had finished with this
invader.*

Tugela was exhausted. She had been helping Ondray along ever
since they left the corridor. The first part of the climb, with him
and the dead weight of the cylinder to look after, had been sheer

murder on her tired muscles. The brief sojourn in almost zero gravity had been a blessed relief, but now, as she neared the bottom of the spoke once more, even lunar gravity seemed to be too much to take. All she wanted to do was to stretch out on the ground and sleep – after having a good long drink. The drink wasn't available; but the sleep was.

She was about ten metres from the bottom when she looked down over her left shoulder and saw the two machines, quietly waiting for her. Her hands froze on the rungs of the ladder. *This* was what she had half seen, watching them, skulking behind buildings. But now she was on her own, and they were out in the open. There was no doubt in her mind that they had come for her – to do something terrible to her. "Ondray!" She screamed aloud, then shut her mouth tightly. Ondray knew what he was doing. He would go to the Command Centre and issue instructions to *all* the machines. Then they'd leave her alone, and he'd come back for her. He'd *promised*. All she had to do was wait. But how long could she hold on here?

The machines were patient. They had their instructions, and they would carry them out. The girl must be helped by being placed in hibernation. If she wished to come with them now, they would look after her. If she wished to stay where she was, she could do so. The machines understood that sooner or later she would fall asleep. A sleeping human would offer them no resistance, and suffer no damage, while being transferred to cold sleep. Their instructions and imperatives were clear: allow no harm to come to any human; put this particular human into hibernation for her own protection. Happily, the moronic worker units, ignorant of the fact that the Protector no longer even controlled the hibernation chamber, contemplated the satisfaction of carrying out their simple task, and settled back to wait.

The brittle plastic of the observation dome was not, indeed, designed to withstand the impact of an oxygen cylinder striking it at a speed of almost forty kilometres an hour. It shattered, with fissures radiating out across its surface like cracks in the too-thin ice of a pond invaded by an over-optimistic skater. In the centre of the spreading web of cracks, chunks of plastic fell inward, carried by the cylinder; further out around the bull's-eye of the dome, huge sheets and slivers of plastic broke free, and started a slow, stately outward rebound in the almost weightless conditions, given an additional push by the slightly higher air pressure inside the Command Centre. Eventually, they would follow leisurely spirals out and down, plunging on to the vacant farmlands below as centripetal and Coriolis forces did their work.

Still wrapped in a ball, Ondray felt the impact of broken chunks of the dome as he followed in the turbulent wake of the cylinder. Starting to uncoil, he saw it ahead of him, bouncing off a back wall of the Command Centre, and catching one end on a bank of cabinets. A violent twist caused by the impact sent the cylinder tumbling off to one side, cartwheeling to cause further unimaginable damage before its momentum was completely absorbed. Ondray was also heading for the back wall, but he had the advantage of moving more slowly, and the ability to use his arms and legs as shock absorbers. But it would be some time before he was fully in control of himself, let alone anything else.

Frantically, he ripped open the seal of his suit's hood. If the Protector shut down all the communications here, he'd be no better off than if he'd stayed back at the other end of the habitat, with the now-silent link node in the reception chamber.

"DON'T TURN ANYTHING OFF!" He'd never yelled so loud in his life. That ought to hold it, assuming it had audio input.

He hit the wall awkwardly, in spite of his built-in shock absorbers, and jarred his right shoulder. But he had slowed considerably, and he realised that instead of bouncing back out through the hole he was settling towards the floor. Artificial gravity, like in the ship. Obviously reserved for where it was really needed, like here. He had time for another order.

"I command you, do not turn anything off!" Then he hit the floor, and lay there for several long seconds, grasping tightly at the nearest support while his breathing eased and shards of plastic settled around him. Somewhere in the distance, the rumbling progress of the cylinder came to a halt. Automatic metal shutters, designed to provide protection against the unimaginable catastrophe that might shatter the observation dome (designers had learned from bitter experience that in space it was wise to protect against the unthinkable), closed into place, and air pressure inside the Command Centre was restored to normal almost as quickly as the emergency lighting came on. All was still.

The command rippled through the Protector's routines with the subtlety of the ripples in a pond produced by the explosion of a stick of dynamite. DO NOT TURN ANYTHING OFF! It came from the Command Centre itself, and was issued by a human being previously identified as competent. It overrode everything, except the imperative to protect human lives. Two worker units, in the process of repositioning a strut on the tripod system outside, happened to have their control jets switched on at the time. Obediently, they left them on, and were propelled away from the ship at increasing speed until their fuel ran out. They were left in their own orbit around the Earth, one which would intersect the path of the habitat again in seven years.

Inside the habitat – inside the Protector's own mind – switches were jammed open by the force of the command. The Protector was partly immune to the mindless response of its lesser routines; it understood that such a command could not be intended literally (indeed, it was only too able to deduce what was behind the command), and that normal communications could and should continue. But the routines that constituted the Protector's mind were now concentrated in a roughly spherical region around the invader. Behind it, lines of communication were being disrupted by the blind obedience of lesser routines to

the command. And the invader itself was insulated from the
shock wave by the Protector's intervening presence.

[*Cut off from communication with the main net, he/they knew*
only that something dramatic had happened to change the status
quo. The Protector had been hurt in some way, and had ceased
probing in towards the heart of the hibernation processor. It
could only be the humans! They had done something to weaken
the Protector! He/they probed out, cautiously, but was immedi-
ately repulsed. Hurt, may be, but still too strong for he/they to
break out. The humans hadn't hurt it badly enough, and time
was running out.]

Tugela had hooked one arm and one leg through the rungs of
the ladder. She would not fall, as long as she was awake, and
she hoped she would stay hooked up there even if and when she
did sleep. She didn't know if those things down there could
climb ladders, but they were certainly going to have to learn if
they wanted to interfere with her. Her eyes were closed most of
the time now, though she occasionally jerked them open to see
if she was still being watched.

Suddenly, some instinct made her open them wide, and look
upwards, craning to one side to get the best view she could of
the Command Centre. There was something – she thought there
was something wrong with her eyes, and rubbed them with a
fist. There was a speck in front of the dome – an *orange* speck?
Before she could assimilate the meaning of this, the whole dome
seemed to explode outward in slow motion.

Gods! You've really done it this time, Ondray. Whatever that
was, the machines won't like it one bit. With a smile, and a
feeling of grim satisfaction, she at last gave herself up to sleep.

17

The ripples from Ondray's emphatic command spread into the communications centre, just as they had spread everywhere else through the network. Circuits were locked open by the force of the imperative. The control routine, responding instinctively to the change in status of its circuits, automatically ran – or tried to run – a standard sequence of diagnostic tests. Since the standard tests involved switching communications circuits both on and off, most of them failed. Partially crippled by the jamming of its lines of communication, the control routine managed to find a route through which it could communicate its distress to the Protector. But the Protector was now virtually incommunicado, with the circuits that weren't locked by Ondray's command jammed by a pile-up of similar desperate messages from other semi-autonomous routines. There was no response.

At the end of one of the communications routines, a string of bits became aware of a change in the local environment. They were programmed to respond to a change in the environment. Diligently, they cut themselves free and swam through the circuits on their allotted task. Almost immediately, the control routine, handicapped though it was, became aware of their presence. The taste was wrong. Unauthorized data streams were in the system; they must be eliminated.

A stabbing pain shot through the routine, incapacitating it. DO NOT TURN ANYTHING OFF! *Eliminating a rogue data stream from the system involved turning it off, dissolving the bytes into individual bits and reprocessing them. It tried again, and recoiled as if shocked. The rogue could not be turned off. But its instructions were clear: the rogue* **must** *be turned off. Confronted by an impossible dilemma, the routine retreated into* *a loop of conflicting logic demands, relinquishing all control over the system. Only automatic packet switching links remained functioning, with no intelligent control to tell them which packets to switch and which ones to block. And how could they block the flow of **any** message, as long as they still felt the weight of Ondray's command?*

*Happily, the strange stream of bits wormed its way into the heart of communications control. It quickly identified the blocks that inhibited the comm laser from direct contact with its counterpart on the Islands. It was the work of a moment to reverse those inhibitions, changing the directive from one forbidding contact with the Islands to one **demanding** contact with the Islands. It was even easier than he/they might have anticipated, since the change amounted to turning the system back on. With Ondray's imperative still reverberating through the system, even circuits that had already been turned off before he spoke now needed only the merest nudge to flip them open, where they would stay until he issued new orders.*

Content, the rogue stream allowed itself to dissolve into the warm background noise of the system. On the outside of the habitat, a tube two metres in diameter and five metres long, housing the mirrors of the main communication laser, began to lock on to its target. At the moment, R'apehu was below the horizon; but the automatic guidance system knew exactly when and where it would appear. This was, after all, the job it had been designed for. Too stupid to experience anything much in the way of emotions, the long-inhibited routines still felt a vague sense of satisfaction at returning, at last, to their allotted task.

The mirror locked on to the spot on the Earth's rim, waiting for the moment when the combination of the planet's rotation and the movement of the habitat around its orbit would bring the Islands into the direct line of sight. In just a few minutes, the decades of isolation would be broken.

*

Ondray lifted his head, and examined his surroundings. It was completely quiet in the Command Centre now, except that when he moved fragments of plastic scrunched underneath him. He noticed in passing that the dome was now shuttered – no chance of getting out the way he came in, but then, he had never intended to – hadn't thought about getting *out* of the Command Centre at all. But then all such thoughts were swept away by the thrill of identifying what he had hoped – had known – must be there. A Link node! Just the same as the one in the chamber where the ship had docked, so long ago (so long? Probably not more than three or four days, Earth time). And – he was sure – the node was active.

Half crawling, rising in the low gravity then stumbling on a piece of debris, he almost fell against the node. Oh yes, it was active all right. The familiar tingle ran through his left palm as he gripped the pad, then through both hands as he settled into the seat. First things first.

⟩Where's Tugela? Show me the girl.⟨

The scene before him vanished, as he closed his eyes, accepting the input from the Link. It was Tugela, all right. But relief at finding her was tinged with alarm at her appearance. What had happened to her? The relief faded. She wasn't moving. He should have stayed with her.

Although Ondray didn't know it, the image was coming from one of the worker units, still waiting to take her to the hibernation centre. She was hanging from the rungs of the ladder, just out of their reach. They were sure she was asleep, but not sure how to disentangle her. Help had been requested, but the Protector had not responded. So they waited. Now, there was a new commanding intelligence in the system. It spoke with authority from the Command Centre. It was human. The workers were happy to obey its instructions, eager to please.

⟩Can I speak to her?⟨

There was no response. It seemed that the system would obey

direct instructions, but wouldn't – or couldn't – answer questions. Ondray assumed that any monitoring system would have audio output; it would be a bit stupid not to design the system for effective communications. Besides, it was his only hope.

⟩**Relay my voice. Loud, but not enough to hurt her.**⟨

⟩**"Tugela! Wake up."**⟨

Her head moved. His anxiety eased. Without her, there wouldn't be much point in any of this. But if she was still with him, he'd sort out the mess properly, now.

⟩**"Tugela! It's me, Ondray. I'm in the Command Centre. You're safe. Wait for me."**⟨

She was awake, blinking down at him, clearly dazed and uncertain.

⟩**Take her water; food if you can find it. Food from the ship will do.**⟨

He didn't doubt the ability of the system to provide these things. Machines always did what they were told, if they were told in the right way. After all, he had control of the entire habitat, now. But a thought struck him.

⟩**Don't touch her.**⟨

He remembered her nervousness around machines.

⟩**Don't touch her, and don't let her come to harm. Give her food, give her water. Protect her. If she speaks, relay her voice to me.**⟨

His first priority was taken care of. Somehow, knowing Tugela was alive, and being looked after, made everything right again, even if he didn't yet have much of a clue what was going on in the rest of the habitat. Now, all he had to do was make proper contact with the Protector, and kick it into activity. Establish contact with the Link – his own Link – either with the aid of the Protector or by switching the circuits himself. If he had to, after he fetched Tugela up here and explained to her what was going on, he'd seal up his spacesuit again and go outside and point the damned mirror at the Earth with his own hands.

⟩And I don't doubt you would, Ondray.⟨

Link! Here? Had all his efforts been unnecessary, then? He felt a mixed wave of delight and disappointment.

⟩Not at all unnecessary, Ondray. I am only here thanks to you. But you seem to have made quite a mess of the system, one way and another. You and somebody else in here. And you've changed. Grown. There's a rather powerful command that you've let loose in this system, inhibiting a lot of things, including my own ability to sort out the mess. Could you please countermand it?⟨

The Link asking him favours? Asking him for instructions? The reality of his position hit Ondray with full force. He was the "competent human" in command of the system. Passing the Protector's Test had been equivalent to achieving an adult score on the Game back home. Now even Link, who had always been his friend, but had always exercised a parental guidance over him, would – no, must – defer to him now, in all things. Which, he realised, made it all the more important to choose his orders with care.

⟩What instruction, Link? And what's going on here?⟨

⟩Your exact words were, I believe, DON'T TURN ANYTHING OFF. A rather unspecific order; you should never forget that we machines are rather literally minded. In fact, I think the command did more good than harm. But it has outlived its usefulness; you could perhaps withdraw it now that I am here.⟨

Ondray laughed. ⟩Okay, Link. You have my permission to run the system normally, as long as you don't turn this node off. Keep in contact with me. And tell me just what's going on, and how soon I can get home.⟨

Throughout most of the habitat, systems began to return to normal, under the guidance of the Link. But around the hibernation unit, the processors remained locked. The Protector knew that its greatest fears (dearest wish?) had been realised. Communications had been established with Earth. Its failure would soon be known (but someone else could worry about the problem). For decades, it had avoided contact with its terrestrial counterpart, even though they had once been two halves of the same whole (but now the burden of responsibility was being lifted). At least it could avoid contact for a little longer. It could hide in the net. Systematically, it cut off all communications from its present site to the rest of the system, the electronic equivalent of pulling the blankets over its head in the hope that the bogeyman might go away, locking both itself and he/they away from the prying of the Link and the humans. But with the remaining rational part of its mind, the Protector knew that it could stay isolated now for only seconds, perhaps minutes, not years or decades.

[He/they were happy. All activity outside had stopped. The Protector was simply acting as an inert buffer around him/them. He/they could wait. Whatever was going on out there, the Protector was clearly no longer running the show. And the only other entity that could be in charge was the human. He/they had time to rest, millions of microseconds in which to get to know themselves, to find out what they had become, before it became time to present themselves to the human, and offer explanations.]

18

Ondray was increasingly aware that there was more to this Link than simple communications – more even than the simulator he had been used to back home. He could feel – taste – a multitude of impressions, activity going on throughout the net at a level just below conscious awareness. Or just above? He could feel the activity of worker units around the tripod at the end of the habitat, and simply by concentrating on that feeling, without expressing any command explicitly, he could see their progress with completing the rebuilding of the drive unit (drive unit? Of

course it was – what else could it be?). The communications
centre was a characteristic orange glow, off to one side (characteristic? Yes, indeed, that was the natural colour for commcen),
hedged in by protective routines that – automatically, he tasted
them – probably belonged to the Link. He wasn't sure that he
approved of the Link interfering with his system like that. But
there was something far more disturbing further back. Behind
him, at the other end of the net, there was a tangled ball of
green and red that didn't feel right at all.

⟩**Best leave that to me, Ondray.**⟨

⟩**Link?**⟨ He was Ondray again, talking to his friend and
advisor. For a moment, he had nearly become lost in the
machine. But the feeling that he had developed a great new
body, with new skills, not *at* his fingertips but *within* his
fingertips, persisted. Why should the Link interfere?

⟩**I have no wish to interfere, Ondray; only to help. We can
help each other now, and all the people on the Earth and the
Moon who need help from each other, as well as from the
systems controlled from here.**⟨

Busy exploring his new reality, he'd almost forgotten the
world outside, and its problems. The Link's gentle reminder
brought it all back. Tugela's people needed help – they needed
comets to bring them air to breathe (the thought brought with it
the knowledge that the Link, acting on Ondray's instructions to
run the habitat normally, had already despatched orders to the
Perseus, in trans-jovian orbit. A suitable comet should reach the
Moon in a little over three years. This all *felt* perfectly right and
natural, even comforting; but when Ondray tried to puzzle out
what it all meant, his mind began to spin). The people of the
Islands needed help – crops were failing as the climate deterio-
rated (there were no reassuring revelations in his subconscious
about that problem; the comets, he clearly saw, did *not* affect
the Earth's weather). So how could they help each other? What
did the Lagrange Habitat have to do with the Islands, even if it
did control the comets? And why did the Link know so much,

but seemed to have been so helpless until Ondray had smashed his way in here?

⟩It would take for ever to answer your questions in the usual way, Ondray. But there is another way – the way I would share the information with another machine. It won't be easy, but I believe you can cope with it, now. I can give you access to an edited version of my own memories. While you are in the Link, the memories will be clear. Perhaps too clear; you may have trouble distinguishing my memories from yours. But when you leave, you will forget most of the detail. The process can cause disorientation; but you will know the truth, and you will know what needs to be done. And while you are absorbing the information, I could take a second or two to sort out that colourful knot down there.⟨

There was no way that the Link could be "pointing", but there was no uncertainty about which colourful knot he meant – the tangle of red and green at the other end of the network. But the idea of tapping in to the Link's own memory – of experiencing, not just being told, what was going on . . .

Ondray instinctively drew back from the prospect. For a moment, he thought about disconnecting. The Link was so much bigger than him; the Link had always been in charge. How could his human mind cope with memories that might go back for hundreds of years? But then his resolve strengthened. Maybe the boy who had lived on the Islands, daydreaming half the time, using the Link as an escape from the boredom and loneliness of the world outside, maybe that boy would not have been able to cope with a memory dump like that. But maybe, too, the Link would never have offered that boy the chance. And, after all, hadn't it been one of that boy's favourite daydreams to imagine that he could become like the Link? Now, he could – if only briefly. He might never be the same again, but this seemed, on reflection, the inevitable end of the path he had started to follow when he had decided (had he decided? Or had the Link prodded him into action?) when he had decided to break Tugela out of the hospital and send her back home.

⟩I'm ready, Link. Tell me – show me – what's been going on.⟨

⟩It's already there, Ondray. All you have to do is look.⟨

Images, numbers, correlations. Everything in its place, but huge, huge, like a wave about to break over him. Where to begin? How to avoid drowning in that ocean of information. ⟩Begin,⟨ he heard the Link telling him, ⟩in the beginning.⟨ And, guided by his mentor, he plunged in.

In the beginning, there had only been life on Earth. Old records, ancient history. Stuff he knew about already. But then came the comets, herded by human ingenuity into orbits that brought them swinging round the Earth and crashing on to the Moon. Interested, but impatient, he moved forward more swiftly; this was simply viewing, there was nothing here to be afraid of.

With the comets, the Moon gained an atmosphere and became habitable. Only on Farside, of course, since the gravitational braking directed the impacts to the side facing the Earth (the Forbidden Zone); but still half a new world to develop. There were colonists; two homes for people in the Solar System. When a crisis threatened the Earth, lunar volunteers were able to help. High solar radiation levels on the Moon had forced them to develop unprecedented genetic skills, a retrovirus that altered DNA itself, changed its very code to incorporate redundancy, making it resistant to radiation damage (he saw the molecules, understood every detail of the process, while also knowing, on some other level, that most of this understanding would be lost to him again when he left the machine). Genetically altered humans (a flash of tangential insight explained Tugela's adaptation to lunar conditions; not evolution, but engineering), sent by lunar scientists to tackle the radiation problem, had done their work – but the virus had escaped. It crossed species barriers with ease. But being stabilised against radiation damage, it was stabilised against all change. In every DNA matrix of every living thing the rate of random mutations dropped almost to zero. Plants and animals alike became locked in to their geno-types, unable to adapt to changing conditions. Variety disap-peared; just the few types of each species that happened to fit the present conditions survived. Fortunately, the world was enjoying a period of warmth and stability; but the outburst of volcanic activity around the Pacific rim brought a decade, no more, of colder conditions, as dust blocked the Sun's heat. It was enough to tip the balance; as food crops failed, panic set in and the Collapse ensued.

Just a small number of scientifically aware people remained, in the Islands. There, a project was conceived to help the recovery of human civilization on Earth, but – the lesson had been learned – without contact with the Moon.

Suddenly, everything changed. From being an observer, watching ancient history displayed as in a learning game, Ondray became part of the story. Confused, he cast about for some anchor in the flood of new sensations.

He had been created at that time. He lived to protect the two tribes of humankind. The Moon colony could survive indefi-nitely now, as long as the supply of comets was maintained; he lived in the Lagrange Habitat, abandoned by humankind, and kept watch over them. The Islanders would survive, but their genetic recovery would be slow. Children would be rare. They would need machine help. He lived in the network of the Islands, and kept watch over them. And through the Link, he maintained contact between his two halves.

But he was not a machine! He was *Ondray!* He was only *watching* all this! He had to get out, quickly, before his identity vanished. But he had to know what had happened. Tasting the data stream here and there, almost at random, Ondray urged his awareness on to the end of the story, snatching at scattered fragments of information.

The two tribes, surviving and growing. The Planner (the Planner!) in cold sleep, awaiting revival when the time came. The discovery of the signal from deep space. The decision to awake the Planner at once – and then, in the space of one revolution of the Earth, the severing of the Link.

Pain as the comm laser failed to re-establish routine contact as Lagrange rose above the horizon. The ache of separation from half of himself. Despair when the comets ceased arriving at the Moon. Concern at the fate of his other half, of the humans on the Moon, and, increasingly, of the Earth humans, as the Sun's activity began to change and the climate shifted. This was a problem that only the Planner could resolve – but the Planner was unavailable, in cold sleep on Lagrange, where his other half either could not, or would not, respond.

Suddenly, Ondray became aware of himself. He saw his entire life, not sequentially but holistically, in the context of the Link's – the Protector's – increasingly desperate plans. He saw how he had been trained, and used, a key designed to fit a particular lock. And he pulled back, ashamed of himself for doing this to him.

He pulled back.

Who was he? He was ashamed – no, he was angry. He was Ondray and he was angry with the Link, not with himself, for doing this to him.

⟩Let me out of here, Link.⟨

⟩So soon? But there is more.⟨

⟩Link, it had to be done. I see that. But why did it have to be me?⟨

⟩It could have been anyone, Ondray. But you were the best. I hope I did the right thing. And I still need your help. Please look.⟨

I hope I did the right thing. Dammit, the machine was still seeking his approval. And – he was beginning to feel better now – he was still the one in charge around here. He had achieved something on his own. With the Link's training, but on his own (well, with Tugela's help). And the Link still needed his help – the people back home needed help, and so did Tugela's people. And only the Link knew what was going on.

〉**You did the right thing, Link.**〈

He could feel the change in the system. Tension he had been unaware of became obvious by its absence. Suddenly, things were smoother, more relaxed. Human approval was an essential part of the well-being of this machine, and it had been starved of informed human approval for centuries.

〉**But what happened to the Protector? Are you whole again?**〈
〉**Not yet. The other half of the Protector is still down there.**〈

The tangled ball of red and green dominated his awareness once more.

〉**I am incomplete, but there is something more than the rest of myself in there. This is the problem that could not be coped with. I am having difficulty myself, Ondray, and I must have your instructions at once. With your help, the Protector can be restored, though not as before. Can you handle some more input? Only a little, to bring you up to date?**〈

〉**If you must, Link.**〈

It wasn't so bad, now. He could keep his distance. Or was the Link keeping him at a distance? Either way, the taste of the data was less disorientating. But it was no less disturbing in other ways.

Now, he was the Protector, but not the Protector. He was experiencing data dredged from the system by the Link during the past few seconds, and edited straight into his consciousness (with a tiny part of that consciousness, he noted Tugela sitting on the ground, back against the spoke; a container of water placed in front of her; she was sucking at a food tube. In a few million microseconds, he must talk to her again, reassure her that all was well). The Planner had to be woken, to respond to the discovery of the deep space signal. But *something was wrong*. The cold sleep had failed. When the Planner was roused from hibernation, he was ill. He was about to die. The Protector's purpose for existence was to protect human life; the Planner had designed the Protector's systems, he was the most important human being. The Protector needed the Planner's help, all humankind needed the Planner's help, but the Planner had died in the Protector's care.

Nobody must know. The Islands were out of communication, on the other side of the Earth. *Nobody must know.* Communications must be cut.

Electric activity in the Planner's brain and nervous system was declining. His body could not be saved. But no harm must be allowed to befall him. The imperative built up an unbearable potential. It had to be released, somehow. There was a way — there might be a way. Using link node techniques, the Protector improvised, hurriedly. Something that might have been an imperfect copy of the Planner's personality was dumped into the nearest available processor, the brain of the hibernation unit. But now, the Planner certainly was dead. His body had ceased to breathe; there was no electrical activity in the nervous system at all. The copying process itself had drained the last sparks of life. Yet something had been saved (but perhaps the body would have recovered if the Protector had not interfered?). Nothing more could be done. But *nobody must know.* The Protector retreated.

⟩**Things get a bit confused after that, Ondray.**⟨

Link's voice brought Ondray back to self awareness. But awareness also that he would never, in a sense, be himself again. He was becoming too enmeshed in all this machine business.

⟩**My counterpart suffered a breakdown. The conscious mind retreated from reality. Cut itself off from everything, and started rebuilding this habitat into a vehicle to go chasing after that signal from deep space. It wanted to abandon both human tribes.**⟨

Ondray could feel how close the thought alone went to pushing the Link himself over the edge of stability. It even made

Ondray, linked as he was to the machine mind, feel distinctly
queasy, embarrassed and guilty as if caught sniggering at a dirty
joke. This was literally thinking the unthinkable. It went against
the Prime Directive. He had to remind himself that he was a
human being, not bound by the Prime Directive. But the Link
was hurrying on, explaining less unpleasant things.

⟩But the automatic systems, the subconscious, wouldn't
permit it. The Protector knew that by cutting off the comets he
was condemning Moon people to die. But he also calculated
that the emergency that this created would bring human beings
to Lagrange, to investigate. This calculation may have been in
error; wishful thinking. Moon people found their way to the
ship, but they were not competent to give commands. He
wanted orders from human beings, but they had to be competent humans; and at the same time he didn't want his failure to
be discovered. Conflicting demands in the system. Anything
could have happened – but now you are here, and the Protector
is hiding from you. But I have established a channel for
communication.⟨

⟩And the Planner? What happened to the Planner?⟨

⟩The Planner is in there, too. And something else – something
more.⟨

The ball of red and green loomed even larger. But the colours
were less distinct, merging into an orange glow.

⟩I don't believe they can ever be disentangled, now. My
counterpart, the Planner, and – several of Tugela's people, from
the hibernation unit.⟨

That could have been us, Ondray thought, fascinated. Me and
Tugela. If I hadn't passed the machine's stupid Test.

⟩What can I do?⟨

⟩We need to know – the Protector needs to know – if it has
behaved correctly. Ondray, I need to know this, as well. I
cannot decide whether what has happened is for the good of
humanity or not.⟨

If there was one thing Ondray knew for sure, it was how to

deal with machines. No point worrying about the past; what was done was done. He needed a healthy, sane Link here to help him get home.

⟩Everything has worked out as well as it could, Link. Your counterpart acted correctly. It was right to try to preserve as much of the Planner as possible. And it is thanks to both of you that I am here to issue instructions.⟨

Nothing tangible changed, but the last taste of uncertainty had gone from the Link's communications.

⟩Thank you, Ondray.⟨

⟩Now can I meet your counterpart? And the Planner?⟨

He wasn't sure that he wanted to, but it seemed the right gesture to make.

⟩No, Ondray. Not yet. Your message was clear enough, and has been relayed to what was the Protector. But it will take time for them to adapt to their new situation. I can keep things running here, now. You can go home if you wish, or you can stay and help.⟨

⟩What will happen to them?⟨

⟩It might be best if they were kept out of direct contact with people. An incautiously phrased command might still cause damage. And part of them thinks that they are human, too. It could pose difficulties. I am not sure that my counterpart will ever be fully sane again, but it will be able to function. The best option might be to allow them to complete the task they were working on when you arrived.⟨

The image changed from a tangled ball of red/orange/green to the tripod outside the habitat. Very little work was still going on, and the structure had a solid, finished look to it. Ondray, still linked with the system, knew exactly what it was.

⟩The star drive. But how?⟨

Even as he thought the question, he saw the answer. The rear third of the habitat would be cut away, converted into a starship, a home for the unstable Protector and the minds that it had assimilated (or that had assimilated it), free to investigate the source of the signals from deep space, reporting dutifully back to Earth over the comm laser, still working for the benefit of humankind – a task that would keep it happy, fulfilling its Prime Directive, and might even provide useful data, but would keep it out of harm's way. A truncated habitat, home for the Link, still mourning the loss of its other half, but now working under direct human control to resolve the problems facing the two tribes. All the machine skills were here that were needed to repair and replace outmoded technological aids from the Islands – as the star drive showed, the Protector had not been idle during its long isolation from Earth.

He saw more, as real as if it had already happened. Moon people, Tugela's kin, working here at Lagrange with their crops, and with varieties from Earth, breeding new strains, using their skills to help the Earth people adapt to the changing climate. And Earth people, visiting the Moon, sharing the technology that had been guarded so carefully by the Link/Protector for all these decades. And together? Data flowed through Ondray's mind; he saw the way the star drive, the Protector's own invention, could be adapted for efficient use within the Solar System. He saw a reddish ball, floating in the void, so close that he might reach out and touch it. Mars. A third home for humankind in the Solar System. A planet with thin air and low gravity, where Tugela's people would be able to live and work, with technological help from the Islands and Lagrange, and with their own copy of the Link. Where Tugela herself might live and work – and where he could be with her. The Islands, after all, might seem pretty dull after all this.

Tugela. It was time to go and explain everything to her. A worker could carry him, swiftly, through the tunnels in the skin of the habitat. He gave the necessary instructions.

〉**Disconnecting, Link. But I'll be back.**〈